ECHOES FADE

DAVID WOLF BOOK 17

JEFF CARSON

CROSS ATLANTIC PUBLISHING

Copyright © 2023 by Jeff Carson

All rights reserved.

No part of this book may be reproduced in any form or by any electronic or
mechanical means, including information storage and retrieval systems,
without written permission from the author, except for the use of brief
quotations in a book review.

ALSO BY JEFF CARSON

The David Wolf Series

Gut Decision (A David Wolf Short Story) – Sign up for the new release newsletter at http://www.jeffcarson.co/p/newsletter.html and receive a complimentary copy.

Foreign Deceit (David Wolf Book 1)

The Silversmith (David Wolf Book 2)

Alive and Killing (David Wolf Book 3)

Deadly Conditions (David Wolf Book 4)

Cold Lake (David Wolf Book 5)

Smoked Out (David Wolf Book 6)

To the Bone (David Wolf Book 7)

Dire (David Wolf Book 8)

Signature (David Wolf Book 9)

Dark Mountain (David Wolf Book 10)

Rain (David Wolf Book 11)

Drifted (David Wolf Book 12)

Divided Sky (David Wolf Book 13)

In the Ground (David Wolf Book 14)

High Road (David Wolf Book 15)

Dead Canyon (David Wolf Book 16)

NEW Echoes Fade (David Wolf Book 17)

The Ali Falco Series

The Como Falcon (Ali Falco Book 1)

1

"Do you see it?"

David Wolf ignored the voice coming from his radio, his head swiveling back and forth as he peered out his SUV windows, trying to get a glimpse of the big cat.

"You there, Wolf?" Tammy Granger said, her words traveling over the airwaves from Rocky Points to his position twenty miles north.

A hundred yards up on the right side of the snow-packed road, he spotted low buildings squatting along the frozen river.

He picked up the receiver. "I'm just arriving. Nothing yet. Stand by."

Deputy Nelson's voice joined the party, scratching out of the radio, "I'll be there in five minutes. I just turned off 734."

"You're not getting here in five minutes," Wolf said under his breath, hooking the radio back on the receiver.

Snow had begun dropping from the sky an hour prior, first as a stray flake swirling over the vehicle, now as a steady shower driving into the windshield, hinting at the big storm forecasted to arrive later in the afternoon. Assuming the mete-orologists were finally going to be correct with this one. Snow-storm predictions this winter had been hit or miss. Mostly miss.

The trees opened, giving way to bushes blowing in the wind, and the full spread of the trailer park came into view. Buildings battered by time and lack of maintenance huddled in a mass along a bow in Cave Creek. Down a slope to the right, the river flowed serene and slow, more rocks poking out than he was used to seeing. The thirsty river seemed to drink the snow from the sky, slurping it into the misting water.

He slowed the SUV and pulled through an arched entrance to the development, crawling forward as he rolled down the two front windows to let sound inside. Snow flowed into the cab, and the wind raked across his face like icy claws.

"Looks like I'm a bit more than five minutes out," Nelson said.

Wolf turned off the radio and took the first left. A battered, gunshot street sign read, *Wildlands Way*. The address he was looking for would be here.

He squinted, searching for numbers through the static-like snow. White picket fences lined the fronts of many of the trailers, addresses painted on them vertically, none of them easy to read due to age and wear.

The sound of dogs frantically barking met his ears. He stopped the SUV and listened, trying to get a bearing.

The front door to the nearest trailer opened, and a man dressed in a sweatsuit came outside, holding a handgun pointed at the sky. With his free hand, he waved for Wolf to stay put, his eyes wild and wide.

"Where is it?" Wolf asked, leaning toward the open passenger window.

"Got us a big ol' wild cat right down there. Dogs been chasin' it for the last few minutes." The man pointed down to the end of the road, the aim of the hulking .45 Glock pistol raking across a half dozen trailers. "I just been holed up in here."

"Please go back inside," Wolf said. "And please watch where you're aiming that. And while you're at it, you might as well put it away."

"Hah!" The man smiled as if Wolf had been joking. "I got yer back if you get mauled."

Wolf looked down the road. About a city block's distance away, Wildlands Way ended in a cross street. Two black dogs ran past, cutting right to left, into view and then out. A huge, honey-colored cat appeared a split second later, its lithe body lunging long in chase.

"That's it! There it is!" the man said.

Two gunshots punched the air.

"Get that thing!" A woman emerged from a doorway on Wolf's other side. "It attacked Tabor. I talked to Sally!" She held up a phone in her hand.

"Stay here! Get back inside!" Wolf accelerated as fast as he could to the end of the road.

He reached the cross street and slammed the brakes, skidding sideways to a halt. Thick woods lined this edge of the trailer park, and running straight out of the trees came the two dogs, veering toward him. In a fluid motion, he opened his door, got out, and pulled his gun.

"Get back over here!" a man screamed somewhere behind Wolf.

The dogs changed direction, shooting past Wolf's vehicle, heeding their master's call, clearly spooked.

Wolf kept his eyes, and aim, on the trees.

"It's up in the woods," the man behind Wolf yelled. "I don't think it went far!"

Wolf went to the back bumper of his idling car and saw two men standing nearby. He started at the sight of blood covering one of them.

"Are you Smith?" Wolf asked, referring to the man who had called dispatch to report the mountain lion attack.

"Yeah. I'm Deegan. That's my brother, Tabor."

Deegan was dressed in sweatpants and a Denver Broncos jacket. Tabor wore a similar outfit in another year's Broncos colors. The biggest difference between the two was the blood-soaked rag Tabor held pressed against his disheveled hair.

"Are you okay?" Wolf asked.

"We're fine," Deegan said. "The thing got Tabor, though."

"Yeah. Are you okay?" Wolf repeated, pointing to the guy bleeding out.

"I'm fine. It's not that deep. Just a scratch on the back of my head. More shook than anything."

"I missed it, damn it." Deegan walked toward Wolf, loading a round into a bolt-action rifle.

Tabor, still pressing the rag to his scalp, followed.

Wolf turned toward the trees, still seeing no sign of the mountain lion. He heard the squeals of hinges and glanced back to find frightened faces looking out the open doors and windows of the surrounding trailers.

"We got to get after it," Deegan said.

Wolf put up a hand. "Just a second. Nobody's going anywhere. To attack a human is not normal mountain lion behavior. We'll wait for Animal Control to take care of it. They're trained to hunt such animals, and they're on their way."

Deegan strapped his rifle to his shoulder, eyes scanning the trees. "Must have finally gotten spooked. It's been hanging around for thirty minutes. If it weren't for this damn snow, and the damn dogs, I'd have got it by now."

"If it weren't for them dogs, I'd be dead right now. That thing had a hold of my head in its jaws. Came out of the snow, out of nowhere, and just tackled me." Tabor's eyes were wide with adrenaline. He pulled the washcloth off his head, and Wolf caught a glimpse of the angry cut in his scalp, a streak of red skin and white bone.

"That looks pretty bad," Wolf said. "You'll want to get to a doctor."

"Like I got the money for a doctor bill right now. I'll be fine."

"Sally will sew it," Deegan said.

Wolf eyed them both, seeing they were dead serious. A pang of pity hit him in the gut.

"They're gonna kill it," Deegan said. "Animal Control. They'll kill it, right? That thing was batshit crazy. Kept coming back for more. In fact, I wouldn't be surprised if it was stalking us right now."

Wolf went to the driver's door, reached in through the window, and shut off the engine, then joined the two men in a huddle once again. He surveyed the trees. The wind had died, and the snow was dropping heavier now, straight down in a screen that was getting more difficult to see through.

"That animal was dead the moment it attacked your brother," Wolf said. "Yes, they'll kill it."

They stood in silence for a beat, listening to the chatter of the people emerging from their trailers.

Wolf searched his brain, trying to remember the last time he had heard of a man, a full-grown man, being attacked by a mountain lion as prey, and came up empty. He eyed Tabor again. Blood streaked anew with the snow melting against his skin.

"Another deputy will be here soon. His name's Nelson. He's a certified medic. He can have a look at that."

"Sally's a nurse," Deegan said. "She'll take care of it. She has all the gear necessary."

Wolf nodded. "Okay. Stay here, please."

His boots crunched the snow as he walked toward the woods. A weave of paw prints led off the ninety-degree turn in the road, heading into the trees, all of them being swallowed by the falling snow. Still, Wolf could see three sets going out, two coming back.

He held his Glock at his side, his hand numb from the cold. He wore jeans and a Carhartt jacket, no hat covering his freshly cut hair. He was dressed for a breakfast meeting up in Brushing with the police chief, which was where he had been returning from when the call had come through, not a hunt.

As he walked backward toward his SUV, he decided there was no sense looking for the rabid mountain lion without backup, anyway. And he certainly had no desire to be the one to euthanize it.

A low rumble cut through the silence, and Deputy Nelson's vehicle drove into view out of the whiteout, roof lights flashing.

. . .

An hour later, County Road 81 outside of the trailer park was lined with cars: three animal control vehicles, a herd from the Sluice-Byron County Sheriff's Department, and a single news van.

Wolf stood by his unmarked SUV and watched the news reporter interview Tabor Smith, who now had a red-splotched bandage wrapped around his skull.

The animal control unit, consisting of four men and one woman, readied themselves, tying up bootlaces, attaching snowshoes, zipping up coats, and checking tranquilizer darts and the specially modified rifles the darts loaded into. Officer Ted Brewer stood in front of them, detailing their hunting plan.

Wolf glanced at his watch, which read 11:20 a.m.

Brewer noticed Wolf, finished up his pep talk, and walked over. The man was short and sturdy, looking even more so bundled in his snow gear. He had a neatly trimmed silver beard, and locks of the same color escaped from his winter cap. His prematurely graying hair made him appear much older than his forty years.

"Hope the weather holds out for you," Wolf said.

The snow had calmed, almost to nothing, opening up a view to the south. The sun was peeking through the clouds for the first time that day, but more white-smeared sky encroached from the north.

Brewer eyed the incoming second wave of the storm. "We'll need some luck. And dogs. Which will be here soon."

"Keep me posted, will you?"

Brewer squinted. "Where are you going? Back to your cushy desk job?"

Wolf chuckled. "Thanks for getting here and securing the

situation when you did. It seems like it could have gotten ugly, listening to those two talk over there." He nodded toward the Smith brothers as Deegan gestured wildly for the camera.

A man walked up behind Brewer, part of the animal control team. He was black, taller than Brewer, and wearing a pair of glasses.

"This is Orlando Charleston," Brewer said, introducing him. "Orlando, this is Detective David Wolf."

Orlando took off his glove and shook Wolf's hand with a warm and sweaty grip.

"Orlando is our local expert on mountain lions," Brewer said.

"What do you think?" Wolf asked. "Rabies?"

He shrugged. "I think if it went down like the victim and witnesses say it did, it's likely. We'll know for sure when we find the animal."

A flake fell between them, followed by a few more.

"We'd better get going." Brewer turned around and whistled. "Let's go!"

Wolf watched the group leave up the road. Orlando took the rear, his own rifle slung over his shoulder.

With the temperature dropping and more snow on the way, he didn't envy the hunting party. All the same, he was excited to get into his warm vehicle, crank the butt-heater, and drive down to his cushy desk job.

2

Wolf turned south on Highway 734, winding at speed along the Chautauqua River. Sunrays poked between the low clouds ahead, but the sky in the rearview was almost black, suggesting the Chautauqua Valley, and the Rocky Points Resort, might finally get the snow they had been desperately seeking for most of the winter.

A mile or so from town, he passed a large sign affixed to a barbed-wire fence reading, *There are more Waze than one to protect our citizens. Vote Gregory Waze for Sluice-Byron County Sheriff.*

No more than a few hundred yards beyond stood another sign. This one was staked into the ground off the shoulder and almost completely tipped over backward due to the wind's buffeting.

Wolf pulled over, picked his gloves and hat off the passenger seat, and put them on. He stepped out into the howling wind and went to the side of the road, kneeling to pick up a river stone that fit in the palm of his hand. He walked down the shoulder slope, then up the hill.

The familiar sign read, *Heather Patterson for Sheriff. Honesty. Integrity. Grit.*

It was a good message that accurately described Heather Patterson, but to Wolf it sounded just as sales-y as Waze's tacky play on words.

He straightened the wooden stake and pounded it deeper into the frozen ground, using the rock as a makeshift hammer, then wedged the stone against the back foot of the stake to keep the sign from toppling again.

Standing, he surveyed his work. The plastic board jittered back and forth, looking like it was seconds from taking flight and landing somewhere in New Mexico. But he'd done as much as he could, so he walked to the SUV, keeping his collar pulled up high on his windward side.

He got back into his vehicle, blasting the heater as he drove the rest of the way into town.

He turned off Main and pulled into the parking lot at the rear of the Sluice-Bryon County Administration Building, a four-floor, glass-encased behemoth of a structure that had been built a decade ago. It housed the sheriff's department, the district attorney's office, a basement full of jail cells, and government offices. At one point in time, the whole sheriff's department had fit into a small building a few blocks up the road that was now a coffee shop and clothing mart. He tended to not dwell on such memories, though.

As he parked, his cell phone vibrated in his pocket. He pulled it out and read the word *Headquarters* on the screen.

"Wolf here."

"Hey, it's Wilson," the undersheriff said in a hushed voice. "Where are you?"

"I just parked. I'm on my way inside now. What's up?"

"I'm trying to get hold of the sheriff, but she's not answering her phone. We have a Mr. Roland Thatcher and his daughter here to see her."

"Roland Thatcher?" Wolf asked. "*The* Roland Thatcher?"

"Yes. And now he's specifically asking for you. Where are you?"

"I'm parking. I'm almost there. Are you in your office?"

"We'll be outside your office when you get here." Wilson hung up.

Roland Thatcher. Wolf rolled the name around in his mind as he made his way through the parking lot. He knew it well. Roland Thatcher was a billionaire—a centibillionaire. One of the richest people in the world.

Gary Connell's former compound, a plot of land covering hundreds of acres, replete with a home and outbuildings that outsized many Colorado towns, had gone up for sale two years ago, and Roland had bought it.

Wolf had never encountered Roland in person, only on television or the internet. Rumor said he had staff that did public tasks on his behalf, like shopping for food, art, and clothing.

So why is he here? Wolf wondered, interest piqued.

He entered the building and rode one of the elevators to the third floor. When the doors opened, he saw three people waiting in the hallway outside his closed office door: Undersheriff Wilson; a tall, well-groomed older man; and a younger woman.

"Hello," Wolf said, walking up.

"Oh, hey," Wilson said. "Detective Wolf, this is Mr. Roland Thatcher and his daughter, Gemma."

Roland turned on his heel, standing a couple inches above

Wolf's six foot three. He outstretched a hand and Wolf took it, shaking with a firm grip.

The billionaire had slicked-back platinum hair. He wore a Moncler jacket zipped halfway down to expose a cashmere sweater and a crisp collar beneath it. A pair of gold chains rested at the base of his tanned neck, and as he pulled his hand away, Wolf caught a glimpse of a gleaming, jewel-encrusted watch poking out from under his sleeve.

"Detective David Wolf," the man said with an appraising glare. "I've heard a lot about you."

"All good, I hope."

"Gregory Waze says you're the best they have in this building. To be honest, I didn't much care to speak to the sheriff, anyway. I was hoping we would be able to speak to you."

"Oh," Wolf said, exchanging a quick glance with Wilson. The undersheriff's expression was blank, but Wolf could tell he was boiling inside. "Well, despite what Waze told you, Sheriff Heather Patterson is by far the best we have in the building."

"I didn't mean to offend," Roland said without inflection.

And yet you did, Wolf thought. But he shook his head, waving it off, and turned to the woman next to Roland. "You must be Gemma."

"Yes," she said, smiling wide, showing a row of brilliant white teeth between unnaturally plump lips.

Gemma Thatcher stood much shorter than her father, reaching only his shoulder. She was attractive, in her early thirties, her skin smooth and covered in heavy makeup. She wore a Moncler jacket, too, one that was fur-lined and worth as much as some cars.

He clasped her offered hand and shook. Her thin fingers were covered in gems that scratched his skin.

"Come, let's go into my office. Sorry to keep you waiting." Wolf unlocked the door and strode in, flicking on the light switch. He gestured to a pair of chairs in front of his desk. "You can sit here."

Wolf went to the blinds and twisted them open, letting in the scant natural light. The clouds to the north were closer now, blotting out the sun. He took off his jacket and hung it on the coat tree.

"Can I take your coats?"

"No, thank you," Gemma said.

Roland shook his head. The man sat stiffly on the chair, looking at Wolf's sparsely decorated walls. He eyed the Colorado State Rams clock hanging above the desk. "Did you go to Fort Collins?"

"Yes, I did. Yourself?"

"Yale."

"Right. Can I get you some coffee?"

"No," Roland said.

His daughter looked at him with an admonishing glare, then smiled at Wolf. "No, thank you."

Wilson went to the couch against the wall, giving Wolf a shoot-me look before he glanced at his phone.

Wolf sat on his well-cushioned chair. "So, what can I help you two with?"

"We have a restaurant up north," Roland said. "It's called The Oxbow."

"Yes. I was just near there. Off of County 81."

"That's right. We've had a robbery. An employee, a man named Brock Wendel, stole three paintings from our restaurant Monday night, three nights ago. He fled town with another woman who works there. She helped him steal the paintings."

Wolf raised his eyebrows. "One moment, please."

He picked up his desk phone, pressed a quick-dial button, then waited.

"Detective Rachette."

"Hey. Can you and Yates please come down here? We have a visitor."

"Sure thing."

Wolf hung up. "I'd like my two detectives in on this meeting." He stood and went to the door, propping it open, then returned to his chair.

Wilson, looking at his watch, stood up and cleared his throat. "Well, Mr. Thatcher, Gemma, you're in good hands now. I have a meeting I have to get to. I hope you'll excuse me."

"Yes," Roland said, not even glancing in Wilson's direction. "Thank you for your hospitality, Undersheriff."

"You're welcome."

"Nice to meet you," Gemma said, turning in her chair and waving.

Wilson nodded to Wolf and left out the door.

Wolf opened up a drawer, moved aside a small felt box, and pulled out a notebook and pencil.

Detectives Rachette and Yates came through the door, knocking on the way in.

"These are Detectives Yates and Rachette. Detectives, this is Roland Thatcher and his daughter, Gemma Thatcher."

Recognition flashed across Yates's face, and Rachette's eyes widened a second later, but the two detectives, to Wolf's relief, let the point go unmentioned as they shook hands with the Thatchers. Rachette perched on the armrest of the two-seater couch while Yates took a cushion.

"What's going on?" Yates asked.

"That's what we were just getting at," Wolf said. "If you'd please continue, sir."

Roland's blank stare was flavored with impatience now. "One of our employees, a man named Brock Wendel, stole three paintings from our restaurant. He was helped by another employee. A waitress."

"Can you spell Brock's last name?" Wolf asked, writing in the notebook.

Roland did.

"And the name of the waitress you think helped him?"

"Clara Abraham."

"You said three paintings . . . Monday night . . . which was February . . ."

"Nineteenth," Yates said.

"Okay." Wolf set the pencil down, leaning back in his chair. "Go ahead."

"The three paintings combined at auction would gather at least two million. In the black market, perhaps one million or three-quarters of a million dollars." The billionaire looked out the window and fiddled with one of his stone-studded cuff links. The stones reflected light in brilliant flashes. "It should be mentioned this man, Brock Wendel, is engaged to my daughter."

Gemma's eyes had been firmly focused on her hands in her lap. Now she looked up and nodded at everyone. "That's right."

"What happened?" Wolf asked.

"We have everything on video," Roland said. "It's easiest if we just show you."

Roland reached into the pocket of his slacks and pulled out

a business card. He set it on the desk and pushed it toward Wolf.

"On the back of that card is a web page where my security manager has uploaded the video. Go there."

Wolf turned to his computer and did as he was told. "It says I need a password."

"Freeloader," Roland said.

3

"How's the campaign going?"

"It's going well," Sheriff Heather Patterson said, smiling even though she could feel the man across the table reading the truth on her face.

"What's going on?" Former Sheriff Will MacLean took a bite of his salad, then looked out the window at the end of their booth, twirling his fork, giving her space to answer. A few short years ago, the same man would have looked at her hard, daring her to give him a response too soft. But since the man had walked away unscathed from a bout with pancreatic cancer and a doctor's death sentence, his gray eyes waited with kind patience.

Patterson set her fork on the edge of her plate and dabbed her mouth.

A waitress smiled as she walked past, disappearing into the chaos of Sunny Side Café's kitchen. The day's lunch crowd had the building bursting at the seams, and there was a group of people milling about outside the window, waiting for tables in the rapidly chilling weather.

"It's a bit of stress," she said finally.

"The job?"

"Yeah, I guess. But this campaign thing is a whole other animal."

"Ah. I see." He eyed her. "Have you given any more thought to what we spoke about last time?"

"What part of what we spoke about last time?" They had covered a lot. They always did.

Not long ago, MacLean had been a vindictive asshole, and she'd avoided him like the plague. Now, she was grateful for the mentor role he had filled in her life, seeking him out for advice once every couple of weeks. It had started with a chance meeting in this very restaurant two years ago on an equivalently crowded day, when he'd offered her a seat at his booth. She had taken the spot reluctantly, but looking back, she was glad she had. The man knew firsthand what she was going through on a level nobody else could.

"The part where you decide to pull back," he said, keeping his eyes on his food.

She chewed, stabbing another bite.

"You said sitting your butt in that chair day in and day out was getting to you."

She shrugged. "I've since decided I'm in it for the long haul. This town and county needs somebody trustworthy, not somebody from out of town, backed by who knows what kind of money from who knows where. Besides, I'm not going to play into the stereotype."

"What stereotype?"

She looked at him, shaking her head. "You wouldn't understand."

"Why?"

"Because I'm a woman, and you're a man."

MacLean's eyebrows stitched together. "Pretend this man has a brain and tell me what you're talking about."

She ate in silence for another beat, then set her fork down. "The stereotype that women—especially mothers—can't handle the stress and responsibility of powerful careers. If I pull back, no matter what the reason, people will say I'm proof that women can't be leaders."

MacLean nodded, but he seemed to be considering the point for the first time in his life.

"Do you get what I'm saying?" she asked.

"I think so."

"Did you have to discuss balancing your family and work life once to anybody in your career?"

He blinked, thinking about it. "No. I never did."

"Well, I have to discuss it all the time. Like my family is going to hell because I've decided to take a job at a certain level."

"It's a bad double standard," MacLean said.

She blew air from her nostrils. "Yeah."

They ate quietly until she said, "Besides, something's off with Waze."

MacLean eyed her. "In what way?"

"I mean, I know he did a good job up in Bend. At least, that's what most people are saying. He was supposedly all aboveboard as police chief, but . . . then again, people would say that if they're being coerced into saying so, right?"

MacLean said nothing.

"I don't know," she said. "His official story is he wanted a change of scenery after his wife's death."

MacLean looked at her, as if to ask, *And so what?*

"And I'm not sure I believe it."

Her aunt, the mayor of Rocky Points and Patterson's self-appointed campaign manager, had solicited the services of a private investigator to dig into Waze's prior professional life up in Bend, Oregon. Although she had every right to conduct due diligence on behalf of the people of the county, something about it felt sleazy, like she was becoming one of those politicians she had grown up hating. To her credit, she had refused to allow Margaret to dive into his personal life. That would be crossing the line for Patterson.

She wanted to tell MacLean about the PI, but she got the sense he would disapprove. Every time Patterson said anything remotely negative about Waze, MacLean seemed to shut down with silence. Just like right now.

"What's with you and Waze?" she asked.

MacLean put down his fork and wiped both hands on his napkin. "Listen, Heather. I have to tell you something."

She put up a finger, stopping him, because her cell phone was vibrating in her pocket. She pulled it out and read the number on the screen, which was a generic extension from headquarters. She also saw several missed calls from the same number. Setting down her fork, she pressed the answer button.

"Patterson here."

"Sheriff, this is Tammy."

"Hi, Tammy."

"We have some visitors here for you and Wolf."

"Uh, okay. Can you have Wolf take care of it? Or Wilson? I'm having a lunch meeting right now."

"Wilson took them up. Wolf is with them now, but I thought you'd want to know who it was."

"Okay. Who is it?"

"It's Roland Thatcher."

She froze. "Like, the billionaire?"

Patterson looked at MacLean, who looked back with a raised eyebrow.

"Yes, ma'am."

"What's he doing there?"

"He says they had an incident up at his restaurant. He was being a bit cagey with me. But he asked for you and Wolf specifically. Like I said, Wilson took him up, and Wolf is with him now."

"Why didn't you call me earlier?"

"I did. Twice. This is the third time."

"Right. Okay. Sorry. Yeah. Thank you. I'll be right there." She hung up and put her phone back in her pocket. "I have to leave. Apparently, Roland Thatcher is waiting to talk to me." She scooted to the edge of the booth. "It would have been better if he was there to drop off a fat check for my campaign. But who knows? Maybe that's in the cards. That is, if I don't leave him sitting there waiting for me all day. I have to go. I'm sorry. Can you get the check?"

"Of course. I got the check."

She stood, gathering her jacket off the bench. "What were you going to tell me?"

He shook his head, pursing his lips. "Nothing."

She eyed him as she zipped her coat. Then, reading his somber demeanor, a shock of realization hit her.

She sat back down, reaching over and touching his hand. His skin was rough, wrinkled like worn leather, and spotted by sixty-plus years of high-altitude sun. "What is it? It's not the . . . the cancer again, is it?"

He straightened. "What? No. It's nothing. Get your ass back to the office and talk to that billionaire waiting for you."

She rolled her eyes. "Fine. You'll tell me next time."

"Good luck."

"Thanks," she said, a bit of nervousness creeping into her gut. "I appreciate it."

4

Wolf entered the password into the text field. *Freeloader.*

"Capital *F*?" he asked.

"No," Roland Thatcher said. "He doesn't deserve a capital. All lowercase."

Gemma returned her eyes to her lap, her face reddening. Wolf typed the password again and pressed enter.

"Okay." Wolf turned the monitor toward the Thatchers. Rachette and Yates stood from the couch and walked over to get a closer view.

The monitor displayed a paused video that was segmented into eight equal squares, each a frozen portrait of a different place within or without a building. The footage was crisp and clear, the color flawless.

"This is the security feed for The Oxbow—Monday night at 11:30 p.m. You can see the timestamp in the upper right-hand corner." Roland leaned, pointing a gold-adorned finger at the third square along the top row. "This is Brock right here. You can see he's standing inside of the kitchen area doing absolutely nothing. Which in itself is maybe not too out of the ordinary for this man. But at this moment in time, for closing, when he has plenty of other duties he needs to take care of before he leaves? It makes no sense." Roland sat back. "Go ahead, press play."

Wolf pressed play, and they watched as the time clicked over to 11:31 p.m.

"Keep your eye on the lower left-hand corner screen," Roland said. "That's the front entrance of the restaurant."

The camera was mounted on a high ceiling, looking down. After a few seconds, a dark figure with a hood pulled over their head approached the front entrance.

Brock Wendel remained in the kitchen, the centerpiece of his tiny portion of the screen. Wolf noted he cocked his head slightly, as if he'd heard a sound. But instead of investigating, Brock continued to attend to his phone, tapping and swiping as if mindlessly scrolling social media.

The dark figure walked into the restaurant in a crouch, as if pantomiming trying to be silent. They passed under a second security camera, and then a third, moving between frames as they seemed to travel with purpose toward a destination.

Wearing black shoes with black laces, black sweatpants many sizes too big, and an equally oversized jacket with the hood pulled up, the figure was unrecognizable. The bulky mass of fabric shrouding their body gave little indication of the shape or thickness of the limbs beneath.

Without pause, with certainty of purpose, the figure walked to a painting hung on the wall, reached up, and ran black-gloved hands along the edges. Two pale wrists bared themselves, both thin, and upon further inspection, Wolf discerned the figure's fingers were just as slender.

They pulled the painting off the wall, dropping it in the process.

"No sound," Wolf said.

"No, there is no sound in our security camera system," Roland said.

Onscreen, Brock Wendel glanced over his shoulder, as if he'd heard something again, but he stayed firmly planted in his spot in the kitchen, looking back down at his phone.

"Seems like he heard it," Rachette said.

The thief picked up the painting, then rushed out of the building and out of sight. In the process, they kept their head down, turning away from the cameras.

"They know where the cameras are," Wolf said.

"Not really," Roland said. "The ones in plain sight are decoys. The real cameras are tiny pinpoints hidden in the ceiling beams. She has no clue where they're mounted. She's just gotten lucky so far. We'll get a good look at her in another minute or so."

"No picture of the vehicle?" Rachette asked.

"No," Roland said. "She knew where to park."

The figure—the woman, according to Roland—walked back in empty-handed, straight to a different spot on the wall, and plucked off another painting.

The second painting was smaller, much easier to handle, and she didn't drop it this time. Instead of taking it outside, she leaned it against the wall at her feet. Moving to another wall and another square on the security footage, she picked off a third piece of art. One painting in each hand, she left out the front entrance again.

A short time later, she came back, hurrying through the restaurant to a small office.

"Here we go," Roland said, a rare smile raising his lips. "She thinks the camera is in the opposite corner of the ceiling."

The burglar walked inside, this time turning directly toward a camera lens, giving them a frontal view of a woman's pretty face.

Wolf paused the video, leaning in.

Roland set his phone down on the desk. "Here's a recent picture of Clara Abraham she posted online."

The woman in the Instagram photo matched the one in the security footage. Online, she looked in her late twenties, put-together and confident. In the security footage, she seemed much younger, perhaps because of the fear tightening her expression.

"You can scroll through her profile." Roland tapped the screen, zooming out to display a higher-level view of Clara Abraham's feed.

Rachette and Yates leaned over to take a look.

Wolf nodded, then started the video again.

Clara continued facing the hidden lens while she opened a drawer and slipped out a blue plastic bag with a Rocky Points Bank logo on it. Fumbling slightly, she unzipped the bag, reached in, and removed a wad of money and receipts. She separated the cash from the paper, returned the paper, and set the bag on the desk, leaving the drawer open.

They watched Clara Abraham leave out the front, still ducking like an overacting cat burglar. A few moments later, a pair of headlights swept across the two exterior video feeds, and then the screens went still once again.

Brock Wendel remained in the kitchen, eyes glued to his phone.

"How long does he stand there?" Rachette asked.

"For another ten full minutes," Roland said. "You can use the slider on the bottom to see yourself."

Wolf scrubbed the slider to the right, verifying that Brock did indeed stand there for another ten minutes, until 11:45 p.m., almost to the second, before turning around and pushing through a pair of double doors, entering the dining area of the restaurant.

"As you can see here, he's definitely in on this whole thing," Roland said.

Brock Wendel went into the office and saw the bank bag had been removed and unzipped. He picked it up off the desk, zipped it closed, and put it back in the drawer.

"See? He ignores the bag, which has clearly been rifled of all cash."

Wolf ignored Roland, watching as Brock walked out of the small office. After swiftly turning off all the restaurant lights, he left out the front door, locking it behind him and walking out of the frame, presumably to his car.

Another few moments passed, then Brock Wendel's car came into view, two piercing headlights sliding down the screen before disappearing.

Roland sat back heavily. "That's it."

Wolf clicked the stop button.

"Do employees usually leave the entrance door unlocked when they are closing up? With one person in the back of the house like that?" Yates asked.

"No." Gemma said. "At least, there's no way in hell I would. I'm the managing owner of the restaurant, and I've always taught closers to lock the door as soon as the final customer is out. The last thing you want is some wacko walking in."

Wolf scrubbed the video back to when the burglar had entered the office, revealing her face for the first time.

Roland put his phone on the desk, another picture of Clara Abraham glowing onscreen.

Without a doubt, she was the burglar.

Somebody knocked on Wolf's door.

"Come in."

Patterson poked her head inside.

"Sheriff Patterson," Wolf said, leaning back.

She walked in, smiling. "Hello, Mr. Thatcher. I'm sorry I'm late. I was in a meeting and just heard you were here."

Roland turned his head, stopping just short of looking at her, as if his neck and eyeballs weren't quite capable. "Sheriff Patterson."

She walked to Wolf's desk and stood next to Yates and Rachette.

"This is Mr. Thatcher's daughter, Gemma," Wolf said.

"It's great to meet you, Sheriff." Gemma smiled genuinely, standing up.

"Please, no need to stand." Patterson shook her hand.

Roland shook Patterson's hand like a member of the nobility might greet a peasant.

Patterson looked at the screen, then Wolf, and then back at the Thatchers. "Well, I heard you've had a theft."

"We've been talking about it," Wolf said. "We just finished watching security footage of the incident."

"Okay." She glanced at the screen again. "Well, obviously, I'm not up to speed, so I'll stop wasting your time. Rest assured, Mr. Thatcher, you're in good hands with our detectives. Wolf, could I speak with you for a moment?" She nodded at the Thatchers. "It was great to meet you two."

Wolf followed her out into the hallway.

"I'd like to know everything about this case the moment they leave, please."

"Of course."

"And I don't need to tell you this man is as prominent as it gets in our little sliver of the world."

And firmly in Gregory Waze's corner, he thought, but he said, "Yes, ma'am."

She nodded and walked down the hall.

Wolf went back inside, where Yates and Roland were in the middle of a conversation, and took his seat.

Roland fondled a ring on his hand. "My security team has been trying to track down Brock and Clara. They haven't come in to work since the theft. They haven't been home. They've shut off their phones. There is no trace of them."

"Do you and Brock live together?" Yates asked Gemma.

"He has his own apartment, but he stays with me a few nights per week. When he didn't show up Monday night, I assumed he was staying at his own place." She shrugged. "I knew something was wrong when I came into work the next day and he wasn't there, either."

"Were you the one who noticed the paintings and money were gone?" Wolf asked.

"Yes. Right away, I saw the blank spots on the walls. I didn't notice the money until later that night."

"So, you saw the paintings were gone, and then what?"

"Well, I called Brock first. But he wouldn't answer. I hadn't been there for a couple days—I took Sunday and Monday off—but I figured it must have happened the night before, or else I would have heard about it from Brock already."

"So he didn't answer," Wolf said. "And then what?"

"I checked the schedule for who was the closing server that night. It was Faith. She's pretty on top of things for me at the restaurant. I called her, and she told me Brock cut her early, around ten, because it was slow. He said he could close by himself."

Wolf wrote down the name. "Did you call anyone else?"

"Clara, since she was working that night, too. But she didn't answer." She gestured to Roland. "And then I called my dad."

Wolf looked at Roland.

"My security manager came to the scene and checked the footage," Roland said. "You know the rest."

Wolf nodded. "Where does Clara live?"

"In a condo north of town," Roland said.

"Did you go there?"

"Yes. She didn't answer."

"Did you go inside?"

Roland said nothing.

"Did you go to Brock's place?"

"Yes."

"Did you go inside there?"

Roland nodded this time.

"I have a key to his place," Gemma said. "We used it."

"Who went in?" Wolf asked.

Roland straightened his sleeves. "My security manager and I did."

"Who's this security manager?" Wolf asked. "His name?"

"Xavier Jorel."

"What did you find?"

"Nothing out of the ordinary. It looks like he just up and left."

"What did you touch?"

"Nothing," Roland said without hesitation.

"You said you've tried tracking them?"

"Yes, but we can't see where their phones were before they shut them off. Not without a warrant for the cellular phone company data."

"Aha," Wolf said. "And that's where we come in."

"That's where you come in."

Wolf swiveled his chair toward the window. Flakes swept up against the glass.

Something felt off about this whole thing. Maybe somebody was playing a game. Maybe it was this billionaire across the desk from him, scenting up his office with his exotic cologne. Maybe not.

He faced Roland and Gemma again. "We'll need to come to the restaurant. We need to know everything we can about those paintings, and we'll need to speak to your employees."

"Of course," Roland said.

"When?" Gemma asked.

They all looked up at the clock on the wall. It read 12:50 p.m.

"When do you open today?"

"I'm supposed to be there at two to oversee prep work," Gemma said. "But our first seating is at five, if that's what you mean."

"How many employees will be there?"

"It's Thursday, our third-busiest night behind Friday and Saturday, so we'll have . . . let's see . . ." She calculated on her fingers. "Eighteen? Maybe I'm forgetting somebody. I'd say twenty to be safe."

"Does everyone come at two for prep work?"

"Some will be there at two, others at three. Everyone will be there at least an hour before the first table is seated."

Wolf looked at Yates and Rachette, then Roland.

The billionaire stared back, watching him think.

He shifted on the chair. His backside was still sore from driving all morning.

"You've seen the forecast for tonight, right?" Wolf asked.

"Yes," Gemma said. "We'll still open, though. If it's getting too bad, we'll close up after first seating. They've been getting the forecasts wrong this year. We don't want to shut down unless we absolutely have to."

"It would be best to get an immediate start on this," Wolf said.

Roland nodded. "Agreed."

Gemma nodded as well. "Okay."

"We'll let you two go on your way, and we'll follow up shortly."

"And the cell phone records?" Roland asked.

"One thing at a time," Wolf said, getting to his feet.

The Thatchers stood, and Wolf shook their hands and led them to the door.

"I won't be there," Roland said. "But I'll send Jorel. If you need any help, any answers, Jorel is your man."

Wolf nodded. "Thanks."

He walked them to the elevator bank, leaving them to ride downstairs by themselves.

5

"Roland Thatcher," Yates said, now sitting in Wolf's chair, manning the computer. It had been over a year since they had established Yates was the best pilot of modern technology between the three of them, so Wolf made no protest.

Through the window, he watched Roland and Gemma leave out the front of the building three stories below. Roland received a kiss on the cheek from his daughter. He didn't return the favor, just ducked into the back seat of a black Range Rover with blacked-out windows. The vehicle zipped away, leaving Gemma standing by herself.

"Sixty-one years old. Born in South Africa to a wealthy mining magnate named Octavius Thatcher. Moved to Connecticut when he was a child, where he was raised. Went to Yale." Yates ran his finger down the screen. "Has honorary degrees from Princeton, Harvard, and Oxford."

Gemma ducked her face into her jacket as she vanished around the building.

"That's good," Rachette said. "If the whole billionaire thing doesn't work out for him, he can fall back on his degrees."

Yates continued, "He owns a mineral extraction company in South Africa; a copper mine in North Africa; three different media companies; a publishing company; oil and gas reserves in North Africa, South Dakota, and Texas; and—"

"He's rich," Wolf said.

Yates sat back. "Ungodly rich."

"What the hell is he doing owning a restaurant?" Rachette asked. "Seems like a chump-change thing to do compared to the rest of that dossier."

"He seems hands-off with it," Yates said, shrugging. "Maybe it's Gemma's thing."

"Let's look at Clara's and Brock's social media," Wolf said.

Yates sat forward and pecked the keys, pulling up their Instagram accounts on separate tabs. He clicked over to Brock's account first, scrolling through the feed.

Rachette whistled softly. "Looks like this guy is living the life."

The man was prolific with his social media presence. There were several hundred photos of him, only a small percentage with Gemma Thatcher: Brock sitting inside a Ferrari Formula One race car; Brock standing outside a Ferrari Formula One race car; Brock standing in the pit garage with his arm around a driver; Brock lying on a beach, scantily clad, body bronzed, designer sunglasses and a Rolex Submariner on his wrist.

"Nice boat," Rachette said as Yates scrolled to the next photo.

It showed Brock standing on a yacht with his arms out, looking at the sky. Behind him, the bleached cliffs and azure waters of a Mediterranean coast were on display. Next to him,

Gemma Thatcher stood in a bikini, smiling, although her smile seemed strained compared to Brock's over-the-top excitement for the high life.

"See, man, look at that," Rachette said. "She's got a nice body, eh, Yates?"

Yates frowned at him.

"What? She's available now, brother."

"What's the most recent post from Brock?" Wolf asked.

They waited while Yates scrolled back up. "Looks like this guy hasn't posted anything in nine days. The last post was a photo of a steak and him saying, 'Cooked to perfection here up at The Oxbow.'"

"Okay. Let me see the other recent ones." Wolf leaned closer. They were mostly selfies in various scenarios of life.

"Not much mention of his fiancée," Yates said.

"What about Clara?" Wolf asked.

Yates clicked over to the next tab, pulling up Clara Abraham's account.

Clara's photos showed off her long blond hair, bright blue eyes, and wide smile that said she either had braces growing up or perfect genes.

"She's a looker," Rachette said.

Yates scrolled through the photos, pausing at one with Clara and Gemma Thatcher. He continued on, revealing more of them together. Clara had been on the same boat out in the Mediterranean that day.

"Gemma and Clara looked like they were pretty good friends," Rachette said. "She didn't mention that."

"Probably because Clara was screwing her fiancé, and she didn't want to mention it?" Yates said.

"Let's look at The Oxbow's website," Wolf said.

Yates returned to Brock's profile and clicked on the link in his bio. The restaurant's home page replaced the Instagram feed onscreen, rotating between photos of mouthwatering steaks and vegetables. There were also photos of the venue, taken during summer, showcasing its view of the Chautauqua River and the millions of acres of untouched wilderness beyond. "I say we have a meal on the department when we're up there."

A tagline read, *When You Expect the Best, You Get the Best*.

"There are no prices," Rachette said. "That means expensive as shit. You ever been here?"

"I went there with Piper once," Wolf said, plucking his jacket off the hook and putting it on. "It was not cheap."

"Yeah, me too. I think it was over two hundred dollars for a couple of hamburgers and a bottle of wine for me and Charlotte."

"You guys got hamburgers at this place?" Yates asked.

"Yeah. Why?"

Yates shook his head.

"Let's go," Wolf said.

"I still haven't eaten lunch," Rachette said, standing up. "We're definitely stopping on the way up."

Wolf eyed his watch, calculating the afternoon. It would take a half hour each way, and then the time spent there.

"You have somewhere to be?" Rachette asked. "Yates and I could go without you. You've already been up north all morning."

"I'll come with you two. I think it's important to Patterson we get this thing right. Not that I don't trust you. Just . . . you know, all hands on deck."

"The dude's worth a billion dollars," Yates said, "and nothing wins elections like money."

Wolf didn't mention that Roland was already friends with Waze, or that no amount of sucking up was going to help Patterson with this man. Wolf had seen the way he'd snubbed her when she had walked in a few minutes ago. They all had.

"I've never seen Patterson's butt-kissing demeanor," Rachette said. "I didn't like it. It was like something was wrong in the universe."

Wolf flicked off his office light, flushing his detectives out.

6

"A mountain lion bit his head?"

"Yeah," Wolf said. "You can see online. Channel two was up there interviewing him."

Wolf leaned forward on the seat as he passed the sign for County Road 81. Snowflakes were falling out of the sky in full force now, making the view beyond his windshield look like that of a starship traveling warp speed and getting faster.

"Jeez." Piper's voice came out of the SUV's speakers, surrounding him. A man's voice said something in the background, and Piper relayed a clipped version of the mountain lion story Wolf had just told. "Well, I'm just glad you're all right. Did they find the lion?"

"I don't know yet. I haven't talked to them again."

"I hear the weather is terrible. Perfect timing for my flight in."

"I don't think it's going to be as bad in Denver."

"How about there? What are they saying?"

"They say up to a foot." Wolf pulled off on County Road 81,

and the cab rumbled as the wheels landed on dirt road. "Maybe more."

"Shoot. Assuming I can make it back into town, are we still on for tomorrow night?" she asked. "I've missed you."

"I've missed you, too. Of course we are."

Wolf turned into the parking lot and parked next to Rachette's vehicle, where his two detectives stood out in the snow with their hands in their pockets.

"Listen. I have to go. I'll talk to you tomorrow. Can't wait to see you."

"Bye. I love you," she said.

"I love you, too."

Wolf hung up and got out, stretching his arms overhead, kicking his feet to get the blood flowing in his legs again.

Snow fell in a silent, windless sheet, obscuring the river next to the parking lot of The Oxbow, but he could hear it burbling. The restaurant loomed tall and dark within the whiteout, though a glow emitted from its expansive windows. It was a sprawling one-story structure, long and skinny, running along the bluff overlooking the river.

"It's going to be a slow drive back," Rachette said.

"Agreed," Wolf said. "Let's get this over with."

Yates led the way across the parking lot. As they grew closer, the details of the restaurant emerged from the snow. Stone walls, likely sourced from local quarries, matched the surrounding landscape, and elegant steel frames supported impressive floor-to-ceiling windows. A grand overhang made of logs sheltered the entrance, a hulking steel door with a wooden handle.

The door opened with minimal effort as Wolf pulled. He stood aside to let his detectives in first, looking at the bulky security camera mounted in the upper corner of the overhang, a decoy as Roland had explained. He failed to see where the real thing was mounted.

Giving up his search, Wolf followed Yates and Rachette inside, entering a large reception area. There was a massive stone fireplace yawning to the left, a stone bench running along its hearth, presumably for people waiting to be seated.

A host stand built from more logs stood to the side, and beyond it, the restaurant opened into its full glory. Brightly lit steel chandeliers hung off chains from a vaulted, beamed ceiling, illuminating dozens of tables tastefully spaced apart, all of them backdropped by a row of windows that looked like blank canvasses at the moment. Any other day, the view of the river, and the mountains beyond, would have been spectacular.

Between the windows were stone walls, and on them hung paintings, large and hyper-realistic, portraying western mountain landscapes enveloped in thunderstorms or aglow in late-day sun. The subjects included cowboys and Native Americans, some depicted in action, others in stoic portraits.

Wolf had known a great artist before, had lived with her and almost married her. He had seen the talent come out of Lauren's hands and onto the canvas, but that had never lessened the impact of a great painting on his soul.

This place was plastered in art that evoked emotions, scents, and nostalgia, but three spaces were conspicuously vacant, empty hooks on the stone all that remained.

"Whoa," Yates said. "I've never been in here."

"Smells good," Rachette said.

The scent of slow-cooking meat and spices filled the air.

Employees, most of them middle-aged or younger, all of them wearing white button-up shirts and black slacks, darted back and forth, setting silverware on tables or passing in and out of the flip doors leading to the kitchen.

Gemma was nowhere to be seen, and the workers shied away from addressing the three cops in the room.

Rachette puffed out his chest, hooking his thumbs on his belt. With each slight, he looked readier to storm into the depths of the restaurant to find their contact himself.

Before he could, though, the kitchen doors opened again, and Gemma emerged, swerving through the tables to greet them. She, too, wore a white button-down shirt and black slacks, looking much different in her work clothing than in Wolf's office earlier. She had a no-nonsense expression on her face and exuded managerial confidence. She seemed to be in her element.

"Detectives, thank you for coming. How was the drive?"

"Not too bad," Wolf said. "But it's getting worse."

She eyed the windows, shaking her head. "I'm still not sure if we'll open or not. We'll give it another hour or so, then I'll have to make a call."

A squat, muscular man with dark hair and tan skin walked out of the kitchen. He spotted them and made his way over, moving smooth and swift like a predator, keeping keen, intelligent eyes locked on them. He wore blue jeans and a turquoise flannel with the sleeves rolled up, exposing hairy, tattooed forearms and a wrist adorned with an expensive watch.

"This is Xavier Jorel," she said. "My father's security manager."

Jorel held out his hand to Wolf. One of the tattoos on his forearm was the Special Forces crest.

"Were you in Group?" Wolf asked.

"Yeah. Tenth. You serve?"

"Seventy-fifth."

Jorel held his gaze for a moment, and then, butt-sniffing over, moved on to Yates and Rachette, shaking their hands.

"Can I get you guys some coffee?" Gemma asked.

"No, thanks." Wolf eyed the employees milling about, then gestured to the empty spots on the walls. "Why don't you start by telling us about the missing paintings?"

"Yeah, sure." She led the group to a painting that remained. "This portion of the restaurant displays my father's collection of Charles Marion Russell's work."

The large painting depicted a group of cowboys on a sage-covered hillside, snow-veined mountains in the background. They were roping a bear, the huge animal thrashing wildly against the feeble-looking constraints.

"I don't think those cowboys made it out of that scenario alive," Rachette said.

Gemma smiled. "This was painted in 1916."

"How much is this thing worth?" Rachette asked.

"Russell's 1918 painting, called *Piegans*, sold for 5.6 million dollars at a 2005 auction, but these would realistically fetch anywhere from five hundred to eight hundred thousand."

Rachette whistled, looking at another painting. This one depicted a cowboy shootout along the dusty road of an Old West town.

Wolf looked at Jorel. "No alarm system for the paintings?"

Jorel shook his head. "Unfortunately, no. Plenty of alarm systems for the building, though. And the structure is a bomb shelter as far as impermeability. All that doesn't matter if you leave the door wide open and unattended, though."

Wolf looked around at the array of paintings, counting over a dozen of them still hanging on the walls. It was a wonder that a robbery hadn't taken place earlier, perhaps with violence.

"It's going to be difficult to get rid of the paintings without us knowing about it," Jorel said. "We have our finger firmly planted on the pulse of the art world."

"And you haven't heard anything yet," Wolf said.

"No."

"And there's the black market. How about your finger on that pulse?"

Jorel said nothing.

Wolf turned to Gemma. "How many employees work here?"

"Forty-one," she said. "At least, I think I have my math right there."

"Forty-two," Jorel said.

"Oh. Forty-two, I guess it is. My mistake."

"How about people working that night of the robbery? Are there any of them here now?"

She looked over at the nearest man walking past. "Tyson."

The man stopped. He was black, thin, and in his early twenties, with short hair sculpted like a helmet.

"This is Tyson Lennox," Gemma said. "He was here Monday night. Tyson, these are Detectives Wolf, Rachette, and Yates."

Tyson folded his arms, nodding a greeting.

"Tyson, these detectives are looking into the paintings and money that were stolen."

"Money?" Tyson asked. "I never heard about money."

"Yes, there was some money stolen that night, too."

"Do you mind chatting with us for a few minutes?" Wolf asked.

Tyson turned to Gemma. "I was just setting section nine."

"Don't worry about that." Gemma put a hand on his shoulder. "I'll do that for you."

"Yeah. Okay." Tyson nodded.

"Why don't you guys go over here?" she said, leading the way to a large, round table at the end of the restaurant. "Is this good for you?"

"This is perfect," Wolf said. "Thank you."

"Do you need me still? Or . . . ?"

"We'll let you get back to work."

They sat around the table, detectives on one side, Tyson on the other, Jorel standing a short distance away.

"What do you do here, Tyson?" Wolf asked.

"Just wait tables."

"And you were here Monday night?"

"Yes."

"What can you tell me about Brock Wendel?"

Tyson shrugged, smiled, and then sighed, clearly a parade of emotions going on in his head. "I don't know."

"Is he your boss?" Wolf asked.

"He bosses people around."

"You don't get along with Brock?" Yates asked.

Tyson glanced over his shoulder at the restaurant. On the other side of the dining room, Gemma disappeared into the kitchen. Tyson looked at Jorel.

Jorel nodded. "Speak freely."

Tyson scoffed, his lips curling into a short-lived smile. "Okay, fine. He's our boss in title, but he's not our *boss*. He's the guy we have to clean up after when he screws a situation. The guy's a piece of shit. A freeloader using Gemma for her money. Everybody knows it. And . . ."

"And what?" Wolf asked.

Tyson leaned forward. "I live down in Rocky Points, and I've seen him around town. You know, with other women."

"And have you told Gemma about this?" Wolf said, eyeing Jorel.

The security manager's face remained impassive.

Tyson lowered his voice. "No, I haven't told her about it. I mean, I guess I haven't actually seen Brock do anything. I've never followed him for proof or nothin'. But he's all over other women. I've seen him leave at suspiciously close times as other girls from the bar. Like, after he was talking to them. Incognito, you know?"

"What about girls here?" Rachette asked.

"Yeah. Clara, for one."

"There are others?" Wolf asked.

"Maybe. Like I said, I don't have proof. He's just sketchy, constantly looking at other women. Flirting when Gemma's not around."

"Are you friends with Clara Abraham?" Yates asked.

"She's pretty cool, I guess."

"You don't hang out with her outside of work?" Wolf asked.

"No."

"Did you hear anything strange over the last couple weeks? Any rumors that now you're looking back on and thinking might explain what happened with the paintings and her and Brock? Any mention of Brock or Clara going somewhere specific? Of them leaving together?"

Tyson shook his head, thinking. "No. Nothing."

"What time did you go home on Monday night?" Rachette asked.

"Let's see, it must have been right around nine. I was cut early."

"Who cut you?"

"Faith," he said, thumbing over his shoulder. "She's the one rolling silverware in the booth."

"And how about Clara?" Wolf asked. "When did she leave?"

"Just before me. We were both cut at the same time."

"And when you left, were there still patrons here? Were there still people eating?"

"Only a couple. A few at the bar. They seemed to be about to leave."

"How many other employees were here when you left?"

"Well, let's see, there was Brock, Faith . . ." He scratched his head, staring in thought. "Sandy. She was here, too. And some back-of-the-house guys."

"Who's Sandy?"

"She's the bartender. She's behind the bar now."

Wolf looked at the long rectangular bar that was the centerpiece of the far side of the restaurant and saw a woman ducking in and out of sight beneath the counter.

"Oh yeah, also Kylie. She was there. She's not here tonight, though."

"Kylie," Wolf said slowly, looking at Rachette.

Rachette nodded and flipped a page of his notebook, revealing his extensive writing.

"When somebody closes, how many people are here?"

"Front of the house? Or back of the house?"

"Both."

"Back of the house usually leaves before the final closers of the front. Basically, the servers keep getting cut until it's the closing server and the manager. Then the closing server leaves, and the manager locks up and leaves."

They stopped talking, turning their attention to a woman who had entered the restaurant. She was in her mid-thirties, wearing a snow-covered winter hat and holding hands with a little girl next to her. She made some kind of announcement to the employees, who then stopped what they were doing and asked questions with piqued interest.

"What's this?" Rachette asked, leaning to see.

Gemma walked to the newcomer, spoke, then walked toward them. "Detectives," she said. "I've just gotten word they're closing the highway north of here, between Cave Creek and Vail. People are calling in, canceling their reservations. I'm going to shut down and let my employees go home before they close the highway back to Rocky Points."

She looked at Tyson.

"You're free to go," Wolf said to the server. "If you wouldn't mind, though, we may have some more questions for you in the future."

"Yeah, sure," Tyson said, standing up and walking away.

"I'm sorry," Gemma said. "I have to get back and shut everything down."

"Yeah, go," Wolf said.

Gemma hurried away, joining the buzz of new activity overtaking the restaurant.

Still seated, Wolf ignored the commotion and looked at Jorel.

The man stared back.

"Sounds like Brock Wendel, Gemma's fiancé, future family member of Roland Thatcher, was screwing around."

Jorel smiled faintly. "Sounds like you've hit the nail on the head, Detective."

"And you're telling me that you weren't looking into this before?"

Jorel said nothing.

"Or maybe Roland Thatcher lucked his way into his money. Maybe he's a moron and doesn't have a clue what's going on in his organizations, or in the personal life of his daughter."

Jorel's smile faded. At that moment, Wolf could see the man was dangerous.

Something about Roland Thatcher and Xavier Jorel didn't feel right, and Wolf still suspected they were getting played somehow. Aside from access to the cell phone records for Brock Wendel and Clara Abraham, Wolf was certain these two men had no use for him and his team.

"I'd better see if they need help," Jorel said, leaving.

Wolf, Yates, and Rachette stood up, making their way back into the main dining area, where the crowd of employees was preparing to leave.

The bartender named Sandy came out from her zone, zipping her coat to her chin. She spoke to Gemma and left out the front door, followed by another couple employees. Wolf and his detectives hung back, watching.

"Yay! Snow day!" The little girl who had come in earlier was seated at a table, vigorously scribbling a crayon across a coloring book. She was four, maybe five years old. She had ditched her winter hat, which was on the floor at her feet, unleashing long, frizzy blond hair pulled into pigtails. The woman who had come in with her was gone.

"This is Faith's daughter," Gemma said, watching Wolf's

eyes. "That was her sister dropping her off. She was the one who let us know the highway was closed up north."

"Hey, kid," Rachette said, picking the hat off the floor and slapping it on the table. "You like snow?"

The girl looked up at Rachette and smiled, showing she had a missing upper tooth. "Yeah!"

"What's your name?"

"Haley!"

"Whoa, you got one volume, huh?"

Haley concentrated back on her coloring.

"I'll be right back," Gemma said.

"Wow, a red tree." Rachette pointed. "That's interesting. You must like fall, huh?"

Haley kept her head down, continuing to color the canopy of a tree deep crimson.

More employees trained out of the kitchen, dressed in coats or carrying warm clothing to put on. One woman and one man wore white chef uniforms. The rest looked like servers. A woman split from the group and came over, nodding to the detectives as she went to Haley.

"Honey, you're making a mess. There're crayons all over the floor."

"You're Faith, correct?" Rachette asked. "Cute girl you got there."

"That's right. Faith Orton. And thanks."

Yates cut in. "We're from the sheriff's department. I'm Detective Yates. These are Detectives Wolf and Rachette."

"Hi." She kneeled, zipping up the tiny pink jacket on her daughter.

Jorel appeared a few tables away, silently observing them.

"We hear you were also closing Monday night. Is that right?" Wolf asked.

"Yeah, that's right." She stood and faced them.

"And when were you cut?"

"I was last cut. Probably about ten—"

"It's getting really bad out there," Gemma said, returning. She ushered them toward the door. "I think we should go sooner than later. I have to finish closing, but I'll be out soon."

Wolf nodded and followed the staff through the front door. He stood under the shelter of the entryway with Rachette and Yates, watching the exodus of cars.

A few minutes later, Gemma came out, pushed the door closed, and locked it by tapping into a keypad. A mechanism whirred inside the door. She gave it a test pull, then turned to face them.

"I'm sorry about this," she said. "This is just abysmal weather."

"It's not your fault," Yates said.

"Right," she chuckled. "Is there anything else I can help you guys with in the meantime?"

"It might be good for us to get an employee roster," Wolf said.

"Of course." She looked at the locked door. "I could email it to you. It would be easier than me going back inside and printing one out."

"Perfect," Wolf said.

"Here you go." Yates handed over a contact card. "You can send it to that email."

"Okay."

"And," Wolf said, "assuming we're not all socked in with

snow, maybe you could let us into Brock's place tomorrow morning."

"Of course. When?"

"Eleven a.m.?"

"Sure. I'll send you the roster this evening, and I'll put his address on there for you."

"Do you have a card?" Yates asked. "So we can check on you in the morning. You know, with the weather and all."

"Uh, no . . . but here's my number." She said it, and Yates added her as a contact in his phone.

"See you tomorrow," Wolf said, leading his detectives out into the snow.

Rachette glanced over his shoulder. "Damn, dog. You move quickly."

Yates frowned. "What?"

"Getting digits already? I like the way you roll."

"I'm just trying to do my job. You know, think ahead. You should give it a try sometime. Hope you didn't lock the keys in your car again."

"That was one time. Never again." Rachette searched his pocket theatrically, pulling out his keys. "Yep. Got 'em."

"Back to the station?" Yates asked.

"Just get yourselves home," Wolf said, veering to his own vehicle. "Let's let this weather pass, and I'll see you guys at the station tomorrow morning."

"You got it."

It took Wolf a few minutes, and a few degrees of body temperature, to clear off the SUV's windows. As he opened his door, he looked past the last few employees leaving the lot and saw a line of vehicles approaching, traveling down County

Road 81. Squinting, he saw they were the emergency vehicles from this morning, including the three animal control trucks.

Wolf climbed into the cab, shut his door, and dialed the cell phone number of Officer Brewer. The man answered after two rings.

"Is that you right now, driving past on 81, right toward the highway?" Wolf asked.

"Uh . . . yeah. Where are you?"

"I'm parked right here in this restaurant parking lot. How did the hunt go?"

"I see you. I'll pull in."

The man hung up before Wolf could react, and he saw one vehicle peel off the train and come into the lot.

Wolf stepped out and met Brewer's truck, stopping at the man's passenger window.

Brewer rolled down the window, looking tired with his disheveled hair and red cheeks. Heat billowed out of the cab, defrosting Wolf's face.

"You look cold," Wolf said.

"Could say the same for you."

"How did it go?"

Brewer shook his head. "We couldn't find it in time. The snow came in too hard. We'll try again another day."

"The dogs couldn't find anything?"

"They struggled. We have a call in for a specialist canine that tracks lions. The nearest one is in Boulder. And funnily enough, that one's busy right now. They've got a pair of pumas attacking dogs every other day near Nederland."

Wolf nodded, slapping the roof of the truck. "Stay safe. I'll be on your six on the way down."

"You too." Brewer rolled up his window, backed out, and drove away.

Wolf followed suit, thinking he was the last to leave the lot until he saw Jorel on the other end, a dark silhouette behind the windshield of a black Range Rover. He considered stopping to talk, but he didn't have the patience right now to crack open the man's motivations.

Instead, he joined the train of vehicles crawling onto Highway 734 and sat back, ready for a long, long ride.

7

"We have to get some dirt on him."

"No."

"Did you just see these numbers?" Margaret tapped the weekly polls report sitting on Patterson's desk. "He's pulling ahead of you!"

"So what? We'll appeal to the masses with positivity."

"Ha! Positivity. What is this, *Sesame Street*?"

Ignoring her aunt, she clicked her computer mouse, opening her inbox to view the seventy-five new emails that had streamed in over the morning. Damn it, it would be more long hours in her chair. She needed to delegate some of this to Charlotte.

Margaret scraped the papers off the desk and put them in her bag. "Do you even want to be sheriff? Because it doesn't seem like you do."

Patterson took her hand off the mouse and looked at her aunt. Margaret's head was tilted.

"What I want is to be able to look at myself in the mirror at the end of this campaign. Don't you?"

"If he's guilty of being an asshole, we owe it to the people of this county to know about it. We're sitting in the dark here because you won't give me the go-ahead to look. If he's a jerk? Yeah. I'm going to sleep just fine."

"I'm not going to start a smear campaign. And that's the last time I want to talk about it."

Her aunt huffed, looking at her with a familiar disapproving glare.

"I didn't like that look coming from my mother growing up, and I don't like it from her sister now, either."

Margaret stood, shrugging on her jacket. "I'll set up some more interviews. I'll come up with some fuzzy, feel-good ways you can appeal to the masses. But I'm not liking the trajectory this is going. None of us are." She walked to the door.

There it was again: the anvil of expectations pressing down on her back.

"Well, I'm sorry to disappoint you. And you can tell all those other disappointed assholes I'm sorry as well."

Slowing to a stop, Margaret shot her another look.

Patterson's face warmed. She felt instant regret for using the word, insulting all the people who had sacrificed so much for her over the last year, who had donated hundreds of hours of their lives to her campaign for sheriff. All those men and women, young and old, were counting on her. Especially all the women.

"I'm sorry," she said. "I didn't mean that. You know I didn't."

Margaret nodded.

"But what would those . . . people, those volunteers, those men and women, think about *me* turning into an asshole? I'm not going to make them join the ranks of a sleazeball politician. I won't ask that of them."

"We'll talk later, Heather." Margaret left, shutting the door behind her.

Patterson looked out the window, watching the snowflakes churning on the other side of the glass, their chaos mounting with each passing moment.

What was she going to do to turn this thing around?

There was a knock on her door.

"Yeah?"

Wilson poked his head in. "How did it go?"

"Hey, come in."

Wilson walked over to her desk. His blond walrus mustache hung limp, the way it always did when his jaw was set in a serious expression.

"She wants to find dirt on Waze," she said.

"Okay. You want me to start digging up in Oregon?"

"No, I don't. I want to win the campaign cleanly. Without flinging poo at one another."

Wilson raised an eyebrow.

She changed the subject. "So, I never got to ask you. How did it go earlier with Roland Thatcher?"

Wilson shrugged, and his eyes darted away, like he was trying to decide how to tell her something delicate.

"What?"

"Nothing."

"Was he nice?"

"He was . . . strange. Like you might expect a billionaire to act. Like everyone on the planet was his employee."

She chuckled. "I'd like to figure out a way to get him in the same room."

Wilson said nothing.

"Do you know who he's going for in the election? Did he mention that?"

There it was again: Wilson's eyes darting back and forth.

"Just spit it out," Patterson said.

"He is friends with Waze."

"How do you know?"

"He mentioned that Waze recommended Wolf." Wilson looked down.

"Waze recommended Wolf? To Roland Thatcher."

Wilson nodded.

"Why? Wolf told me he hasn't spoken to Waze for more than a sentence or two since he's been in town."

Wilson shrugged. He scratched his closely shorn head.

"And?" Patterson asked.

"And nothing . . ."

"You think I can't read that you're holding back? Just tell me."

"Roland said something to the effect that he was glad you weren't here. That he wanted to talk to Wolf, anyway, because Waze said Wolf was a good detective. There. That's everything."

She stood up, facing the window, her insides dropping. "Okay. Thank you for telling me that."

"Yeah. And just so you know, Wolf told him you were the best we had in this building. He put him in his place."

Silence filled the room. She turned back toward Wilson.

"I don't think it's a bad idea to look into Waze," he said. "If he's buddy-buddy with billionaires, then he's probably taking money from them. If you find something bad, you don't have to be the one to fling the poo."

"He hasn't filed any campaign contributions," Patterson said. "He maintains he's running with the money he inherited from his wife."

"He's gotta be hiding something."

She sat down, breathing out heavily. "Thanks, Wilson."

"For what?"

She smiled wanly. "For making my day better."

"I shouldn't have told you any of that," he said. "I'm sorry, Patty."

Yeah. You're right, she thought. But she said, "No. I want you to tell me these things. Thanks for keeping it real."

He turned and went to the door. "Let me know if you need anything."

"How about a miracle?" she said, but the door had already closed behind him.

8

Wolf squinted behind his sunglasses, his retinas burning from the sun reflecting off the freshly plowed snow in the parking lot of Brock Wendel's apartment complex.

The forest-green building had been built two or three decades ago. Located on Edelweiss Road, just on the western edge of town and on a hill, the parking lot afforded a good view of Rocky Points and the Chautauqua Valley sprawling out in its snow-blanketed splendor to the north.

"Here she is," Rachette said.

Wolf shielded his eyes from the sun with a hand, watching a silver Range Rover turn into the parking lot, breaking through a small barrier of snow the plows had left near the entrance. It drove toward them and parked, wheels squealing in the packed powder as they came to a stop.

Furry brown boots emerged from the vehicle first, followed by the rest of Gemma Thatcher. She was decked out in an outfit that was all fur and elegance, sparkling jewelry dangling off any piece of exposed skin.

"Hello, detectives." She gestured to the building. "Here it is. Number 319. Top floor."

They walked across the lot, making small talk about the storm and its abrupt passing the night before. As it was, the low-pressure system that had dipped in from the north had dropped six inches of powder onto the valley, falling short of the forecasted foot.

The air was still, and the faint sound of traffic floated up from the town. Snow dropped from the pine trees lining the lot.

They climbed an external stairwell in silence to the third floor, then walked down an open-air hallway, Gemma leading the way as she pulled out a set of keys. She went to the door labeled 319 and stuck the key in.

"I don't know. Should I knock?" she asked.

"Would you usually knock if you came over?" Rachette asked.

She shrugged. "He usually came over to my place."

Yates walked up, raising a fist, and knocked. When nothing happened, he stepped aside.

She twisted the key and opened the door.

The door squealed on its hinges as it pushed inward, and she reached inside and flicked on the light switch. Not that they needed it. The window blinds were open, letting in plenty of natural light.

To the right was a kitchen with a small circular table against a window. From three stories up, the Chautauqua Valley was even more of a spectacle.

"Quite the view," Rachette said.

"Yes," she said.

Her boots squeaked on the linoleum floor of the kitchen as she flipped on another set of lights.

The place was warm, so Wolf shut the door, keeping the cold out.

The left side opened to a family room, where a worn couch sat with a folded blanket. Next to it was a newer, much more expensive BarcaLounger and an end table with an empty beer can on it.

The walls were sparsely decorated with just an *Indiana Jones* movie poster, a blown-up photo of a man jumping off a cliff on skis, and a large flat-screen television. The place oozed bachelor pad ambience.

"Let's take a look around," Wolf said. "Glove up."

They took out latex gloves from their pockets and put them on.

This clearly spooked Gemma. "Do you want me to leave?"

"How about you take a seat at the table there," Wolf said, not wanting to send her out into the cold, but aware they were probably stepping into a crime scene.

"Okay." She sat, pulling out her phone.

Wolf walked through the living room, eyeing the space closely, then went into the kitchen. He opened the refrigerator, letting out the smell of five Asian takeout boxes, an open container of milk, and a bag of mystery meat.

"His bedroom," Rachette said from behind him.

Wolf shut the door, following the two detectives.

The bedroom was large for an apartment, and a king-size bed fit with plenty of space to spare along one wall. The frame was hand-carved wood, and the sheets looked designer. *Perhaps Gemma's touch*, Wolf thought.

"Got an en suite," Rachette said. Then, under his breath, he added, "I could have used a place like this during my single days."

"For what?" Yates asked, pulling open a drawer in one of the nightstands.

"Getting busy."

"Is that what you call stumbling home and passing out with your clothes on?"

Wolf entered the bathroom, his eyes transfixed by a charging electric toothbrush. "Look at this."

"What's that?" Rachette asked.

"What's his toothbrush doing here?"

"Good question," Yates said. "You pack your toothbrush when you leave on a trip."

"Maybe he was forgetful," Rachette said, making his way to some accordion doors opposite the bed. "Maybe he was in a hurry and packing didn't occur to him."

Wolf pulled open a drawer, revealing a tube of toothpaste.

Yates watched, exchanging a look with Wolf.

Wolf checked the shower, seeing a wire shelf fully stocked with shampoo, conditioner, body wash, and some shaving supplies. "Same thing all over the place. You think he would have packed some of this."

"Pretty full closet," Rachette said.

Wolf turned around and went to the closet, verifying Rachette was right. The rod was jammed with clothing all the way across.

Brock Wendel was apparently a neat freak, because the clothing was meticulously sorted into type. First jackets, then button shirts, then long sleeves, then short sleeves, and finally pants. He had a clear taste for darker clothing, all of it black or gray.

"The guy dressed like an undertaker," Yates said.

Wolf stared at a duffel bag on the ground. Next to it stood a rectangular piece of Tumi luggage.

"There's the bag he didn't pack," Yates said.

Wolf went to the nightstands and looked in the drawers, finding ripped-open boxes of condoms, lube, and chewing gum.

Yates scoffed. "Be glad you're gloved up."

Wolf returned to Gemma, who was tapping a text message on her phone.

"Does Brock own this place?" he asked.

"No, he rents it."

There was a noise outside, and through one of the windows, they watched a man directly across the exterior hallway come out of his own door, shut it, and begin walking away.

Wolf pointed at Rachette, then outside.

Rachette opened the door. "Excuse me, sir?"

The man turned around, startled. "Oh my God, you scared me."

Rachette stepped out, followed by Yates and Wolf.

"What's going on?" the man asked, looking at the badges and guns on their hips. "Is something wrong?"

"We're looking for Brock Wendel."

The guy removed his sunglasses and put them up on his head, revealing puffy, bloodshot eyes. "I haven't seen in him days. Oh, hey, Gemma."

Gemma waved sheepishly from the doorway. "Hi, Rick."

"What's happening?" Rick asked. "You're looking for Brock?"

"When exactly was the last time you saw him?" Rachette asked. "Do you remember?"

"Jeez, must have been Monday."

"And what was he doing?"

"He was standing out here, locking his door when I was leaving."

"Did you happen to talk to him?"

"No," he said. "He was on a phone call. He was pretty into it, actually. He nodded at me, then walked away talking to whoever he was talking to."

"Has he said anything about leaving town this week?" Wolf asked.

Rick shook his head, hands rising. "I really don't hang out with him much. We'll say hi and bye, but that's about it."

They stood in awkward silence for a few moments until Wolf nodded. "Great. Well, thank you very much. Appreciate it."

Rick left, his feet clanking the metal grate stairs on the way down.

They turned to Gemma.

"How often does Brock stay with you?"

She shook her head, thinking. "A few times per week. Three or four. Sometimes twice, I guess."

"And where do you live?"

"Third and Alpine. A few blocks up from Main on Sunnyside."

Locals referred to anything east of Main Street as Sunny-side because that's where the sunrays hit last during the day. West of Main was often called The Icebox or Coldside, usually by people who didn't live there.

Wolf pictured the houses where she lived. They were on

large lots—at least, relative to the rest of the downtown properties. Her house undoubtedly had a ten-yard buffer zone all around it, probably with large, old-growth trees. Probably costing multiple millions of dollars.

"That's a nice area," Yates said.

"Does he keep a toothbrush at your house?" Wolf asked.

"Yes."

"Like, a travel one?" Wolf asked.

"No. An electric one."

"Is it still there?"

She nodded almost immediately. "Yeah. I put it away last night. I was sick of looking at it."

Wolf saw Yates looking at him from the corner of his eye, but he didn't meet his gaze.

"Why?" She shivered.

"Let's head back to the cars, back out in the sun, shall we?"

Gemma locked up the apartment, then Wolf led the way down to the parking lot.

Halfway to the cars, Wolf said, "Gemma."

"Yes?"

"Did you suspect that Brock was cheating on you?"

She remained silent until they reached her vehicle. Turning toward him, she crossed her arms, her eyes obscured by the mirror lenses of her Gucci sunglasses.

"I suspected it, yes."

"With Clara?" he asked.

"Yes."

"This is difficult to ask," he said, folding his arms, emulating her stance, "but were there others?"

She didn't respond for a good ten seconds. "I'm not stupid. Really, I'm not. I just . . . he's good to me. When he's with me, that is. He's fun. And I used to like that he didn't come from money. It was refreshing to be around somebody who saw a boat and was a kid in the candy store, not some snob demanding the caviar be chilled to a certain temperature before they serve it on the helipad or whatever."

A tear streamed down her cheek.

"But yeah. Things were getting bad. I was already having second thoughts about marrying him. If he wouldn't have done this, I probably still wouldn't have gone through with it."

"Were there others at the restaurant?" Wolf asked.

She cried steadily now, her face twisting in agony. "I don't know."

Yates produced a travel pack of tissues and handed it to her.

"Thank you," she said, wiping her nose. "I've seen some suspect behavior between him and Sandy."

"The bartender?" Wolf asked.

She nodded. "And . . ." She shrugged, not finishing her sentence.

They waited, knowing from previous interrogations that sometimes silence was all somebody needed to get out their thoughts. Whether they wanted to or not.

". . . there's a newer waitress," she said. "Her name's Kylie. She's young and beautiful. All the boys at the restaurant love her. And that includes Brock. I'm not sure if he's done anything with her, but I wouldn't be surprised. Other than that, I have no idea."

Wolf nodded. "Thank you, Gemma. We know that was very difficult."

"Yeah," she said on a sigh. "He's a real jerk."

They said nothing, though Wolf silently agreed.

"We'll try our best to find him and bring him to justice," Yates said. "Slapping cuffs on him won't fix the hurt he caused you, of course, but maybe it would be a consolation prize."

She nodded at Yates. "Thank you."

"You got it, ma'am," he said.

"Am I free to leave?" she asked Wolf. "I have to get up to the restaurant now."

Wolf nodded, and she climbed into her SUV and left, leaving a puff of exhaust swirling around them.

"'Slapping cuffs,'" Rachette said. "Nice."

"Shut up."

"You're into her. Did you guys exchange any texts or anything yet?"

"Shut up."

"Man, I love that you're into her. Because one day, I'm going to be in a picture next to you on that yacht in the Mediterranean. And on that day, I'm going to be drunk on Italian prosecco."

Wolf popped open his door.

"Where to?" Yates asked.

"Back to the station."

9

The rest of Wolf's workday passed uneventfully. Brock Wendel and Clara Abraham were covering their tracks well. Neither of them had used a credit card since Monday, their phones were still off, and their social media accounts remained unchanged.

Wolf, Rachette, and Yates spent the afternoon making calls to friends and family, yielding no clues regarding the fugitives' whereabouts. Clara's mother seemed genuinely upset about her daughter's crime and disappearance. Her father, on the other hand, who had remarried years ago and now lived out in New York City, barely reacted to the news.

Brock's family was more of an enigma. His father had died twenty-three years ago, and his mother, who lived in Portland, Oregon, showed no interest in speaking about her son.

"He's in trouble? Figures," she said when they introduced themselves.

When they finished their call list, Rachette and Yates sent local uniforms to conduct quick passes of all the parents' homes to make sure they weren't harboring Brock or Clara.

Meanwhile, Wolf reached out to Summit Wireless for the cell phone records. They were characteristically dragging their feet, and Wolf knew not to hold his breath on getting anything from them until after the weekend.

Satisfied with their initial progress, Wolf packed up at 4:15 p.m. He showered in the locker room, changed his clothing, and left the office to meet Piper down the street for their first date in over a week.

Black Diamond Pizza thrummed with patrons. The air was muggy, smelling of alcohol and freshly baked pizza. The atmosphere felt more like that of a frat party than a restaurant, which was no surprise given it was a Friday night in February after the first powder drop in a while.

That was why Wolf and Piper had decided to meet here so early: so they could maximize their chances of snagging a booth along the wall.

Upon seeing the commotion, he immediately assumed Piper was waiting by the door to inform him they were going to have to eat someplace else. But she wasn't. Instead, Wolf saw her seated alone in one of the booths.

"Can I help you?" the hostess asked.

Wolf pointed. "I'm meeting her."

"Oh, okay. Enjoy your meal."

Wolf smiled, walking past, and noticed that Piper was not alone.

A man stood over her, talking, gesturing with a glass full of copper liquid on ice. He wore dark slacks, a button-up shirt rolled to his elbows, and a Breitling watch with a blue face. He was tall, muscular, and had long, wavy hair that fell over a tanned, chiseled visage.

Piper tilted her head back and roared with laughter as Wolf

arrived at the table. He dropped his coat on the bench, remaining standing next to the man.

"And then, after that, he—" the man cut off his sentence when he noticed Wolf. His face was bright red with fading joviality. "Oh, hi. You must be David?"

"Hi."

"David, this is Austin," Piper said. "Austin is one of the partners at the law firm."

"Ah," Wolf smiled.

Austin grasped his offered hand. Wolf noticed he wore no rings.

"So, you're Austin. I've heard a lot about you," he said, telling the truth.

Not many days went by without Piper mentioning the man's name while discussing a case she was working on. Austin had been the one to hire her, and apparently, he was a good boss to work for. He was fair and honest and amicable, not one to fly off the handle.

"Thanks for being such a great boss to Piper," he said. "And for giving her the chance to work at the firm."

"Please. She's a great employee. We're lucky to have her. In fact, she is singly responsible for us retaining our client in Boston. If it weren't for her, we'd be out on our asses, and out of an eight-figure retainer."

Wolf raised an eyebrow, looking at Piper. "Is that so?"

Piper blushed, looking down.

"She has a great future at the firm. That is, if she wants it."

"That's awesome," Wolf said.

Piper smiled at Wolf, beaming with pride.

After a few silent seconds, Austin backed away. "Well, anyway, nice to meet you, David. You two have a great night."

Wolf nodded and slid into the booth across from Piper. She reached both hands across the table and grabbed his forearms, massaging them gently.

"How are you?" she asked. "Long day?"

"Long couple of days. But enough about me. I want to hear about how you saved the firm."

She waved a hand. "He's exaggerating. They were just getting in a pissing match, and I reminded them of something that rendered their bickering pointless." She shrugged. "I might have cracked a joke at the right time. The president of the firm liked me, and . . ." She twisted a hand. "It was boring." She leaned forward, her eyes hardening. "Tell me more about man-eating mountain lions."

He laughed, then told her the full story about the mountain lion incident up north, including the gaping wound on Tabor Smith's head. She listened with rapt attention, reacting at all the right spots.

"Can I get you two a drink?" A waiter stopped at their table, flipping open a notebook. "Oh, hey, Mr. Wolf. How's it going?" It was Chris Webb, a childhood football teammate of Jack's. Now in his early twenties, the young man had been a staple employee at Black Diamond Pizza for years.

"Hi, Chris."

"How's Jack?"

Wolf shrugged. "Last I heard, he's good."

"That kid of his is getting big already."

Wolf smiled, thinking of his grandson, Ryan, and the last video he'd seen of him sledding down a hill, screaming bloody murder.

"What can I get you?"

"You go ahead," Piper said, looking at the drink menu.

Wolf ordered a Sprite, and while he waited for Piper to choose her beverage, he eyed the crowd near the bar, spotting Austin. The lawyer was with a similarly dressed man. He raised his glass, nodding to Wolf, and Wolf nodded back.

He slid his gaze to the mirrors above the bar and spotted Roland Thatcher sitting in one of the booths across the restaurant. Odd to see the man in town twice in two days, Wolf thought, considering he'd never seen him in person until yesterday.

"David, are you listening to me?"

Wolf blinked, turning to Piper. Chris was long gone, and she stared at him expectantly.

"Sorry, what?"

"I said, I visited my dad today when I got back. He says he likes it." She shook her head. "But I don't know."

Piper's father had recently moved into a nursing home facility. Or rather, Piper had moved her father in.

"I know you're worried," Wolf said, reaching across the table and stroking the back of her hand.

But she was more than worried for her father. She was racked with guilt for putting him in the home, even though it was the best thing for them both. Wolf had said it plenty of times: she didn't have the bandwidth to give him the care he needed, not while trying to work full time. And even with traveling nurses coming to help him, the man had been lonely. He'd needed to be around more people. The home was good for both father and daughter.

"How's your mom doing?" she asked.

He shrugged. After the long drive back to town during the snowstorm yesterday, he'd stopped to see his mother for a few minutes and make sure she was all right. She had been napping when he had shown up, and she had seemed less than enthused to see him.

"She's doing okay," he said.

She read his face. "Maybe it's time she goes in, too."

"Maybe."

"My guilt aside for doing it, I really do see an improvement in my father's mood. They're always socializing in there. There's always something going on every morning, every afternoon, every night."

He nodded. "Maybe you're right." But when he thought about broaching the subject with his mom, the idea lost a bit of its luster.

"Here you go." Chris placed a beer and a Sprite on the table. "You ready to order?"

They ordered a pizza and some salads.

"I have to use the restroom," Wolf said, scooting to the edge of the booth.

Piper raised her beer and took a sip. "I'll be here."

He stood up and walked through the crowd, threading a route between Austin's spot at the bar and Roland's booth. Sneaking a glance as he passed, he recognized the man sitting across from the billionaire as Gregory Waze.

Wolf made it to the skinny hallway leading to the bathrooms without being noticed.

After relieving himself, he washed up, looking at his reflection in the mirror. The man he saw there lacked Piper's vitality. While her skin was radiant, tanned from her business trip, his was the color of ash, carpeted with stubble that was more salt than pepper these days. His hair, which had also grayed over the last few years, stuck up in back, the result of a cowlick that had formed when he had grown out his hair for the winter.

At least he smelled good, he thought, checking his pits, making sure.

He pictured Austin, the power lawyer, the partner in a multinational firm, with the physique and dashing good looks of a man a decade younger. He remembered the way Piper had been laughing when he had walked in. Then, he reminded himself that she had laughed at his jokes, too. She was just like that: personable to anyone and everyone. It was a big reason he loved her.

Reaching into his pocket, he pulled out the ring box and cracked it open, revealing a platinum band with a Tiffany diamond sparkling between delicate prongs. It was no crown jewel, but it was the best he could afford.

He had been rehearsing the proposal in his head for a few months now. He'd taken the ring on their last two dates, and despite chickening out both times, he'd psyched himself up about doing the deed tonight. The reason he had stopped to see his mother yesterday had been twofold: to see how she was doing, and to get encouragement for asking Piper.

His mother had asked who Piper was, then made a big production about remembering, which had not filled him with enthusiasm.

His plan was to ask her after dinner. Of course, he wasn't going to ask her here in this place, overcrowded with people the likes of her boss, Roland Thatcher, and Gregory Waze as witnesses. He intended to pull over the car on the way home, in a quiet, secluded place with a view of the valley lights, and just ask her.

Previously, he had pictured going on a beautiful hike. And then that had seemed like a bad idea because of the cold air that had blanketed the area for the past month and their conflicting work schedules.

But now, as he stared at himself in the mirror, he knew his pulling-over-the-car idea was dumb. The hike was way more romantic.

Damn it, he was waffling, and he knew it. But the truth was, right now he just wanted to sit down with his girlfriend and enjoy a meal, content with where they were at.

Unbidden, a memory of Lauren driving away from his house, little Ella's raised hand in the back window, flashed in his mind.

The door opened, and a pair of kids pushed inside, breaking his thoughts with their squealing laughter. After drying his hands, he went back out, deciding he would plan the hike. His blood pressure dropped with each step closer to Piper.

As he walked past Roland Thatcher's booth, he slowed because he had to. Roland had seen him coming from ten yards away. To ignore him would've been more than awkward.

"I didn't think you would be caught slumming in a place like this," Wolf said, nodding to Roland.

"Detective Wolf, you know Gregory Waze, right?"

Waze raised his glass of scotch in a hello gesture. He wore a flannel shirt rolled to the elbows, displaying a luxurious Rolex and thin, tanned forearms. His eyes rested on Wolf for a moment before lowering to his drink.

The last time Wolf had seen Waze had been at the grocery store. They had exchanged pleasantries, but for a year now, Wolf's intention had been to avoid long conversations with the man trying to steal Patterson's job, so he had walked away without saying much.

Wolf had always been suspicious of the man's real intentions, and the strings pulling and tugging behind the scenes. Seeing him now, out in public with such a rich and powerful figure, only strengthened those suspicions.

"How did it go at Brock's apartment?" Roland asked.

"We didn't find much."

"How about the cell phone records?" Roland asked.

"We're getting them."

"When?"

"When we do."

Roland's eyes flashed, and his face dropped all pretense. "You met my security manager, Jorel, yesterday."

"I did."

"I'd really appreciate it if you could brief him as you progress with the case."

Wolf smiled. "I will keep you and Gemma posted. Now, if you two would excuse me, I'll let you get back to whatever it is you are doing, and I'll get back to my date."

Wolf turned away and walked to his booth, sliding onto the bench across from Piper again. Their food had arrived in his absence.

"What was that?" Piper asked.

"Just saying hi to a billionaire and a sheriff candidate."

Her eyes widened, and she peered at the two men. "Wait, that is Roland Thatcher? *The* Roland Thatcher? And that's Waze with him?"

"Yep. Don't stare." Wolf grabbed the spatula, extracted a piece of pizza off the pan, and put it on Piper's plate. He then did the same for himself.

"Wow. I thought they were familiar. You should have seen the way they looked at you when you left their booth."

"What can I say? I'm a likeable guy."

She smiled and took a bite of her pizza. "You are, you know that?"

Austin strolled up and knocked twice on the table. "I'm out. I'll see you next week. Good to meet you, David." He left without waiting for a response, staring intently at his phone as he went through the front door, which his companion held ajar for him.

Wolf wanted to make a wisecrack about Austin's brisk exit, but he decided to keep his mouth shut when he saw Piper concentrating on her food.

They ate in comfortable silence, Wolf inhaling two pieces without even thinking. It had been a long day, and he'd saved his appetite for this moment. As he went for a third, he noticed Piper struggling to chew a too-large bite, her hand over her mouth. He smiled.

"What? Why are you looking at me?"

He gave no answer, just smiled wider at her mock anger.

Across the restaurant, Waze and Roland stood from their booth, putting on jackets. They walked past Wolf and Piper, Roland's gaze fixating on a far point on an imaginary horizon, Waze nodding at them with pressed lips.

Wolf raised a finger in acknowledgement.

The two men parted ways outside after exchanging a handshake.

"You'd think they'd be more discrete with their relation-ship," Piper said. "I mean, it just looks bad."

"Yeah," Wolf said. "It does."

Piper's hands came to rest on his, and he turned to see her smile. "Listen, why don't we get the rest of this pizza to go and take it up to my place?"

He nodded, feeling the ring box stretch the fabric of his pants pocket.

"What's wrong?" she asked.

"Huh? Nothing." He mustered a smile. "That just sounds . . . perfect. Let's do it."

10

FOUR MONTHS LATER...

Wolf reached the apex of the hiking trail and looked down upon the valley that stretched out in front of him. His lungs pumped vigorously for the little oxygen saturating the high-mountain air, and he bared his teeth, squinting toward the sun piercing the blue sky above the peaks.

Unshouldering his pack, he plucked out his water bottle from the side sleeve and took a long, greedy swig of ice water. The wind licked his back with a cold tongue.

Rachette stepped up next to him, his boots scraping on the rocky ground. He put his hands on his hips and looked around. "Finally. That was a climb. Damn, it's beautiful up here. You think living surrounded by the things, I'd have been up on these mountains more. But no."

Wolf looked at him. Not long ago, Rachette had been over-weight and low on energy. Now, the man looked chiseled from the granite that surrounded them, and his breathing wasn't stressed in the least after the hard five miles, mostly uphill, they had just done.

"What?" Rachette asked.

"Nothing."

"They're fast," Rachette said, gesturing ahead.

Two members of their hiking party had come into view from behind a rock outcropping, already halfway down the scree-covered slope.

"You good?"

Wolf nodded.

"I'm going to keep going." Rachette continued along the path.

A minute later, Yates walked up huffing. "Damn, I haven't been up this high in a long time. Whew." He pulled off his backpack and put it down, withdrawing his own water bottle. "This is it, right? This is the valley. I mean, this is the top. Right?"

Wolf nodded, smiling. He pointed toward the thin tendril of a dirt road at the bottom of the valley, where they were due to meet Dr. Lorber and his forensic investigation team. They had at least a thousand feet to descend.

"Ready?" Yates asked.

"You go ahead. I'll wait for Brewer."

Wolf watched his detective leave as he stood in place, taking in the view. The sun blazed high in the east, and the sky was as clear as it got. Grass carpeted the bowl-shaped valley below. A jagged line of peaks, still capped with white sheets of snow, surrounded their position for 360 degrees. At lower levels, the snow was melting off, water draining down with a percolating noise that came from all sides.

Animal Control Officer Ted Brewer walked up. Though he brought up the rear of their party, he breathed strong and steady and wore his hulking pack like it was nothing.

"Looks like Orlando and Joan are almost there," Brewer said. "Have you talked to your team?"

Wolf shook his head, checking his watch. "Not since we left the parking lot."

Hauling in the forensic equipment on foot would have been possible, but Lorber had insisted his team make most of the trip in their vans, approaching their destination from the Roaring Fork Valley side to access the two-track road below. Driving meant their total journey would be longer, but their hike at the end much shorter and less strenuous.

Looking at the rocks dotting the valley floor, Wolf wondered if Lorber had made the right choice. The four-wheel-drive Mercedes-Benz Sprinters had been up some of the most treacherous terrain before, but Wolf knew from experience that the road below was particularly hairy.

"After you," Wolf said.

Brewer nodded and led the way.

Fifteen minutes later, after a handful of switchbacks, Wolf veered off the trail to where the group had gathered near a bulge in the mountain.

Officer Brewer and Orlando stood next to Dr. Joan Cornell, a resident geologist with the Colorado Geological Survey who specialized in abandoned mines. She was of medium height with a muscular build, and the combination of her demeanor and worn boots said she was capable and comfortable in this environment.

Yates sucked on his water bottle, and Rachette munched on a protein bar.

After a brief rest, they formed a single-file line and followed Brewer around a rock outcropping, skirting the base, to a dark hole framed by old timber in the side of the mountain. The opening had been invisible from the trail.

"This is it." Brewer took off his pack and stretched his back.

"The Blue Corners Mine," Dr. Cornell said.

Wolf eyed the mouth of the abandoned mine shaft. At one time, it had been rectangular, but now it was a triangle, the upper left side of the entrance having caved in.

"What's it look like inside?" Wolf asked, turning to Dr. Cornell.

"It's pretty brittle in there." Dr. Cornell took off her sun hat, revealing a flop of curly black hair beneath. Her eyes were small and green, surrounded by a wrinkled web from years of working in the sun. "The mine ran for twenty years following a vein of silver, but then it became unprofitable a hundred and twenty years ago and disappeared. The timbers inside are original. If you're going in, I'm telling you now—do not touch the ceiling. Do not touch the walls. There was a recent cave-in. In fact, I'll go in first to take another look, just to make sure things are still stable enough for us to enter."

"Sounds good to me," Wolf said, but she was already moving.

She unzipped the top of her backpack and pulled out a headlamp and a climbing helmet, pulling both over her frizzed head, clicking on the light. She ducked, entering the hole on muscular legs that stretched the fabric of her cargo pants.

Wolf and the rest of the group donned their own helmets

and headlamps, eager to get inside, minus Rachette, who stared after the geologist with a stricken face.

"You can stay out here," Wolf said.

Rachette blinked, like he was forcing away a memory. "Thanks."

"Glove up," Wolf said to everyone else, putting on a pair of latex gloves.

A moment later, Dr. Cornell emerged.

"It's the same as yesterday," she said. "Two people, tops. Me and one other. I don't feel comfortable with all of us packing in there."

They all looked at Wolf.

"I'll go in with you first," he said.

She nodded, ducking back inside and out of sight.

Wolf clicked the button on his headlamp and walked to the hole.

He kneeled on the hard ground, pointing the light inside, illuminating a wider and taller space than he had expected.

"Careful in there," Rachette said.

Wolf nodded and crawled forward. Once inside, he rose, able to stand all the way up.

The mine shaft extended straight inward at no grade. It had a rounded ceiling made of thousands of hard angles, all hand-carved by a band of ragged men one hundred forty years prior.

Dr. Cornell was a looming shadow ahead, standing a few paces inside, pointing her headlamp down the tunnel. The light pierced deep into the maw, illuminating a wall of rock— the collapse she had talked about.

There were streaks of black along the ceiling, and the

sound of trickling water echoed around them. It smelled like wet earth, along with animal dung.

He pointed his headlamp at the ground to find the reason why they were there.

Immediately, he saw signs of wildlife activity. Fur lay everywhere, brown and gray, of varying lengths, probably some of it from prey, some from predator. Bones littered every inch of the mine shaft floor, some of them large.

Kneeling, he identified two deer skulls. None of the bones looked to be human.

"Over here," Dr. Cornell said, indicating a spot in front of her.

He stood, walked over, and saw another few bones on the ground.

"That's a human tibia and fibula, right?" Dr. Cornell said. "You know, lower leg bones."

Wolf kneeled again, verifying she was right. The bones were long and slender. Human. And they were attached by a piece of sinew at one end. It only took a little mental puzzle-piecing to recognize that if they were straightened and put next to one another, they would be a human tibia and fibula.

"And there's still tissue attached to them," she said. "These aren't a hundred-plus years old. These are newer."

"That's good forensic work," Wolf said.

"I was pre-med for two years before I copped out and went to geology," she said. "And just in case we need more proof, there's more down here."

She got up and moved, stopping a few paces closer to the collapse, her headlamp illuminating another swath of ground.

Wolf followed her and saw over a dozen bones within the pool of light. Almost all were remains of rabbits and deer, but one, directly in the center, demanded attention—the jawbone of a human.

He picked it up with his gloved hands, turning it. A silver tooth filling glimmered in his headlamp's beam.

"If you want my un-professional opinion—I mean, I spent a lot of time staring at these bones yesterday, and I told you, you know, I'm not a doctor or anything, I just did pre-med—"

"What?"

"They look female to me. Or perhaps juvenile. A teenager. If you go over there and put those bones next to yours, they're short."

Wolf set the jawbone down gently and went back to the leg bones, seeing she was right.

"You have any idea who this is?" Dr. Cornell asked. "Any missing people you're looking for?"

Wolf stared into nothing, thinking about the case they had been presented four months ago, and the zero progress they had achieved in solving the whereabouts of Clara Abraham and Brock Wendel.

According to the cell records Summit Wireless had eventually handed over, both Clara's and Brock's cell phones had shut off nearby. Not just nearby, but in the exact same parking lot where this expedition had begun two hours earlier.

"Maybe," he said, feeling almost certain he was staring at Clara Abraham's bones right now.

"Can I come in?" Officer Brewer's voice echoed into the space.

Wolf looked at Dr. Cornell. "Do you mind?"

"I'll see you outside," she said, walking out, disappearing into the brightness outside.

Brewer ducked into the cave, shining his light in disorienting flashes across the ground.

Wolf continued studying the bones in front of him.

"Human?" Brewer asked.

"Looks like it. We'll get confirmation when forensics arrives. But yeah."

Brewer pointed a latex-covered finger. "You can see all the chew marks. The scraping. The lions definitely fed."

Brewer turned full circle.

"We've gathered a lot of evidence lately," he said, "showing mountain lions will use these abandoned mines for shelter, usually during the winter months. But even the summer. Lots of other animals, too. A team down in the San Juans put up a system of cameras, and you'd be surprised what you see. Mountain goats come in and lick the salt off the walls."

Brewer walked toward the mound of rock and earth abruptly ending the tunnel.

Wolf joined him, aiming his light at the gaping hole in the ceiling left by the collapse. Water dripped rhythmically through the opening, each drop a falling jewel illuminated by halogen bulbs.

He remembered the last time he had been in a mine shaft. He hadn't liked it then, and now was no different. Suddenly, he felt the weight of the millions of tons of mountain above him. But he held still, watching the water hit the ground at his feet.

"What the hell?" Brewer crouched down and began removing rocks from the mound, setting them aside.

"Hey, what are you doing? We're not supposed to be touching anything."

"Look at this." Brewer ignored him, or didn't hear him, continuing to move rocks. "Look."

Wolf saw a large cat paw protruding from the mound.

"There's a lion underneath this collapse," Brewer said, displacing another rock, revealing more leg and blood-covered fur. "Holy cow." He grasped the leg, then combed the blond hair of the animal, as if checking it for ticks. "It's under here."

A pebble fell from the ceiling.

Wolf shone his light up as a stream of dust followed the pebble's path. He pulled on Brewer's shoulder. "And it's going to have to stay here. Let's get out."

"How was the drive?" Wolf asked.

Dr. Lorber, the medical examiner of Sluice-Byron County and the head of the forensic investigation team, climbed out of the driver's side of the second van, stretching his long, spider-like arms overhead. "Ah, maybe the hike with all this equipment would have been better. Either way, my butt's going to hurt tomorrow."

Wolf watched the six-foot-seven man limber himself up, wondering if his giant frame would fit inside the hole up there.

"You need to put some shoulder straps on these things," Yates said, taking a metal box full of gear from the rear of the first van.

"There are shoulder straps on those things," Daphne Pinnifield, Lorber's first assistant, said, unbuckling the lid and producing two lengths of fabric.

"Oh."

After the initial flurry of activity of unpacking the vans, they all turned and looked up at the steep terrain ahead of them. The winding switchbacks were barely visible, just slight discolorations of the gray, scree-covered mountain slope.

Wolf slapped Lorber on his shoulder. "You'll get that hike after all."

Lorber lowered his John Lennons on his nose and looked up. "Shit."

Wolf, Rachette, and Yates each took a load of gear, which wasn't much because the forensic team had packed light in anticipation of the hike, and set off.

Once again, Rachette led the way, keeping a blistering pace that proved his workout routines were effective, or that he had a new masochism that needed to be addressed with a therapist.

Thirty minutes later, they arrived at the mouth of the mine shaft.

Wolf took the forensic gear off his back and set it down, catching his breath and wondering how much he was going to be able to move his legs the next day.

Dr. Cornell stood near the hole, brushing some dust off her pants.

"How's it look in there?" Wolf asked.

"Still stable. As long as nobody goes moving rocks again." She looked at Brewer.

"My mistake," Brewer said, holding up a hand with a sandwich in it.

"Show me the way," Lorber said, wasting no time zipping up his forensic suit and gloving his hands.

Dr. Cornell repeated her speech about the brittle state of the mine shaft for the newcomers, warning them to enter in pairs and to be careful not to touch the walls or ceiling. Everyone agreed, and the forensic team began working the scene.

Camera flashes came out of the hole, along with bags of

bones, some of them human, many of them not.

Meanwhile, Wolf, Rachette, and Yates sat a few yards away, stuffing their lunches into their mouths with greedy bites. Wolf was comfortably lethargic as he sat on a warm pile of scree, listening to the whistles of a nearby marmot. Above, an eagle circled in the sky, pestered by a smaller bird.

Clouds had sprouted in the couple of hours they had been on this side of the mountain, and they were growing larger and darker by the minute. This late in the spring, they could be looking at a soaking rain, a full thunderstorm, a brief snow, or anything in between.

Lorber came out of the hole like a daddy longlegs emerging from a thimble. He walked over to them, stretching his back with a wince.

"Any way of knowing if it's her?" Wolf asked.

"I'll have to get it back to the lab for the match," Lorber said. "But I'd say the remains look a few months old. Kind of difficult to tell with the elements, of course."

"Can you tell if they are a woman's remains or not?" Yates asked.

"I'll have to do a DXA scan for the bone mineral density. But the tibia and fibula are short in length. Could be. We'll know more later. We're about done in there. It wasn't much to go on. The mountain lion did a number on those bones."

"I'll bet this explains the lion attack on that man down in Cave Creek a few months ago."

They all turned and saw Brewer standing a few yards away.

"Sorry, I couldn't help but overhear," Brewer said. "So, you do have a missing person. A woman."

They looked at one another, not answering the question.

"If you could keep your voice down about that," Wolf said.

"Yeah, sorry." Brewer glanced over his shoulder. Dr. Cornell and Orlando were too far to hear.

"What explains the lion attack?" Wolf asked.

"Well"—Brewer edged closer—"if the woman was dead before the mountain lion ate her."

"How's that?" Rachette asked.

Brewer shook his head. "I'm not sure. It's just a theory. But maybe the mountain lion was hungry and came across her body. This winter was one of the warmest and driest on record, and that means it was more difficult for the mountain lions to catch prey."

"How so?" Rachette asked.

"Mountain lion paws are basically big snowshoes. The opposite of a deer's hooves. When it snows a lot, mountain lions get the advantage, and they can catch deer easier. This winter, the weather made it difficult for them, so they were resorting to other means to eat. We saw a lot of lion attacks on dogs and other household pets over in Boulder County, up near Nederland. Instead of hunt, they would case people's back-yards and wait for the prey to come out to them."

Lorber shook his head. "Shit."

Brewer nodded. "It's unfortunate. Also, it's why we could never find the mountain lion involved in the Cave Creek attack. All the specialist tracking dogs were busy up in Nederland. By the time we got our hands on one, the trail was cold, and we finally had some snow." He shrugged. "It became difficult."

"And you think this is the mountain lion that attacked?" Lorber asked. "The one sandwiched under that rock in there?"

"It would make sense."

"But why does the victim have to be dead first?" Lorber asked. "I don't follow."

"Well, for how hungry mountain lions can get in bad years, it's still very rare that they attack humans. Unless they are rabid. And I got a blood sample from that mountain lion's leg in there, and it tested negative for rabies."

"You tested that mountain lion's blood?" Yates asked.

"Yes. We have a portable test. It takes thirty minutes. I did it while you guys were down the slope."

"Okay," Wolf said. "So, continue with your point, if you would."

"Right. I'm saying that if this lion came across this woman's body during a point of desperate starvation, I could see it becoming opportunistic. Scavenging. And then possibly getting a taste for human flesh. Which I think might explain why it came down to the valley and started attacking humans as if they were viable prey."

Wolf nodded. "I understand."

"But, like I said, it's just a theory. But it's a good one. Without rabies, it's unclear why it would attack a human."

"Maybe it's just psycho," Rachette offered.

Brewer said nothing.

"Listen," Wolf said. "Could you please keep what we've been talking about under wraps?"

"Of course."

Thunder cracked and rolled through the valley.

"Shit." Lorber clapped his hands, getting the attention of his team, who were milling about outside the hole. "Let's get a move on. We have everything packed up?"

"Yes, sir," Daphne said.

Lorber looked at the rest of them, upturning a hand. "You guys going to be okay? We don't have room in the vans for more people."

"It's okay," Wolf said. "We'll shelter here until it passes, if need be, and then make our way back to our vehicles. You guys need help?"

"No, we're fine. It'll be much easier on the way down."

Wolf and his detectives, and the three others with them, watched the forensic team descend the mountain, verifying they made it back to their vans all right. By the time the vehicles were turned around and heading down the valley, the rain was hitting quick and hard, with frequent lightning.

The six of them, to the chagrin of Dr. Cornell, packed themselves into the mine shaft to wait it out, keeping carefully away from the walls and the collapse.

The storm, as was often the case in the Colorado high country, only lasted a few minutes, and soon they were out, packed up, and on the hiking trail.

It took about two hours to get to their vehicles. When Wolf finally sat in the warm cab of his SUV, he swore he was going to have a chat with Rachette and figure out how to get back in shape soon.

11

Wolf pulled into Piper's driveway, edging his SUV up against the closed garage door, then shifted into park.

He pulled the ring box out of his pocket and opened it. The spring, worn from constant use, let out a tiny shriek.

The ring inside told him it wasn't a good time again. Not tonight. His legs ached from the day's activity, and his mood was tanking fast, probably from lack of calories. And oxygen. And water. And strength.

He was just excited to lie in bed. He didn't really want to be here right now, if he were being honest. But they had planned on this dinner for three days, and Piper had spent all evening cooking for him, and he didn't have the heart to break their date.

He stared at the ring some more.

Then again, maybe tonight he would finally do it. Sometimes, it took completely breaking the body for the mind to submit.

Smacking the box closed, he put it in his pocket and hopped out of his SUV, wincing at his tight hamstrings.

He rounded the house toward the front door. The clouds blazed orange overhead as the sun set across the valley.

Through the windows, he saw Piper padding around the house on socked feet, wearing sweatpants and a long-sleeve shirt, her dark hair straight today and resting on her shoulders.

"Knock, knock," he said, poking his head past the door.

"Hi. Come in."

"Wow, it smells really nice in here," he said, his mouth watering.

"Are you hungry?"

"I've never been hungrier in my life."

She laughed, looking at him. "Oh my God, you're so sunburned."

"Yeah. I guess I didn't put on enough sunscreen up there."

He took his boots off at the front door, teetering on one leg and then the other.

"Are you okay?" she asked, walking up and embracing him in a hug.

"I probably smell," he said. "Is there time for a quick shower?"

"There's about ten minutes left on the potatoes."

"Perfect."

She kissed him on the lips. "You look beat."

"It was a lot of hiking."

"I can't wait to hear about it," she said, moving to the kitchen, then out the door to the back deck, where she had set up a table with plates and silverware.

He hobbled upstairs and took a shower, savoring the warm water flooding over his body. A few minutes later, he was wearing the underwear, shirt, and pair of sweatpants he kept in the closet of Piper's spare bedroom, the ring box tucked inside the pocket of the pants.

He paused at the top of the stairs, looking at the conspicuous, cube-shaped bulge in his pocket, then shoved it down his underwear.

Deciding that was just too weird, he pulled it out and stuffed it into his sock, pulling the leg of the sweatpants over it.

When he made it downstairs, he went into the kitchen, where he was met with soft music and the scent of delicious food.

"Here, will you take this?" Piper handed him a tray of steamed asparagus.

He took the food outside and set it on the table, noting the glass of red wine in front of one plate and the tonic with lime in front of the other.

The air was cool but not uncomfortable, with a gentle breeze flitting through the aspen leaves overhanging the side of the deck. A hummingbird zipped past, a tiny shadow disappearing into the darkening sky. A deer stood inside the tree line, fifty yards away, across the expanse of manicured lawn, feasting on grass.

Piper removed the lid of a centerpiece bowl, unleashing a cloud of steam from the plate of vegetables, rice, and strips of flank steak.

"I hope you like it," she said sheepishly.

"Wow," he said. "I promise there is no chance in hell I won't."

She laughed. "Sit."

They sat down, served themselves, and tucked into their meal.

"So?" she asked, leaning toward him. "What happened up there?"

He smiled at the flash in her eyes. She was genuinely curious. Almost desperately so. She had once been a cop, and she always would be.

He told her about the jaw and leg bones they'd found, and the possibility that they could belong to the remains of Clara Abraham. He also told her about Brewer's theory that the lion had chanced upon her dead body.

"Holy cow," she said. "So, you think it was Brock Wendel?"

Wolf nodded, then shrugged. "I don't know. But, if it's her, it would make sense Brock killed her."

"Where is the rest of her, I wonder? Back in that mine?" Piper frowned, shaking her head. "You said the entrance was a five-mile hike in, over a mountain. No way Brock carried her there, right?"

"The mine burrows through that mountain in all directions, according to Dr. Cornell, a geologist who was with us. There are ventilation shafts all over that mountain, on both sides of it. There could be something closer to the parking lot where their phones last pinged."

"That makes sense. The cat was wandering the mine and found her body."

Wolf shrugged, smiling.

"What?"

"You just . . . you know, you could still work at the department if you want. I'm sure Patterson can find you an opening."

She scoffed. "Yeah. On your detective squad? That would

be fun for us, right? Spending every waking moment together?"

He smiled, conceding the point. "Anyway," he said, "we'll be taking up cadaver dogs tomorrow, along with some maps of the mine. Hopefully, we'll find something."

They ate in silence until Piper shook her head. "Well, I can't wait to hear what you find tomorrow."

"How about you?" he asked. "How's work?"

She sat back, sighing and wiping her mouth. "Not bad."

"Anything interesting going on?"

"Not really. Just that divorce case I'm working." She put down her napkin on her plate. "That was good. Have you had enough?"

He nodded, content.

They stared at one another, as they tended to do during quiet moments. Her eyes shone in the deck's lighting, like pools of molten chocolate.

She leaned forward and kissed him. Her lips tasted like wine.

"I have to use the bathroom." She got up and walked away, leaving him by himself.

He took the dirty dishes in, set them in the sink, and went back out to the porch table. Hearing the toilet flush inside, he took the ring box out of his sock and put it in his pocket.

Something had shifted inside of him. Perhaps in response to the evidence of death he'd seen earlier today. Whatever had caused it, he knew now was the time. It wasn't going to get any better than this.

Piper came back, holding her cell phone, smiling at the screen. She typed something and then put it face down, leaning toward him. She looked like she was going to say something, but the phone vibrated, and she picked it up, reading the message, shaking her head with a smirk.

"Who's that?" Wolf asked.

"Austin. He needs a deposition transcript, and he's an idiot."

"Ah."

"IT changed the login system, and now every time he has to get in, he's a helpless baby." She put her phone in her pocket. "I'm sorry. I'm being rude."

Wolf said nothing, putting the ring box, which he had taken into his hand when she had come outside, back into his pocket.

He balled his fist around the felt cube. The discussion of work, and the thought of Austin, had ruined the moment.

"What's up?" she asked.

Wolf's earlier dark mood returned with a vengeance. He needed to extricate himself from this situation before he said something he regretted.

"I'm dead tired. Thank you for dinner. It was so good. I'm going to head in and finish the dishes." He stood up.

"You're welcome. And no, you go up and sleep. I'll finish the dishes."

"You sure?"

"Yes." She pecked him on the lips. Backing away, she glanced down at his hand still planted in his pocket. "I'll be up in a bit."

Wolf sighed, watching as she walked to the kitchen, her hair trailing in silken waves. "Good night."

12

Sheriff Heather Patterson sat with her legs crossed, watching the Chautauqua Sentinel reporter scribble frantically in her notebook. The digital recorder lying between them had a blinking green light. So what was she writing?

"And what do you say to the people who are calling you too soft?" The reporter looked up from her notes.

Margaret, sitting in the chair adjacent to the reporter, scoffed.

The reporter did not react. A hard hitter, apparently.

"Who's calling me that?" Patterson asked.

"The opposition."

Patterson knew Waze had never called her that, but plenty of his supporters had. It was a distinction she decided to skip over.

"Well"—she hesitated, forgetting the woman's name—"I stand firm in what I believe in the moment, given the information I have. And if I need to change my mind, I change my mind, often to the delight of my opponents. That's what they call soft. I call that strength of character to admit when I'm wrong. But I'm not worried about what my opponents think."

There was another long pause as the reporter wrote. Margaret winked at Patterson, giving a subtle thumbs-up.

Patterson kept a blank face, but she was crawling inside her skin. Margaret's good-little-candidate gestures were getting old, and she was sick of these interviews. She knew every single word she said could and would be used against her in some caricature of her real thoughts.

"That's a good answer," the reporter said, looking up from her notebook with a smile.

"It is, isn't it, *Cindy*?" Margaret emphasized the reporter's name a little too much. She had clearly picked up on Patterson blanking. Once again, Margaret covered the open base.

"Now for the big news that's just coming out," Cindy said. "I would be reprimanded by my boss if I didn't ask about the current event unfolding now at the Blue Corners Mine. Can you tell me about the human remains you found up there?"

Patterson smiled, wondering how the hell she had heard already.

"I'm sorry," she said. "Some of the details are still uncertain, and I wouldn't want to give you any misinformation on the record. I'll be giving a press conference later today. You'll be able to learn all we know at that time, along with everyone else."

"Okay. Yes, ma'am. Well, is there anything else you would like to say? On the record?"

Patterson shook her head.

"Let the record show Heather Patterson is an honest candidate," Margaret said.

Cindy turned to her. "Are you saying you don't think Mr. Waze is honest?"

Margaret opened her mouth to respond, but Patterson cut her off. "We're not saying anything about Mr. Waze at this time. Isn't that right, Margaret?"

Margaret held a frozen smile. "That's right, Sheriff."

Cindy looked between them. "Um, okay. Well, I guess that's it." She poked the stop button on her recorder, then put the tiny machine and her notebook in her backpack. "Just so you know—off the record, in case it wasn't already obvious—I'm rooting for you, and you have my vote. You give that slick talker and his male cronies hell in the election. We don't need some outsider stuck in the pocket of billionaires running our sheriff's department. We need a strong local. And quite frankly, we need a woman in charge."

"Damn right, sister," Margaret said.

"I'll do my part by writing the best story I can, Sheriff."

Patterson nodded, keeping her expression neutral. "Thank you."

"Let me walk you out," Margaret said, getting up.

Patterson stood and shook the reporter's hand, then watched as they both left. The door shut quietly behind them, leaving Patterson alone in her office. She walked to the window and looked outside, down at the sun glaring off the rain puddles left by the morning's showers. She wiped her hands on her pants, then drew her forearm over the sweat beading at the edge of her hairline.

"Well, that went well," Margaret said, barging back into the office and sitting down in front of her. "She was sweet. I think she'll do a good job with the write-up. And she told me she would let us look at it before it goes live."

Patterson kept her eyes outside.

"Heather."

"What?" She turned around to face her aunt.

"You all right?"

"Yep."

"Good. Let's talk next weekend."

"What about it?"

"Scott will be there, right? You have a babysitter lined up for the boys?"

Patterson took her seat. "Yeah, yeah. We'll be there."

"Good. We need to make a good appearance."

"Versus what? A bad appearance? Where I get drunk and start swearing at everyone at a fundraiser for sick children? What does that even mean, Margaret?"

Margaret wiped an imaginary piece of lint off her pant leg. Her smile vanished, and she pulled out a piece of paper from her shoulder bag. "It means we're behind in the polls again."

Patterson ignored the piece of paper on her desk. Last week, she had been ahead by a point. The week before, ahead by two. The week before that? She forgot, but it had been neck and neck for months.

"So what?"

"A good speech at a fundraiser dinner is just the thing we need. Have you got it memorized?"

"I have another eight days until the thing."

Margaret shook her head. "Start looking at it now. If you make a good speech, and we have some nice pictures taken by a top-notch photographer, that will go a long way with a well-written piece in the Sentinel. We're doing good work. Half a point. Half a point."

Good work. The election was her work now, not her sheriff

duties. She was just a piece of clay being molded by those around her, following blind, ridiculous orders.

She rubbed her eyes.

"Heather?"

"Yeah?"

"I said, make sure you wear the pantsuit."

Patterson blurted out a laugh. "Yeah. Okay. The pantsuit. I know. You don't want me looking too girly with a dress."

"That's right," Margaret said, staring her down.

Ever since Patterson had shot down her aunt's plan to investigate Waze's personal life, Margaret had been ruthless, unapologetic with what she had asked of Patterson. They had sat through interview after interview over the last four months, attended event after event, made speech after speech. The cold-hearted look in Margaret's eyes right now taunted Patterson, dangling a way out with a silent invitation: *just sign here in blood, and I'll dig up some dirt. And it can all stop.*

Patterson's inner turmoil settled, and she met her aunt's stare. "I'm excited for it. It will be fun."

A chipper smile assaulted Margaret's face. "Oh yeah, and your mom and dad will be there, too! They're coming from Aspen."

Patterson's vision glazed over.

Two knocks hit the door.

"Yeah?" Patterson said, inviting whatever hell was on the other side to rescue her.

The knob twisted, and the door opened. Wolf's face, deeply tanned, appeared in the crack.

"Oh, hey, David," Margaret said. "How's it going? Jeez, you look like you've gotten some sun."

Wolf walked inside.

"Piper's still looking beautiful as ever," Margaret said. "I saw her at the store yesterday. She said she was buying you two dinner. Getting pretty serious, eh?"

Wolf said nothing, though discomfort at the onslaught of questions soured his face.

"Margaret, we do have actual work to be doing right now," Patterson said.

"Time to put a ring on that finger, David," Margaret said, leaving.

"Bye." Patterson shut the door.

They stood in silence, letting Margaret Hitchens' wake settle.

"What's up?"

"You heard the DNA match showed the bones are Clara Abraham's?" Wolf asked.

"I did."

"I just wanted to check in and let you know we're headed back up in a few minutes. The cadaver dog is on its way from Brushing."

Patterson looked at the bronzed skin of his face, then out the window at the slow-passing, cotton-ball clouds back-dropped by blue sky.

"You . . . want to come?" Wolf asked, reading her mind.

She did, but she had sheriff things to do. First, a lunch meeting with a local rancher and potential donor to her campaign. After that, she'd have to be back in the office for the press conference. And then there were the three phone meetings she had on her calendar.

"No, thanks," she said. "But keep me posted."

"Yes, ma'am."

Patterson followed Wolf to the door. She stood there,

observing him join Yates and Rachette, who had been waiting in the hall. As they walked away, Rachette slapped Yates on the shoulder and cracked one of his dumbass jokes. Yates pretended Rachette didn't exist, while Wolf pretended neither of them did.

"How did the interview go?" Wilson appeared next to her, jolting her out of her thoughts.

"Jeez, you scared me. It was fine."

He looked down the hall at the departing detectives. "You want to go with them? I could cover for you."

"What? No. Did Wolf tell you to say that?"

"Wolf? Tell me to say what?"

She shook her head. "We have a call with the election committee, remember? Speaking of, did you get those Com Portal stats yet?"

"No."

She raised an eyebrow at him.

"I'll get on it." He hurried away.

She remained in place, watching Wolf, Rachette, and Yates disappear behind the elevator's metal doors. In moments, they would be outside breathing fresh air. Something she hadn't experienced for weeks.

With that depressing thought, she turned and went back into her office.

13

Wolf arrived at the Silver Vein Wilderness lower parking lot five minutes after the 11:00 a.m. meet time, parking his SUV last in a line of three vehicles. He got out and stretched, noting his flexibility was half that of the previous day. Hopefully, his aching muscles would hold out on their hike through the rocky terrain.

Opening the hatch of the SUV, he pulled out his backpack, which was complete with water, protein bars, emergency equipment, and sunscreen. He now took the time to liberally apply the sunscreen to his face, neck, and arms.

Rachette and Yates were both standing by the front vehicle, holding packets of paper. They sounded like they were in a heated discussion. The uniformed officer and his K-9 companion beside them seemed happy to look away.

Grabbing his pack, Wolf shut the hatch and walked over, feeling the sun beat down. The fragrance of the sunscreen, a blend of ocean breeze and coconuts, tainted the scent of pine trees saturating the warm air.

Cave Creek rushed just beyond the tree line, the sound

echoing in the stillness along with the cawing of crows and the excited panting of the German shepherd sitting patiently by its handler's side.

Rachette and Yates stopped talking and turned toward him.

"What took you so long?" Rachette asked.

"Sorry. Food."

Yates gestured to the Brushing K-9 police officer next to him. "You know Officer Lake?"

Wolf nodded. "It's been a while, Jon. How's it going?"

They exchanged handshakes and pleasantries, then Wolf turned to the dog.

"I don't think I've met this guy."

"This is Shirley," Officer Lake said.

"Ah. Excuse me." Wolf gave her an affectionate scratch.

"We were just filling him in on the cell phone data," Yates said. "And how Brock Wendel's and Clara Abraham's cell phones shut off here at the same time, the same night, four months ago."

"But you found the human remains on the other side of that mountain," Lake said, pointing to the looming mountain that peaked at over twelve thousand feet.

Wolf looked up, hoping Shirley wasn't about to guide them all the way back over the rise. His legs would barely be able to take it.

Yates shuffled the papers in his hands, turning a stapled page. "This is the best we could come up with for a map of this mine."

Wolf had seen the map already. He'd received it earlier this morning from a contact at the United States Geological Survey, thanks to a rush request put in by Dr. Joan Cornell.

The mine had never been officially mapped with modern equipment, so all they had to work with were the original drawings made in 1886, digitally scanned into a database. The mine shafts were represented by a grid of wobbly lines that crisscrossed the page, intersecting at varying angles.

"These are entrances," Rachette said, pointing to locations on the map where horizontal lines ended. "And these are ventilation shafts." He pointed at three vertical lines. "Dr. Cornell said this shortest line is on this side of the mountain, just up the road near the upper Silver Vein Wilderness parking lot. If Clara Abraham's body was dumped into the mine, and that's how the mountain lions got ahold of it, then it's logical we might find the rest of her remains inside that shaft."

"Then again," Yates broke in, "this is where her phone shut off, so it might be logical we find her near here. That's what we were just discussing when you pulled up: where do we start? Up there? Or down here?"

They looked at Wolf for the answer.

He scanned the trees, thinking of the night Clara and Brock had driven up here and shut off their phones. It had been a clear, cold night, according to historical weather data.

"What are you thinking?" Yates asked.

Wolf shook his head. "I think we need to let the dog do what it does."

Officer Lake nodded. "We're ready to go if you are."

Shirley lurched to her feet, sensing her time to shine was near.

Lake bent down and took off the leash, saying something under his breath.

Shirley sat back down and stared patiently at her handler.

Electric tension filled the air for a moment, and then Lake told her to go.

Shirley took off, swerving between the vehicles and stopping near the end of the lot. She faced uphill with her nose tilted into the air.

"Hey, just a second," Rachette said, opening the door to his SUV. He pulled out his backpack and put it on, tossing Yates another bag, which he caught and put on as well.

They reconvened and followed Shirley, who turned and started pawing uphill again, this time at a faster clip.

"What I wouldn't give to have superhuman smelling power like that," Rachette said.

"You wouldn't be able to live with yourself," Yates said.

"Walked into that one."

Shirley left the lot and crossed the dirt road, lunging up the forested slope on the other side.

Wolf's legs strained as he followed behind.

"Looks like she's headed straight toward the upper lot," Yates said.

"It must be a mile up the road," Wolf said. "Is it possible she's smelling something so far away?"

Huffing, Officer Lake nodded. "Under perfect conditions, she could smell something twenty kilometers away. Bury a body fifteen feet deep, and she'll still catch the scent."

"And a hundred feet down a mine ventilation shaft?"

"Well, that's not buried. So, yeah, I think so."

Wolf glanced up the hill at Shirley's rear end flitting in and out of view between the trees.

Officer Lake whistled and yelled, "Hold!"

Shirley stopped, sat, and looked back, panting.

"You want to drive up?" Rachette said to Wolf. "You could

go back and drive up to the top lot and wait for us. If we find anything, you could hike down to us instead of up."

Wolf shook his head, very much wanting to drive but not liking the pity in these younger men's eyes. "Let's go."

They continued, following the dog making steady progress on a straight line up the hill. Wolf's legs protested with each step, but there was only one way to get them in shape, he decided, watching the backs of the trio thirty yards ahead.

When the others reached the top of a rise, Yates put his hands on his hips and turned around to face Wolf, who was still far behind. "You going to make it, old man?"

Wolf looked over his shoulder. "Who are you talking to?"

He pressed on, doubling his speed.

"I don't think there's any doubt she's headed to the top lot now," Rachette said. "We're more than three-quarters of the way there. You can see the clearing in the trees."

Wolf made it to the flat point where they were waiting for him, then kept going without stopping, leaving them in his wake. He could see the clearing Rachette had mentioned. *Just a quarter mile to go*, he told himself.

"Oh, okay," Rachette said. "I like it. We'll follow you."

Ten minutes later, with Wolf back in the rear, the terrain began leveling out, and the forest thinned to a wide opening. Shirley sat at the edge of the upper lot, waiting patiently for them. Past her, they could see the glimmer of vehicles.

Breaking out of the trees, Wolf cherished the flat grade.

Two SUVs sat silent and empty, parked near one another. A trail led out of the parking lot, winding up into the trees in the opposite direction from which they'd come, toward a peak north of the one they had climbed yesterday via the lower lot.

"Let's have some water," Rachette said, taking off his pack, producing a water bottle.

Wolf pulled his own container and drank, feeling every cell in his body suck in the cool liquid.

They looked at Officer Lake, who turned to Shirley and gave her another command.

Shirley rose, pivoted, and left the parking lot, trotting away from the SUVs and the trailhead, back into the trees.

"She'd better be headed to the ventilation shaft and not the other side of this mountain again," Yates said.

The terrain was easygoing, sloping gently down to the start of a rocky incline that rose above the trees a hundred yards into the forest.

Shirley began barking, so they picked up speed, jogging through the widely spaced lodgepole pines toward the base of the hill, where Shirley was pacing back and forth near a black opening in the ground.

"This is it," Yates said. "Gotta be one of the ventilation shafts."

A broken chain and a frayed cable, along with a few short lengths of decayed, splintered wood and a rusty pulley wheel, lay on the dirt. Nearby, two old posts leaned out of the ground.

"This was more than a ventilation shaft," Wolf said.

Yates kicked the cable. "They must have pulled ore out of here."

Wolf looked at Officer Lake, gesturing toward Shirley.

Lake nodded. "She's hit a mark."

They walked up to the side of the hole. It was rather large, stretching the width of two men lying end to end, the length just short of the same, giving it a rough rectangular shape.

Sunlight reached a few yards into the nearly vertical shaft before being swallowed up by darkness.

"Hello!" Rachette yelled.

An echo answered him.

With the toe of his boot, Wolf kicked a rock over the edge and into the black maw. A full two seconds later, a loud metallic clank rang out of the hole.

Everyone straightened, looking at each other.

"Do it again," Yates said.

Rachette picked up a rock and threw it down. This time, there was a different, even louder noise. Still metallic, but hollower.

Shirley growled, a stripe of fur sticking up along her back. She bared her teeth, eyeing the hole. Then she turned away, whimpering.

"What's wrong, girl?" Lake asked, walking over and putting a leash on her.

Shirley seemed to snap out of her trance, licking her lips and wagging her tail.

"We need to see what's down there," Wolf said.

"Well, we got to get search and rescue up here," Rachette said.

Wolf glanced around and saw a long log, dead and bleached white, close by. He walked over and picked up one end. "Give me a hand."

"Why?" Yates asked.

"Put it over the hole."

They dragged the log over, then placed it on the ground so it made a bridge over the hole.

"Okay, what are you thinking here?" Rachette asked.

Wolf took off his backpack, set it on the ground, and pulled out a throw bag containing seventy feet of quarter-inch, bright-yellow polypropylene rope.

"You're going to lower yourself down on a water rescue rope?"

Wolf looked at Rachette.

"What?"

Wolf pulled out his phone and began tying one end of the strand around it.

"Oh," Rachette said. "I get it. You're going to lower your phone down."

"That's clever," Lake said.

"It's also clever to use words to explain your plan." Rachette shrugged. "Just saying."

Wolf finished tying a parcel knot around his phone, keeping the camera facing down, and then unlocked the screen, turned on the camera flash, and hit record.

Carefully, he draped the rope over the log and lowered it down, letting the length out slowly at first, then faster as he got the hang of it. It took almost the entire seventy-foot rescue line until he felt a bump, and then slack.

Wolf started reeling the phone back up, hoping he wouldn't catch a snag like a fisherman who'd hit the bottom of a lake. After raising the rope a couple of feet, he stopped and let the line settle, waiting a few seconds for the camera to take whatever footage it could from the new distance. He repeated the process a few times on the rest of the way up.

When the phone finally resurfaced, Wolf slipped it from the knot and held it in his palm.

They gathered around, heads jammed together to get a look as Wolf pulled up the video.

He pressed play, and they watched the disorienting footage of Wolf slinging the rope over the log.

"Skip ahead," Yates said.

Wolf hesitated for too long, apparently, because Yates put his own finger on the screen and scrubbed forward.

The footage remained black for a long time, and then something came into view.

"It's a car," Rachette said.

"Maybe. The camera is too close to tell for sure." Yates removed his finger from the screen, letting the video play. "We gotta keep watching until the part where you lifted it up."

As the camera ascended, the back of a vehicle came into view. It was covered by a thick layer of rust-tinged dirt. The color and texture matched the earth near the edge of the hole. Despite the coating, every nuance of the vehicle was still discernable, including the make, model, and license plate.

"It's . . . not her car," Rachette said.

Wolf and Yates knew he was right. They had been trying to track two different license plate numbers for four months now, and they had memorized them both in the process. One stamped on a Colorado plate, and the other on a California.

Wolf nodded. "It's Brock's."

14

Chad Gilpin of the Chautauqua search and rescue team tugged on the harness cradling Wolf's crotch, snugging it around his inner thighs.

"That good?"

"Yes." Wolf nodded.

Lorber appeared over Gilpin's shoulder. "I wish you'd let us do this instead of you."

Wolf shook his head. "I'm going down first."

"How's that helmet?" Gilpin asked.

Wolf shook his head around, rattling his rock helmet. He tightened the strap until the rattling stopped.

"Headlamp's working," Gilpin said.

Wolf put his hand in front of the beam, seeing a circle of yellow.

The area near the hole was now doused in the shadow of the mountain. It would remain that way for the rest of the day. The question was whether storms would roll in. So far, the clouds had held no rain.

Vehicles crowded the nearby forest, two of them from the

search and rescue team, two from Lorber's crime scene unit, and two from the detectives, who'd shuttled to the lower lot earlier to bring them up.

Gilpin and his team had set up a rescue tripod over the hole. A climbing rope was threaded through the pulley, one end leading to Wolf's harness, where it was firmly attached via carabiner, the other leading to a rescue winch manned by Gilpin's second-in-command.

"You ready?" Gilpin slapped his shoulder.

"Yep."

A few seconds later, after some delicate maneuvering, Wolf dangled over the hole, shining his headlamp down the shaft.

The powerful beam illuminated the vehicle far below, and it also showed the shaft was actually angled toward the mountain by a few degrees.

Smooth and slow, he descended in a half-seated position, gently bouncing his feet off the walls to keep his body centered in the tubular space. Thirty or so feet down, his foot slipped on a loose rock, and the rock tumbled, hitting the rear windshield of the vehicle with a dull thud. Impressively, the window remained in place, although a few more cracks joined the web in the tempered glass.

"You okay?" Gilpin called down.

He gave a thumbs-up. "I'm fine."

"Careful."

"Yeah, yeah," he said under his breath.

The deeper he went, the higher the temperature and humidity rose. Sweat began beading in his armpits, running down his temples and spine.

Finally, the tips of his boots softly touched the back of

Brock Wendel's dirty BMW X5. The vehicle had seen better days.

"Stop," he said, thumbing the radio attached to his chest.

His descent halted, and he pulled on the rope with both hands to help him straighten. Still dangling an inch or so too high to stand up comfortably, he stretched his foot out to scrape some of the caked earth from the BMW, revealing a black paint job.

"Down another six inches, if you could," he said.

They began lowering him again, and he planted his feet. With his full weight on the vehicle, he paused for a moment to get his bearings—and to sense if the vehicle beneath him was moving or not. It seemed to be wedged solidly into position.

He wiped dirt away from the cracked rear windshield with a gloved hand, then crouched down, putting his headlamp to the glass. The light scattered and reflected back at him, obscuring the inside.

His next order of business, as decided with Gilpin, was to figure out what was under the vehicle. Had it stopped mid-plunge, wedging into place, or had it hit the bottom of the hole?

He moved to the edge of the vehicle and aimed his light down, noticing the driver's side door was hanging open. Beyond it, he saw the dusty floor of the mine shaft a short distance away.

But something didn't look quite right. The open door was farther down than it should have been. He stared in confusion for a beat until he realized he was looking at the open door of a second vehicle.

"What do you see?" Rachette's voice came through the radio.

"There are two vehicles."

"What?"

"Give me a minute." He stepped out into the space between the cars and the shaft wall, using a foot against the BMW to stay suspended over the open door.

"Okay, descend again. Half speed, please."

"Copy that," Gilpin said. "Descending at half speed."

The search and rescue team started letting out the rope again, and his headlamp illuminated the side windows of the BMW as he passed. They were less covered in dirt, but not by much. Through streaks of dried mud, he could see into the empty interior. The windshield was caved in.

He checked below and saw he was going to land on the open door of the vehicle beneath unless he moved. Not wanting to put any more weight on the vehicles' *Jenga* game than he already had, he delicately gripped the small notches in the shaft wall to direct his trajectory.

Safely on the ground, he pulled a Fenix TAC flashlight out of his pocket, raking the high-powered beam across the demolished car beside him. The silver body was crumpled and mangled like a smashed aluminum can. He probed the interior of the vehicle with the light, stopping at the front passenger seat.

"What do you have?" Rachette's voice came over the radio again.

Wolf ignored him, inspecting an ivory skull with a missing jawbone. The skull was lying on the floor mat, and it had been gouged by sharp teeth. Long blond hair billowed next to it, attached to a dried, shriveled scalp. The front seats and dashboard were littered with claw marks and shredded pink clothing.

Wolf used his flashlight to trace the path of the claw marks, finding paw prints in the dirt by his boots. He imagined the hungry mountain lion stealing the body from the crashed vehicle and taking it somewhere else, but not before gnawing off the head.

"Wolf, talk to us," Rachette said.

"Yeah. I'm here. I found Clara Abraham's skull in her car. The rest of the body has been removed. Looks like by the mountain lion."

"Copy that," Rachette said, his voice somber.

Wolf studied the side of Brock's vehicle above, spotting claw marks in the paint. Almost like the mountain lion had wanted to get inside.

He unscrewed and unclipped the carabiner from his harness, then pointed the beam of the Fenix flashlight down both directions of the horizontal mine shaft. A cave-in blocked the shaft on the other side of Clara's vehicle. On his side, there was a mine cart track. It continued for the visible length of the shaft, which was flat and long, gradually bending out of view to the right.

"Stand by. I'm going down the tunnel."

"What?"

"Stand by."

Wolf walked, crouching slightly to keep under the ceiling, his light leading the way.

Between the rails of the mine cart tracks, a smattering of paw prints proved the lion had been back and forth many times.

All in all, the shaft was in good condition. The support timbers on either side appeared strong, minimally damaged.

Intrigue pulled him forward, beyond the turn in the tunnel,

to a new section that led straight into the heart of the mountain.

Wolf paused, transfixed by the way the powerful beam of his flashlight reached so far into the long expanse ahead of him. He pictured miners from another century wandering these tunnels with feeble oil lamps, groping in the dark.

A hundred or so feet beyond where he stood, the shaft split. The mine cart tracks disappeared into a hole to the left while the main tunnel continued straight. Another hundred feet on, an object sat on the ground.

He moved his hand higher, pointing the beam slightly down, and saw the object was pink, like the clothing he'd seen shredded inside Clara's car.

Continuing forward, he listened to the sound of his boots scraping on the ground. The air was stale and humid, smelling faintly of animal feces. Just like the day prior, he now felt the mountain above him.

"Wolf, you there?" Rachette's words were garbled this time, barely audible as the radio signal broke up.

"I'm on my way back. Give me a minute," he lied. He would check out the pink object first.

"Wolf. Do you copy?"

He ignored the radio. He would be back in a matter of two minutes if he moved fast—and maybe with the whereabouts of Clara Abraham's body.

Wolf stopped at the split, catching his breath, feeling the tension in his lower back from crouching slightly. Curious, he shone the light into the left tunnel.

He froze, his breath halting in his lungs.

Two mountain lions stared back at him, their eyes gleaming like tiny full moons.

"Oh . . . shit."

He kept his light locked on them, the beam shaking, and remembered the way Shirley had spooked earlier. She had sensed the danger lurking below.

The two cats were both sitting on their haunches, facing one another, heads turned to look at him. One of them had blood-caked fur along one side, the other a dusty coat.

He was no wildlife biologist, but they looked extremely thin. The way their heads bowed and jaws hung slack said they were starving.

Instinctively, Wolf reached to his side to draw his Glock. He cursed upon realizing it was topside, taken off when he'd put on the harness.

The distance between him and the exit multiplied with each thumping heartbeat in his chest. He walked backward slowly and deliberately.

A growl vibrated the air, spiking his adrenaline.

He bent down and picked up two jagged rocks, one for each fist, putting his left hand on double duty with the flashlight and rock.

He checked if his headlamp was going strong by moving the beam of his Fenix away for a moment. It was still shining, albeit not as powerfully.

What was a better weapon? A handheld flashlight or a rock?

Asking himself that question, he kept his feet moving, starting the long trek back to the ventilation shaft. He took deep breaths, his pulse racing in his neck.

"Wolf here, do you copy?"

No answer came through the radio. He wasn't sure what he was going to say, anyway. They were two hundred fifty horizontal feet and seventy vertical feet away. They couldn't do anything for him.

He turned and walked faster, keeping the Fenix pointed back.

A formidable rustling sounded behind him, then another growl, this one murderous.

He spun, pinning the two cats with his flashlight. They had emerged from the left tunnel and were no more than twenty paces from him. They stared at one another, looking to be in the midst of fighting. Their lips peeled back, revealing gleaming white teeth, and their paws swatted one another with brutal force.

They were quarreling over their next meal, he realized with a sick drop of his stomach. Whether or not he would fight back seemed to be the least of their worries.

He decided to change their outlook. Lifting his right hand over his head, he swung it back and launched the rock at the lions like a professional softball pitcher.

It flew fast, careening high, striking the ceiling above them. Debris rained down on the two predators in an explosion of earth.

With satisfaction, Wolf watched as they raced away.

But after only a moment, one of them stopped and turned, baring its teeth. A second later, the other one stopped and turned, too, acquiring some bravery from its sibling.

In the back of his mind, Wolf realized that's exactly what they were: two juvenile mountain lions, locked in these caverns to starve by a roof collapse that had taken their mother. One of them was bigger than the other.

He shifted the other rock to his throwing hand and hurled it, this time missing them completely. Neither cat flinched.

Shit.

Wolf reached down and picked up two more rocks, putting the flashlight in his pocket. Projectiles were feeling like a better defense than photons right now, but he needed a real weapon, damn it. The thought spurred him into action.

He walked backward toward the ventilation shaft at full pace, not daring to turn and run even though his instinct was telling him—screaming at him—to get out of there as fast as he could.

The two cats followed, prowling lazily, their bony shoulders rippling.

He reached the curve in the tunnel. Far down the next section, he saw daylight stabbing from above, marking his entry point. And hopefully, his exit.

"Wolf here," he said, pressing the radio button. "Do you copy?"

This time, the answer was clear and immediate. "Yeah, he's here, guys," Rachette said. "He's here. Where the hell are you—"

"I need you to throw down a gun."

"Excuse me?"

"Throw down your gun! Throw down any gun! I've got two mountain lions coming after me!"

"Are you kidding me?"

"I need you to throw down a gun."

"Yeah, yeah."

Within three seconds, something clanked on the ground beneath the ventilation shaft, just under fifty yards away.

"Did you get it?"

Wolf looked at the four shining eyes pointing right at him. The cats' bodies were sleek and low to the ground now. They had been maintaining their distance at about twenty paces, but the one on the right began moving faster.

He threw another rock as hard as he could, again using the underhand method. It hit the ground short and bounced over the mountain lions, not slowing either in the least.

"Hey!" he screamed at the top of his lungs, his voice straining. "Get the fuck out of here!"

He hurled the second rock sidearm and caught the left cat in the center of its face, making it howl in pain as it fell backward.

The other remained unfazed, gaze still tracking Wolf.

He picked up one more rock and threw it, missing the lion but hitting the wall right next to it, stopping it in its tracks for a moment.

Glancing over his shoulder, Wolf saw he was just twenty yards from the cars—and Rachette's gun.

"Wolf, are you okay?"

He continued walking, keeping the still-stalking cat, which was now only ten paces away and gaining on him every passing second, in his peripheral vision as he scanned the ground for the firearm.

The other cat reappeared, skulking close to the tunnel wall opposite its sibling. They were splitting up, preparing to attack on both sides.

He kicked dirt at them. Picked up another rock and threw it, aiming at the more aggressive one on the right, hitting it in the chest.

Both cats stopped, and the one on the right loosed a long, loud mountain lion growl that Wolf had only heard in movies.

"Throw another gun," Wolf said into his radio. "Try to hit the left side of the hole at the bottom."

Nobody answered, but there was a big metallic clank on Clara Abraham's open door next to him, and a pistol skidded to a stop at his feet.

He picked it up and fired into the dirt, the gunshot deafening his ears in the confined space.

The two cats turned and ran, disappearing into the darkness.

"Are you okay? Talk to me! You alive down there?"

Wolf grabbed the rope and hooked it to his harness. He pushed the radio button with a clumsy, trembling finger. "Yeah."

15

"My God, I'm glad you're okay. That's crazy."

Heather Patterson pulled her car to the side of Main Street, parking in front of an art gallery, and shut off the engine.

"Yeah." Wolf chuckled through her car speakers. "I won't be sleeping much tonight, I suspect."

She shook her head. "So, what's happening with the mountain lions?"

"Brewer and Orlando went down and shot them with a tranq gun and then lifted them out of the hole with special harnesses."

"Probably destined for a zoo," she said.

"That's best-case scenario."

She sat in silence for a beat, watching the traffic pass down Main Street. Throngs of people were on the sidewalks, coming in and out of the row of restaurants and bars and shops, seeming like they were enjoying the mild late-spring evening.

Poor cats, was all she could think. There she was, being soft.

"I left Lorber and his team there, and I'm headed home. Rachette and Yates are on their way home, too."

"I don't blame you," she said.

"They have a long night ahead of them trying to get those vehicles out of the hole."

"Let them do their job. You go get a good night's sleep."

Wolf said nothing.

"Okay," she said. "Looks like we're on call for the weekend. Keep me posted on Lorber's progress."

"You got it."

The speakers clicked, and she opened her door, stepping out. The passing cars reflected the fiery sunset in their windshields as they whipped up the cool air around her.

She went to the sidewalk, looking up at the peaks above Sunnyside, which glowed with an orange tint in the final hour of daylight. The street smelled like comfort food and the flowers hanging in pots from the lampposts. Bluegrass music floated out of the open barn door of a tavern across the street.

She entered Black Diamond Pizza, stepping into a bustling dining room backdropped by a semi-crowded bar with few open seats.

"Hi, Sheriff." Veronica, the hostess, greeted her with a bright, youthful smile. "You and the family eating in or taking out?"

"I'm just taking out. I called it in a minute ago."

"Okay. You know the drill. You can wait at the bar if you like."

"Thanks, Veronica. I will."

She walked through the dining room, nodding at John Bergstrom, a ski patrolman, and his family as she went by their booth.

"Sheriff," he said, returning her nod.

She wondered if Bergstrom and his wife were voting for her or Waze. A good politician would have stopped and asked.

Instead, she continued without pause, sitting on an empty stool.

The bartender, a heavily bearded, long-haired man with tattoos strafing every inch of his wiry, rock-climber physique, came over.

"Hello, Sheriff. Your pizzas just went in. It'll be a few minutes. Like something to drink while you wait?"

"No. Thanks, Jim."

"I'll be right back with the bill."

"Sounds good." She looked up at the television, where a mountain biker barreled down a steep slope with zero regard for his life.

Letting her bored gaze drop, she eyed the mirror behind the bar. With a start, she recognized Gregory Waze sitting in a booth, talking to two people on the bench across from him.

Turning on her stool, she could see the profile of one of Waze's dining companions. The man was dressed in a sharp suit, two gold rings adorning his gesturing hand. On his far side, a woman's hand came into view, chopping the air, and then the booth erupted in laughter, Waze's smile cracking as he noticed Patterson's observation.

She turned back to the television and watched some more death-defying bikers.

But then her eyes slipped down to the mirror, where Waze caught her stare. She gave him a toothless smile, and Waze nodded back.

Awkwardness mounting, she pulled out her phone and flicked through it idly.

She allowed herself another look and noticed Waze was wearing a corduroy jacket over a hooded sweatshirt and jeans, certainly underdressed compared to his companions. She couldn't make out who they were, but she saw a white envelope appear in the woman's hand, pointed toward Waze.

Waze ignored it, sipping his drink. And then the woman set the envelope down and pushed it toward him.

Patterson pretended she was looking at her phone as she snuck more glances.

The envelope was conspicuously placed in the center of the table. The man sitting across from Waze poked it while he spoke emphatically.

Waze nodded, smiled, picked up the envelope, and put it in the breast pocket of his jacket.

Patterson turned back to the bar.

"You sure you don't want a drink?" Jim asked, putting the bill in front of her.

She added a hefty tip and signed the receipt. "No. Thanks. I'm fine."

"Hey, thanks, Sheriff." Jim walked away.

"Don't mention it," Patterson said, watching a waitress come to Waze's booth and deliver a salad and sandwich in front of him. The waitress spoke to the two other people, but they waved her off, and she walked away to another table.

Waze's companions held out their hands, which he shook one by one. Then they got up and left out the door.

Patterson watched in the mirror as they departed, and after raking her eyes back to Waze, she saw he was looking at her, his glass raised in a toast.

"Hi, Sheriff," he said.

Here we go, she thought.

She turned and smiled, sliding off the stool and walking over.

Waze gestured to the bench across from him. "You want to join me?"

She slid into the booth, settling onto the warm wood, cologne and perfume still thick in the air. "Wow, they smelled nice."

Waze smiled, forking his salad.

"I was wondering if you were going to come over or just watch me all night," he said.

The waitress came by again. "Hi, Sheriff. Would you like me to get you something? A drink?"

"No, thank you. I'm not staying. I'm just waiting for a pizza."

"Oh, okay. I'll check on it for you. Mr. Waze, can I get you another one?"

He smiled, looking down at his now-three-quarters-drunk scotch. "Yeah, it looks like I need another one, doesn't it? Thank you, Tracy."

Tracy left.

Waze took the rest of the drink down in one gulp, the ice sloshing against his stubbled upper lip.

"Hope you're not driving."

"No, I most certainly am not," he said. "I have firsthand knowledge of the kind of damage a drunk driver can do." He placed the glass on the table and forked his salad again.

"Right. Sorry."

Tracy came over and set down another drink, picking up the empty.

"Thank you, doll."

"You got it."

When Tracy walked away, Waze picked up the glass, slurping the first sip with a smack of his lips.

It didn't look like there was much ice in the drink.

"Who were you talking to?" Patterson asked.

"Who, them?"

"Yeah. Them."

"They're with a lobbyist group named Alpine Heights. We've been working together for a number of months now."

"That's funny. We haven't noticed any reports of you receiving donations from them for your campaign."

"That's right."

"Hmm," she said, flicking her eyes to the breast of his jacket.

"You got a question for me?" he asked.

She decided there was no reason to hide it. "Yes. What was in that envelope they just gave you?"

"I have no idea. I haven't opened it yet." He pulled the envelope out of his pocket, slapped it on the table, and pushed it across. "You can open it if you want. Let me know what's in there."

She smiled, keeping her gaze on his.

He looked down at his salad, unperturbed. He pushed it aside and forklifted the sandwich off the other plate with one hand. "They have the best food here. I'm here all the time."

She said nothing.

"Come on. Just open it. You've piqued my interest."

She almost ignored him, but since he was insisting . . . She picked up the envelope and pulled out an ornate invitation. She opened it, marveling at what appeared to be handwritten calligraphy.

"What's it say?"

"It's for a state dinner at the White House."

"When?" He sipped his drink.

"Does it matter?"

His face remained blank.

"July nineteenth."

He took another bite of his sandwich, looking at the television screen above the bar. "My God, these kids these days are crazier than ever. Those jumps they have up at the mountain are bigger than the house I grew up in."

She turned the invitation in her hand, shaking her head.

"You can drop that on the ground," he said. "They'll clean it up later."

She scoffed. "An invitation to a state dinner is a big deal."

"Not to me. I hate politicians."

She set the card down and leaned back. "And yet here you are."

He shrugged. "Touché."

"Let's backtrack a bit," she said.

"To where?"

"To the part where you're receiving backing from this lobbyist group and not reporting it."

He plopped the sandwich on the plate and slurped his scotch again, making no attempt to explain.

"Here you go, Sheriff." The waitress arrived at the table, placing two steaming pizza boxes in front of her.

Patterson nodded. "Thank you, Tracy."

"You're welcome. I saw you already paid. You have a good night, Sheriff." Tracy smiled and left.

Patterson watched Waze poke at his salad.

"Okay, well then." She slid to the edge of the booth.

Waze put a hand on the pizza boxes, stopping her. "Me and the lobbyist group—it's not what you think."

"Then what is it?"

"Alpine Heights gives money and support to candidates who show commitment to changing the lives of impoverished people. You know, the hungry, the poor, the disadvantaged."

She blinked. "That sounds great. But I wasn't asking about the group. I was asking about you and your relationship to them."

"I've been donating to them." He removed his hand, picked up his fork, and dug into his salad. "Not the other way around."

She paused on the edge of the booth for a few moments, watching him stuff his mouth as if she were invisible.

"My wife had a lot of money. I don't know if you know that. She left it all to me and my daughter. I've been trying to put it to good use."

"I thought you hated politicians."

"Just the bad ones." His fork wavered as it reached his mouth.

"Like me, huh?"

He looked at her. "I never said you were one of the bad ones."

"But you're trying to oust me from office. You're trying to take my job."

He shrugged, sipping his drink again. Some of the liquid dripped out onto his lap. He didn't seem to notice.

"So, are you taking a car ride service back home or something?" she asked.

"Nope. My condo's not that far."

She knew where his condo was, and it happened to be over

a mile north, out of town and across the river. She imagined he'd take the path along the river, where he might fall in and drown with how drunk he looked.

"Be careful," she said.

That got a snort out of him, like he was laughing at an inside joke she had stumbled upon. "I always am," he said, eyes on his food.

"Well, have a good night."

"Until next time." He raised his glass. "Have a great night, Sheriff."

She walked away.

Once back to her car, she sat inside, staring out at the darkening sky and the first few stars shining above the town. She had the feeling she'd just been duped, and she sure as hell wasn't going to take Waze's explanation of that invitation to a presidential state dinner at his word.

She pulled out her phone and scrolled to Margaret's number. After staring at it for a moment, she put the phone down and dug into her laptop bag, producing a business card.

Dialing the Oregon number, she listened to the ring come out of her speakers.

"James Long," a voice said.

"Mr. Long, this is Heather Patterson. I'm Sheriff of Sluice—"

"Yeah, I know who you are."

"Right. Listen. Margaret Hitchens gave me your contact information. I was supposed to call you if I wanted you to look into a person here in Rocky Points. I'm running for—"

"Gregory Waze. You're running for sheriff against Gregory Waze. I know all about it from your aunt."

"Oh. Okay. Wait, have you been looking into him already?"

"No, ma'am. I just know your aunt from . . . I guess a previous life. We got to chatting a few months ago when she called me."

A previous life. Patterson decided she didn't want to know. "Okay, well, I'd like you to look into him now."

"Professional? Personal? Financial?"

She shifted into drive. "All of it."

16

Wolf stood outside the Sluice-Byron County Medical Examiner's Office with his hands shoved inside his pockets, his chin tucked into the zipped collar of his fleece. Despite it being only days until the official beginning of summer, winter didn't seem ready to relinquish its hold yet.

The sky was clear, and sunrays reached over the eastern wall of the valley, melting the layer of frost carpeting the ground and pine trees. Still, the office of the medical examiner was doused in shadow.

Traffic passing by on 734 was light, as it was no longer ski season and not yet the height of summer tourist season—a great time to be a resident.

He eyed his watch: 7:41 a.m. He was early, but so were the others. Rachette's SUV pulled off the highway and into the lot, followed closely by Patterson's duty truck.

That surprised him. He hadn't expected her.

They parked, Rachette and Yates climbing out of Rachette's SUV and Patterson from hers, all of them sipping travel mugs.

Rachette had a folder tucked under one arm.

"You're just standing out here in the cold?" Patterson asked.

"It's either fresh air or dead bodies."

He looked at the building. The single-story structure had finished construction at the end of last year and been put into use over the winter. Filled with brand-new, hardly used equipment, it had had little time to accumulate the scent of death. But it was still a morgue.

"I can't say I blame you," Rachette said, already dipping his finger into a jar of Vicks VapoRub, dabbing some underneath his nose. He held it out, and when nobody took it, he shoved it in his pocket. "Fine, suit yourselves."

They walked into a clean, fresh lobby with white floors and walls, sterile of any style. Bright fluorescent light banks hummed overhead. The reception desk was unmanned, so they pressed a button on a call box and waited until they were let into the inner door remotely.

Just as Wolf had expected, the temperature inside the morgue was about the same as outside, the air laced with the pungent scent of formaldehyde and other embalming agents.

Patterson led the way down the hall to an office, where she stopped, knocking on the open door.

Daphne Pinnifield sat at her desk, looking like she had just woken up from a nap. She straightened in her chair and rubbed her eyes.

"How's it going?" Patterson asked. "Long night?"

"Yeah, just trying to catch a little shut-eye."

"Well, don't mind us. Is Lorber in his office?"

She nodded.

"Okay, you go back to sleep. We'll talk to him."

Daphne didn't need any more coaxing. She rested her head on folded arms.

Rachette lagged behind as they continued down the hall. The man had never tolerated the morgue well, not before, when it had been down south in the county hospital, and clearly not now in the new building.

Lorber was sitting at his desk, his John Lennon glasses reflecting the screen of his computer.

"There you guys are. Right on time." He stood up and walked past them, out of his office, skipping formalities. "This way."

They followed him to a set of double doors, which he pushed open.

"Thanks for coming over," he said, flicking on two bright lamps, illuminating a gurney underneath each one.

"Yeah, as much as we like the secrecy," Patterson said, "what's happening that you couldn't tell us over the phone?"

Lorber stared at her with an unreadable expression, then went to one of the gurneys and pulled back its sheet, revealing gnarled, broken bones devoid of tissue, picked clean by mountain lions. A scalp with hair streaming off it was splayed out above the skull. The remains clearly belonged to Clara Abraham.

"Jeez," Patterson said, moving closer to the carnage. If anybody could hold their own in the face of death, it was Heather Patterson. She pointed. "This hole, here in the upper back part of her skull. That looks interesting."

"Yes, it is. It's an entrance wound. Thirty-eight caliber. We pulled a slug out of the dashboard. The exit wound peeled off one side of her jaw. The lions did the rest, as we saw in the cave. Inside her vehicle, fluorescein testing showed trace amounts of blood spattered on the dashboard and inner wind-shield. The angle of the bullet entering the dashboard, along with the rest of the forensic evidence, suggests she was seated in the passenger seat when she was killed."

"So, she was shot inside the car," Patterson said, "and the killer was outside of the car."

"Yes."

Patterson gestured to the remaining gurney and the considerable bulk underneath its sheet. "Okay, let's have it. Who's under there?"

Lorber walked over and unveiled a twisted corpse, its neck craned at an odd angle, face pulled up on one side and sagging on the other, lips wilted, teeth brown. Both eyes were closed and caved in, but one eyebrow was upturned and the mouth was open, as if the corpse had just heard some interesting news. A jagged hole pierced the left cheek, revealing bone and tissue beneath. Even with the face so deformed, locked in a gruesome expression of death, the man was recognizable.

"Brock Wendel," Lorber said. "He was stuffed in his own trunk." He pointed a gloved finger close to the hole in Brock's cheek. "Exit wound here. The entry is on the back of his head. And there's another entry wound in his back." Lorber grabbed the corpse and lifted it straight up, showing them the entry wounds in Brock's head and torso.

Rachette made a noise and edged toward the exit, looking out the windows into the hallway.

"You gonna make it, buttercup?" Lorber asked.

Rachette raised a middle finger.

"We have DNA matches for both of them, confirming we're looking at Brock and Clara, in case there was any doubt." Lorber gestured to what was left of Clara's body. "We found her remains down in the tunnel. The two lions had a little den down there. It looks like they had been trying to get into Brock's trunk to no avail. Which is a pity. They might have been less desperate to eat you yesterday."

Wolf remembered the scratch marks on the side of Brock's car. "Any DNA under Brock's nails? Signs of struggle?"

"No."

"Did you get any slugs from him?" Yates asked.

"The head shot went through and through, and I couldn't find it on-scene. But, yes, the second shot he received in the back lodged in a rib. It matches the bullet that killed Clara Abraham. Same twist rate. The unique rifling pattern of a thirty-eight Smith & Wesson revolver."

"What's happening with the vehicles?" Wolf asked.

"Underhill's still up there overseeing the extraction. We've got two tow companies doing their damndest to get them out, but Brock's vehicle is wedged in tight. It's going to take a lot of manpower to get those cars out. Or cutting them into pieces, which I'm trying not to do." Lorber took off his glasses and rubbed his eyes, revealing they were bloodshot and darkly ringed.

"But," he continued after a moment, "we've done a thorough processing of the scene on-site. The mountain lions, and the open elements, destroyed much of Clara's vehicle. Brock's vehicle, on the other hand, was a time capsule. We found chemical cleaner residue and only a few prints on the driver's side of the vehicle, suggesting it was wiped. We did find Brock's prints in various other places, though, along with Clara's. Hers were around the front passenger seat—and both of theirs were all over the back doors, seats, and windows. Even the ceiling."

Lorber handed some pictures of the prints to Patterson.

She nodded, then handed one to Wolf. "Looks like they really were having an affair."

"You doubted that they were?" Lorber asked.

"Until now, we've only had the suspicions of Gemma Thatcher to go on."

"And Tyson Lennox," Rachette said.

Patterson handed another picture to Wolf. "If Gemma Thatcher knew about this, which you guys told me she did, she could have been very angry."

"You think Gemma did this?" Yates asked. "No way. She's not . . . She didn't seem angry at all. Sad? Maybe. But not angry."

"Easy," Rachette said. "We know you dig her, but . . ." He waved his hand, giving up on talking as his eyes landed on Brock's body.

"She would have motive," Wolf said. "And so would her father. This man was coming into a lot of money by marrying Gemma. A lot of money that Roland Thatcher might not have been too happy giving up. Especially to a guy screwing around on his daughter."

A bag containing shredded pink fabric caught Wolf's attention. It matched the clothing that Wolf had spotted before being chased out of the mine by the mountain lions.

"Clara's sweater," Lorber said. He pointed at two other bags. "There's her jeans. And her jacket. They were on the ground down in the lions' den."

"Phones?" Wolf asked.

"No phones."

"What about the cars' event data recorders? Did they reveal anything interesting?"

"Yes. The data is in my office, on my computer."

"I'll lead the way." Rachette left.

The rest of them stayed in place, watching the doors swing shut.

"Is that all we have?" Patterson asked.

Lorber nodded, yawning. "I think. I'll do a thorough write-up, but I'll need to catch a few hours of sleep first."

"Of course," she said. "Let's see that EDR data, and then we'll get out of your hair."

Lorber led the way out, down the hall, and to his office.

They crammed inside, Wolf and Patterson taking the seats in front of Lorber's desk. Light streamed in through the window now that the sun had risen above the eastern mountains.

Lorber tapped his keyboard, then twisted the screen for them to see.

"February twentieth, 12:39 a.m., was when Clara's vehicle shut down after massive impact."

"That's about an hour after she took the paintings," Yates said.

Lorber nodded. "You can see on the pre-crash data that for a number of minutes, the car was idling at low revolutions per minute. The passenger side airbag was turned on, meaning somebody was sitting in the passenger seat upon impact. As mentioned before, the angle of the bullet entering the dashboard and the blood spatter found in the vehicle suggest Clara was shot and killed while seated there."

"There's a gradual slope with spaced-out trees leading from the upper parking lot to the ventilation shaft," Wolf said. "It makes sense the vehicle would have been driven down with low RPMs. It could have coasted most of the way."

"And then they pushed her in," Yates said.

"Leaving the car in gear to propel it over the edge and into the hole," Lorber said, pointing at the supporting data.

Rachette looked at Yates. "You said, 'They.' But that all could have been done by one person."

"Maybe in Clara's case, yes, but Brock's is another matter," Lorber said. "He was shot twice, one of the wounds producing spatter. But there was no spatter found inside his vehicle, which means he was shot outside, picked up, and put into the back. His DMV weight had him at one hundred ninety pounds two years ago. That's some heavy lifting for one person."

"Maybe not so heavy for a guy like Xavier Jorel," Rachette said.

Lorber tapped some keys, bringing up Brock's EDR data.

"You can see Brock's BMW's numbers are similar, minus here, where you can see there's nobody in the passenger seat. Again, the car is idling, running at low RPMs. Nobody's touching the brake upon impact, which shuts off the car at 12:45 a.m., also February twentieth. Six minutes after Clara's car was put in the shaft."

"And exactly an hour after he closed up the restaurant," Yates said.

Rachette placed the leather-bound folder he'd been carrying on Lorber's desk, opening it up and pulling out the cell phone records for Clara and Brock.

They were silent while Patterson took the stack of papers and thumbed through the pages, separating them into two piles.

Wolf was still stuck picturing somebody edging Clara's car up to that hole, jumping out, and watching it career into the darkness, then hurrying back to the parking lot, where another vehicle, and another body, awaited the same fate.

"According to their GPS readouts," Patterson said, "both phones shut off in the Silver Vein Wilderness lower parking lot minutes before their cars plunged into that hole."

Wolf had seen the cell phone records many times. They had gotten access in late February. Back then, they had assumed the lower parking lot for the Silver Vein Wilderness area was a rendezvous point for Brock and Clara, a location of some unknown significance. Back then, they had assumed Brock and Clara were on the run with their expensive paintings.

Patterson flipped the page to show the last phone calls Clara had made. Wolf had memorized this information, but he slid his eyes down the list, anyway.

Clara had called Brock twice the week before their disappearance, speaking for three minutes and seven minutes, respectively. She had also called a smattering of other numbers, all but one of them belonging to fellow restaurant employees. The odd one out belonged to someone living in New York City who seemed to have been Clara's go-to friend for long, drawn-out conversations.

When Wolf had called this number, a woman named Tricia had answered. She'd had no idea where Clara had gone, but Clara had told her she was planning to run away with a man. When Tricia had asked about the man, Clara had said that he was her boss and they were in love. But Clara had apparently never shared that the relationship was secret in nature, or that the man was engaged to be married.

Clara had also called the restaurant landline once or twice per week during the month leading to her disappearance, then twice the weekend before she'd stolen the paintings.

Other than her conversations with Brock, nothing stuck out as significant.

Patterson flipped to Brock's call records, and Wolf skimmed those, too.

In Brock's final week of life, he had made many calls to the restaurant landline, much more often than Clara. Some had lasted seconds, others upwards of fifteen minutes.

He had also called Gemma, Clara, and Kylie Jones—the young, beautiful waitress who Gemma had mentioned was all the rage among The Oxbow's male employees—twice each. That piece of information lent credibility to Gemma's suspicions that her ex-fiancé might have been a serial cheater.

Beyond the restaurant and the women, Brock had received one interesting call that they'd circled in red. It had come from a cell phone registered to one of Roland Thatcher's companies, lasting two minutes and five seconds, seven days prior to his disappearance.

"What do we know?" Patterson asked, leaning back in her chair.

Wolf spoke up. "We know that on Monday, February nineteenth, Brock Wendel sent everyone else home from the restaurant before close. He stayed back, leaving the front door open for Clara Abraham to come in and steal three valuable paintings.

"We know Clara drove to the lower parking lot of the Silver Vein Wilderness area after that, and at some point, she was made to sit in the passenger seat of her car. Then she was shot, probably unsuspecting, in the back of the head.

"We know Brock locked up and left the restaurant ten minutes after Clara left with the paintings. We know he also drove to the same parking lot. We know he was shot twice, once in the head, once in the back, then shoved into the back of his car.

"We know Clara's and Brock's phones were turned off at exactly 12:26 a.m., and that their cars were shoved into the ventilation shaft at exactly 12:39 a.m. and 12:45 a.m., respectively."

"Do the times tell us anything?" Patterson asked.

Wolf sat forward, a thought coming to him. "How long does it take to drive from The Oxbow to the Silver Vein Wilderness area's lower lot?"

Lorber opened Google Maps on his computer and plugged in the locations. "Twenty-one minutes, assuming all speed limits are obeyed."

"Brock left the restaurant just after 11:45 . . . 11:47 according to the video. He would have gotten there at 12:08, give or take a minute or two."

"So, between 12:08 and 12:45, someone drove both cars to the upper lot, coasted them to the hole, and pushed them in," Rachette said. "Also, they killed two people. And wiped the prints off the driver's side of Brock's car."

Yates frowned. "That's a whole hell of a lot of stuff for one killer to do in thirty-seven minutes. Especially since they would've had to move the vehicles one at a time, running a mile back down the rocky mountain terrain in the dark in between. Sounds like at least two people to me."

"Don't forget that Clara left the restaurant before Brock," Wolf said. "If she went straight to Silver Vein Wilderness, she might have already been dead when Brock arrived, making the timeline more feasible. Still hard for one person, but not impossible."

"We could debate this all day. For now, let's move on."

Patterson tapped Brock's cell phone records. "We know this phone number that had a long, drawn-out conversation with Brock a week before his murder is registered under Roland Thatcher's umbrella of companies. I'm interested in that."

"And we know that it was Roland and Gemma Thatcher who came to us," Wolf said. "They wanted us to go looking for them. Why do that if you just killed both of them? Why bring suspicion to the situation at all? Why not just let them rot in the mine?"

"Yeah, that doesn't make much sense," Rachette said.

"To not report it would have made less sense," Patterson said. "Two people go missing after stealing paintings from your restaurant, you have to report it to the cops. Whether we like it or not, the Thatchers have motive. We have to know what was said on that call. It's time we talk to Roland Thatcher again."

"Excuse me," Lorber said, clearing his throat, "but if you're done with me, I'd like to excuse myself to go pass out. I've been up for almost twenty-six hours now."

"Right, of course." Patterson stood up, gathering the papers into the folder, handing them to Rachette.

They exited Lorber's office and went out into the parking lot.

The sun was higher overhead now, warming the air to a balmy fifty degrees.

"Let's go stop by Thatcher's place now," Patterson said. "I'll drop off my vehicle and you can drive me, Wolf."

Wolf, Rachette, and Yates exchanged glances as she opened her truck door.

"Assuming he's home," Wolf said.

"He is. Margaret was out to breakfast with him this morning."

"And if he doesn't answer? It's a waste driving all the way up there. I mean, for you. You could just send us."

She shrugged. "If he doesn't answer, then we'll go to the mine. I still haven't been up there to see everything yet, and I needed to do that today, anyway. We'll stop by Thatcher's, and then we'll go check out that hole. See you in a few minutes."

Patterson climbed into her truck, fired it up, and left.

"What the hell's with her?" Rachette asked.

"I don't know," he said, watching her speed down the highway toward town. "But I guess we'd better get going."

17

"Have you ever been here?" Patterson asked. "I mean, you know, since Thatcher bought the place?"

"No."

About halfway between Rocky Points and Cave Creek, the giant gate loomed up on the right.

"Jeez," Patterson said. "I didn't think you could get a gaudier entrance than what Connell had out here. I stand corrected."

Wolf slowed, pulling off the highway and up to a thick iron gate set between two spires of gray native rock that continued up, meeting in an arch. A large, blocky *T* hung down, made of shiny black metal.

Rachette's SUV followed as Wolf coasted up to a huge boulder that had been trucked in to serve as the backdrop for a flush-mounted, flat-screen television.

"State your name," a pleasant female voice said, accompanied by words scrawling across the black screen.

"David Wolf."

"State your reason for visiting."

Wolf looked at Patterson. She shrugged.

"We have news about Clara Abraham and Brock Wendel. New news."

That seemed to stump the computer because nothing happened for a full thirty seconds.

"Hello?"

A loud click sounded from the iron gate, and then it silently, slowly, swung open.

Wolf drove through, Rachette tailing his bumper.

The dirt road was the same as it had been all those years ago, still rising up a gradual hill that obscured the view on the other side.

Wolf thought about the last time he'd been here, and the proposal Gary Connell had made him, and the way his refusal had created a shitstorm he had narrowly survived. That was back when Wolf had wanted to be sheriff. Back when he had pined for his ex-wife and high school sweetheart, Sarah, who had just come out of rehab, and when Jack had lived with his grandparents.

"What are you thinking about?" Patterson asked.

"Just how old I am."

"Yeah."

Wolf looked over at her. She had her eyes out the window, a troubled expression on her face.

"Everything okay with you?" he asked.

"Yeah. Fine."

They rode in silence for a while, the cab humming as the tires steadily climbed toward the apex of the hill.

"Margaret hates Thatcher," Patterson said.

"I thought they were at breakfast this morning."

"They were. But just because she wants him to back me in the election."

"Why does she hate him?"

"When Thatcher first came into the area, she was working with him. You know, acting as his realtor. She was showing him a bunch of places up on Sunnyside, a couple up by you, and some large homes in town. And then this place.

"After coming here, he ghosted her. Stopped taking her calls. She thought he'd lost interest in the area. And then, bam, a few months later, she got word he'd done the transaction himself, without her help. The listing price was over a hundred million, and he cut her out of the commission."

Wolf whistled softly. "That's a lot of money."

"It's her fault, though. She never had him sign a buyer's agency agreement. She says she thought he was above that kind of thing. That somehow, billionaires worked on a different level or something. She expected him to be a man of his word." Patterson snorted.

"They sure did a lot of work up here. It will be interesting to see what's changed."

Wolf had passed by the property a number of times over the last couple of years, often seeing large earthmovers traveling up and down this hill. He'd heard rumors that the place had been completely gutted and overhauled. Apparently, Connell's extravagant monument to himself hadn't been good enough for Roland's extravagant monument to himself.

They settled back into silence as the mountains came into view over the rise, their thirteen-thousand-foot peaks shining in the midday sun. A minute later, the road flattened out and the hidden valley below appeared.

"Wow," Patterson said, leaning into the windshield.

Wolf leaned forward, too, mirroring her sentiment with a silent gasp.

It had significantly changed. Some of the outbuildings were still there—a horse stable, two maintenance-looking buildings probably housing large machinery, and a barn—but the house, which had once seemed like an unmovable monolith entrenched in this earth for millennia to come, was gone. Erased completely. Replaced by a sweeping, smooth hillside covered in grass, sage, and wildflowers.

The new house was a long distance to the east, toward the vast expanse of mountains looming over the property, near a wall of pine trees that led into the wilderness beyond.

"Wow," Patterson repeated.

They descended the hill, then made their way up a road that hadn't existed before.

As they neared the new home, Wolf saw it had all the fixings of its predecessor, including large wooden beams taken from old-growth pines, rock ornamentation, and plenty of glass on all sides, allowing the inhabitants to take in the majestic view sweeping out around them.

Wolf parked in the covered circle in front of the home's entrance.

Jorel, dressed in his usual combination of jeans and a flannel shirt, sleeves rolled up to display his Special Forces tattoo, walked out to meet them with a hard gaze.

Wolf and Patterson got out.

"Sheriff," Jorel said, shaking Patterson's hand.

Jorel and Wolf nodded at one another in greeting.

Rachette pulled up behind Wolf's vehicle, parked, and he and Yates got out.

"Quite a place you got here," Rachette said, rounding the front bumper of his SUV.

"It's not my place," Jorel said. "Mr. Thatcher will see you inside."

The iron front door was huge and inlaid with glass, resembling the one up at the restaurant, and it opened at the hands of some unseen force.

They entered a tall, cylindrical foyer with a glass ceiling, which let sunlight stream in. The sound of gently trickling water pulled their eyes to a waterfall coming out of a stone wall covered in tropical-looking foliage. The room was humid, smelling of sweet flowers.

"Hello, detectives," came Roland Thatcher's booming voice as he appeared from behind the water feature. "And Sheriff. First your aunt, and now you? To what do I owe the pleasure?"

"Hello, sir," Wolf said, offering a hand.

Roland shook his and Patterson's hands, then backed away, ignoring the two detectives with them.

"Come," Roland said, turning around.

They trailed after him over an impressive stone floor that could have been sourced from Stonehenge itself. The rock was ancient and colossal, showing striations, and it had undoubtedly been put into place with huge cranes, leveled to perfection, and smoothed to a glossy shine. The work involved must have rivaled Egyptian tombs.

The next room featured a thirty-foot-tall rock wall with floor-to-ceiling windows framing the mountains to the east. Display cases decorated the stone, filled with a number of oddities that only somebody with billions of dollars of extra money lying around could have collected. The skull of a tyrannosaurus rex smiled its huge dagger teeth at them as they walked past. A saber-toothed tiger skull did the same, along with a half dozen other species. All were labeled with engraved copper plates.

In a nook carved into the rock sat a round stone as large as a medicine ball sliced in half. An unseen light source shone down on it, illuminating a glossy silver matrix inlaid with greenish crystals. Its copper plate read, *Stony-Iron Meteorite.*

"The stony-iron meteorite is the rarest of the three meteorites found on earth. Those are olivine crystals contained within," Roland said. "It's much longer than it appears. Half of the mass extends into the wall. It weighs over a ton."

"How much does something like that cost?" Rachette asked.

"It's priceless."

"Yeah, but it cost something to acquire, right?"

Roland's wistful attention on his galactic masterpiece wavered, and he turned to Rachette, clearly displeased. "It takes focused attention. A lot of it."

"Oh, okay." Rachette saw the look Wolf was giving him and nodded. "It's beautiful."

"Thank you, Detective Rachette," Roland said, using perfect French pronunciation.

"It's Rachette. Like a hatchet."

"No, it's not."

Rachette's eyes hardened, and his pecs flexed underneath his checkered shirt.

"How about that?" Wolf asked, pointing to a hunk of solid metal gleaming in its own nook. Sun glared off the inscription, obscuring the letters.

"It says, 'Ag,'" Roland said. "For *argentum*, which is the Latin word for silver."

Wolf and Yates exchanged a glance.

"They pulled this specimen out of a Colorado mine not far from here."

"The Blue Corners Mine?" Wolf asked.

"No. Nothing as spectacular as this was ever found in that mine. This came out of the ground near Silver Plume."

"You know your Colorado mines," Wolf said.

"I own a copper mine in North Africa, and I have a diamond mine in South Africa. As far as my knowledge of Colorado mines goes, I've visited a few. I'm somewhat of an enthusiast, I guess you could say. But I'm a dunce compared to some of the people I know."

"Are you a restaurant enthusiast, too?" Rachette asked.

"What's that?"

"You own a restaurant."

"That's right."

Rachette smiled amicably. "Isn't that a little small-time for you? I mean, you own mines. Oil companies. Media conglomerates. And a steak-and-potato joint?"

Roland laughed heartily. "Yes, I own a restaurant, but it's not my baby. It's Gemma's. She's always been infatuated with cooking. She started playing chef when she was just five years old, so I made sure growing up she got to spend time with the greatest chefs in the world. She's on the hook for the success of that establishment, just like any other people I invest in."

"Oh," Patterson said. "That sounds great."

"What do you know about the Blue Corners Mine?" Wolf asked, trying to bring the topic back around.

Roland hesitated for a moment, then answered, "They

found a silver vein running through that mountain back in the 1880s. It ran out, and they abandoned it, but not before hollowing out much of the . . ." His sentence faded to nothing as he narrowed his eyes on Wolf. "Jorel tells me you have news regarding Clara and Brock."

Patterson cleared her throat. "Yes, sir. We do."

"Please," Roland said, sliding his gaze to the sheriff. He walked to a leather chair near the windows and gestured to a formation of matching couches. "Sit."

Wolf sat next to Patterson, and Rachette and Yates took the couch perpendicular to them. The cushions were pristine, smelling fresh out of the furniture factory.

"You found them," Roland said to Patterson.

"Yes, sir. We did."

Wolf interjected, "Before we get into the details, we were hoping you could tell us what you and Brock spoke about a week before his disappearance."

Roland looked at him blankly. "I didn't speak to him a week before his disappearance."

"He received a phone call from a number associated with an organization called Thatcher Holdings on February twelfth. One that lasted just over two minutes."

Roland flicked a look to Jorel, who stood behind Rachette and Yates's couch. They shared some silent communication, and then Roland shook his head, a look of puzzlement crossing his face. "I own over two dozen companies worldwide. How many employees are we up to, Jorel?"

"Over three hundred and fifty thousand."

"That much?" Roland scoffed, astonished. He folded his hands in his lap, crossed his legs, and looked at Wolf.

"When were you first aware that Brock was sleeping with Clara Abraham?" Wolf asked.

Roland said nothing.

"And did you know that he was possibly sleeping with other women as well? Including a newer employee named Kylie Jones?"

"Where are they?" Roland asked Patterson. "You said you found them. Where are they?"

Patterson hesitated, then let out a sigh and said, "They're dead."

Without a moment's hesitation, Roland uncrossed his legs, got up, and strolled out of the room without saying another word.

Jorel rounded the couch, standing in front of them. "It's time for you to leave."

They rose and walked out, ushered by Jorel's silent presence on their heels.

Three minutes later, they were back in the SUVs, driving out of Roland Thatcher's personal chunk of the world.

"He's following us out," Patterson said, looking in the side-view mirror.

Wolf inspected the third stream of dust in the rearview. It came from a familiar jet-black Range Rover with tinted glass, maintaining a far distance behind Rachette's vehicle.

When they got through the front gate, Wolf pulled over and rolled down his window. Rachette stopped alongside him with his passenger window already open.

"Where to?" Rachette asked. "The restaurant or the hole?"

"I'd like to see the hole first," Patterson said.

Rachette glanced at where Jorel's Range Rover had stopped

on the hill on the other side of the game fence surrounding the property.

"They're a little skittish," Yates said. "What do you make of it?"

"I think Roland's a smart man who knows when to shut his mouth," Wolf said. "Let's go."

He rolled up his window, and they joined the midday traffic heading north.

18

Wolf watched as Patterson twisted in place in the dirt of the lower parking lot, scanning the forest in all directions. She was holding the cell records in her hands, her eyes bouncing between the papers and her surroundings.

Near the entrance to the Silver Vein Wilderness area, a pair of barricades had been set up, closing the road. A deputy named Granby had been stationed there to turn away any hikers coming up to use the two parking lots.

From where their group stood, the upper lot was invisible behind the folds of the forest, but a loud whirring sound echoed through the valley, proving the forensic team was still hard at work extracting the two vehicles from the mine shaft.

"She's getting into this," Rachette said under his breath.

"It's been a while since she's been on a case," Yates said.

"She's not on the case. She's on a ride-along."

Patterson turned around and walked back toward them. "Let's go up."

They got back in their SUVs and drove to the upper lot,

where a tow truck was parked near two forensic department vehicles. Brock's BMW X5 was perched atop the back of the tow truck, dented and just as dirty as the day prior.

"They're making progress," Patterson said.

Wolf continued through the lot and into the woods, following what now looked like a well-worn road due to all the tires that had traveled down the gradual slope to the hole. He parked his SUV among the mass of official vehicles and got out.

A large group of uniforms were gathered near the hole, keeping their distance from a heavy-duty tow truck and the taut cable it had lowered into the shaft. The air smelled like diesel fuel and burning rubber as the driver revved the tow truck's engine, inching the vehicle forward. The winch mounted on its back whirred and screeched like a dying yeti, straining to bring Clara's vehicle to the surface.

Deputy Nelson walked up, nodding in greeting. "I'd stay back. That cable could snap at any second. They got the BMW out."

"We saw," Wolf said.

"They had to remove some rock from the walls with jack-hammers while preventing a cave-in and keeping the debris from damaging the cars further. It was a whole ordeal all night."

Wolf didn't envy them. But then again, he was the one who had almost been eaten by two mountain lions.

They observed for a few minutes as men yelled and scrambled, and the truck and winch pulled. Finally, the tail of Clara Abraham's mangled Mazda lifted into view, lurching out of the hole.

The driver of the tow truck shut off the engine, and the group of uniforms cheered.

Wolf turned to Patterson and saw she had been ignoring the spectacle, instead wandering the woods behind them.

"What's up?" Wolf asked.

She rejoined the detectives. "It does seem highly unlikely one person did all this."

"Agreed," Rachette said.

She nodded, eyeing the action near the hole. The Mazda was being dragged onto the ramp of the tow truck. "Let's take off," she said. "There's nothing we can do here but get in the way. I want to visit that restaurant."

"Yes, ma'am." Rachette followed Patterson, seemingly energized by her presence, leaving Yates and Wolf behind.

19

Patterson relished the scenery on the way down. She appreciated how the trees opened up, giving her a view of Cave Creek and the Chautauqua Valley to the south. She couldn't remember the last time she'd been on this road, and as she stared out the side window of Wolf's vehicle, the rumbling tires lulled her into a calm, content state.

They arrived at The Oxbow at 3:15 p.m. The parking lot had a few vehicles in it, undoubtedly servers and cooks getting ready for the restaurant to open for dinner.

She got out and stretched her limbs. The afternoon sun was directly overhead, shining down on the modern building and reflecting off the rippling Chautauqua behind it. It was warm, though a few dark clouds to the south told her Rocky Points might be getting rain right now.

Patterson inhaled deeply, savoring the smells of sage and river water and slow-cooking meat. A hawk circled overhead, reminding her how much she loved being out of the office.

Rachette and Yates exited their SUV and came to stand beside her.

"Now, how about you let us lead the way in here, Patty?" Rachette said. "It's been a while for you. And besides, we've got the lay of the land from our earlier visit."

"Back in February?" she asked.

"Yeah."

"Can you even remember back that far?"

"Not really. But I don't need to." He brandished a small notebook.

She plucked it from his hand and flipped it open.

"Disorganized, unintelligible chicken scratch," she said. "Just what I expected to see."

Smiling at his rare loss for words, she gave it back and followed Wolf across the parking lot to the entrance.

"Gemma Thatcher's here," Wolf said, nodding at a Range Rover in the parking lot.

"Ah."

Wolf opened the front door for them, and they streamed into the restaurant, Patterson letting Rachette and Yates take the lead. She was enjoying herself, stepping right back into her old detective role as if she'd never left it, but she had to remember this was their case. Not hers.

She stood at the host stand, taking in the interior of the establishment. It was majestic, designed with tasteful opulence, and had stunning views of the valley outside.

Gemma Thatcher was speaking with a server in the middle of the dining room as employees rushed about in preparation for the evening. When she noticed their arrival, she patted the server on the back and walked toward them.

"Hello, detectives. Oh, and Sheriff."

"Hi, Gemma," Patterson said. She had never spoken to the

woman outside of their quick introduction in Wolf's office four months ago.

Gemma looked upset. Her eyes were puffy, twinkling with tears. "I just heard the news from my dad."

Wolf stepped forward. "I'm sorry."

"Is it true?" Gemma asked. "They're both dead?"

Wolf nodded. "I'm afraid so."

Gemma shook her head, looking at the floor. "That's just crazy. I can't believe it. I spent all this time thinking he ran away with that . . . with Clara. And now this?"

They watched her dab her eyes with a tissue.

"Now that the case has changed," Wolf said, "we're stopping by to let you know we'll have to talk with you and your employees over the next several days."

Gemma nodded, sniffing. "Right. Yes, of course."

"The few interviews we did earlier with some of your staff were short and had to do with the robbery. Back then, we were merely searching for clues of their whereabouts. Now that we know they're both dead, we have two homicides to investigate."

"How were they killed?" Gemma's voice was a whisper.

"We'd prefer to keep the details to ourselves for the time being," Wolf said. "It's crucial for a case like this."

"Right. Of course."

Patterson hung back, watching Gemma closely. The woman seemed anything but guilty. She was genuinely upset. At least, that's how Patterson's trained eye read the situation. But it had been a while.

Wolf continued talking to Gemma, asking her something about back-of-the-house workers, and Patterson let her gaze wander.

"They replaced the paintings," Yates said, gesturing to the walls.

"Not surprising, given how long it's been," Patterson said. Then, quietly, she asked, "Who should I pay attention to here?"

"That guy's name is Tyson," Rachette said under his breath. "Behind the bar, delivering the glasses. He made it clear he distrusted Brock from the beginning. He was telling us he'd seen him in town, screwing around with other women."

"He didn't say that." Yates came closer, matching their volume. "He said he suspected Brock was screwing around. When we pressed him if he knew, he said he wasn't sure."

"Whatever." Rachette eyed the dining room. "That woman behind the bar is Sandra."

"Sandy," Yates said.

"Right. And there's that woman sitting at the booth rolling silverware." Rachette flipped open his notebook, studying a page. "Faith Orton."

"And that's her kid over there," Yates said.

Patterson saw a little girl, about four years old, sitting alone at a table in the center of the room, coloring with crayons.

"We're going to go get an updated employee roster," Wolf announced.

"Sure thing," Patterson said.

Wolf followed Gemma to her office.

A young woman came out of the kitchen's double doors. She had long blond hair, big brown eyes, and a body that would have made Patterson's eighteen-year-old self envious.

"Who's that?"

"That's Kylie Jones," Yates said.

"The same Kylie Jones who Brock called twice the week before he disappeared?"

"Indeed. We had a brief conversation with her during a follow-up visit here. She was working that Monday night. But yeah, looks like she might have been involved with Brock as well."

"She also has a cat," Rachette said.

"What?"

"She told us about her cat. She was all over the place."

Yates nodded. "Now that I think about it, she was stuttering. Blushing. Hurrying her words. Clearly had some inner turmoil when the subject of Brock came up. At the time, we suspected she was just trying to hide her involvement with him and was a terrible liar."

"But maybe she was upset because she'd just whacked him and put him in a hole," Rachette said.

"And Clara." Yates shook his head. "I don't know. I don't see her being the double-homicide-mastermind type. I'm telling you, the carpet we're standing on has a higher IQ."

"She could have been the accomplice," Rachette said. "Somebody else could have been the mastermind."

Wolf and Gemma came around the corner and into view, Wolf holding a piece of paper.

Rachette walked toward them, followed by Yates, then Patterson. She noted the way the bartender, Sandy, stared at them between tasks. Faith, the woman rolling the silverware, also looked at them often, almost invitingly.

"Hey, it's you again. What was your name?" Rachette asked, pausing beside the little girl. "Flippy? Flappy?"

"Haley!" The girl giggled.

"Oh yeah, that's right. You're still sitting here coloring all these months later. One day, your art will be on the wall, kid."

Haley ignored Rachette, shading a mountain scene in angry red, her hand making a fist around the crayon.

Wolf and Gemma reached them.

"We'll be in touch with everyone soon," Wolf said to Gemma. "In the meantime, we'd like to start by speaking to you."

Gemma's eyes narrowed. "You don't think I had something to do with this, do you?"

"Of course not," Yates said. "But we'd like to start from the top and work our way down."

"When?" she asked, looking at Yates.

Wolf handed the paper to Patterson. "Now, if you could."

There was an awkward pause, so Patterson studied the paper, observing Gemma with her peripheral vision. Roland had walked away without saying a word once the mention of death had reached his ears. She knew Wolf wanted to talk to Gemma before her father shut her up.

Gemma nodded, but her eyes were wide, and her chest was heaving a little. Clearly, she was wondering what to do.

Patterson looked down at Haley and noticed that Faith had left her booth and was walking their way.

"Hi," Patterson said. "You must be Faith."

Faith smiled, nodding. "Yes. Haley, dear, why don't you come over here with Mommy? We can let these people chat, okay?"

"Your daughter's a great artist," Rachette said. "Sees things differently. You ever think about testing to see if she's colorblind?"

Patterson's insides flipped. The breath left her body, and her eyes bugged as she looked at Rachette.

Rachette held steady, unapologetic eye contact with the woman. "It's passed on by the parents, you know. Are you colorblind?"

"No," Faith said, frowning at Rachette. She scraped the art utensils into a box, dropping one. "Let's go, honey."

"Hey, I'm sorry. It's just that—ah!" Rachette stepped back, using his foot to rub his shin, which Patterson had punched while picking up the stray crayon.

"Sorry, ma'am," Patterson said. "Here's your crayon, Haley."

"Haley can stay," Gemma said, eyeing Rachette. "We can go talk over there." She strolled toward a bank of windows looking out over the river below.

Face burning, Patterson smiled sheepishly at the girl and her mother before trailing after the detectives. She joined them at a table by the windows, sneaking a glance at Rachette. The blood had drained from his face.

"You told us you were not working on the night of the thefts," Wolf said.

Gemma nodded. "That's right."

"Do you remember what you were doing?"

"Oh . . . it's been so long. But usually—"

"Excuse me," a male voice cut in. "Gemma, stop talking, please."

It was Jorel. The man had somehow entered the building and approached their table unnoticed.

"She's done talking to you," he said. "Gemma, come with me, please."

Gemma looked at Jorel, a hint of anger, followed by resignation, flashing in her eyes.

"I'm sorry," she said to them, threading her way between Rachette and Patterson.

Jorel whispered to her as she passed.

Gemma halted, confronting him. "Why?"

He responded too softly for them to hear.

She shook her head, storming away, and Jorel faced them.

"What's going on?" Patterson asked.

Jorel gestured to the entrance, just like he had at Roland's house. "It's time for you guys to leave. The restaurant's closing."

"Closing?" Patterson asked.

"That's right."

"Why?"

"I'm not at liberty to discuss with you."

In the center of the dining area, Gemma was making the rounds, talking to employees. Most people looked confused, some of them disappointed.

Patterson and her detective squad sat in silence for a beat, then made their way toward the door.

"But I am at liberty to discuss with you," Jorel said.

Patterson turned around, seeing Jorel had stopped Wolf.

Wolf raised an eyebrow at her.

"It's okay," she said. "We'll see you back at the station."

Not waiting for a response, she went to catch up with Yates and Rachette.

"What the hell was that all about?" Rachette asked as they crossed the parking lot.

Patterson ignored him, climbing into the rear seat of his SUV.

When Rachette sat down, she lurched forward and grabbed him by the earlobe.

"Ah!"

"'Colorblind'? Did you really just say that to that woman?"

"What? Tommy's red-green colorblind. Ah! Patty! I wish somebody would have given us a heads-up like that! I probably just saved that girl a shitload of hard times!"

She let go, collapsing hard against the seat, whipping the seatbelt over her shoulder and buckling it.

"Jeez, Patty. Easy."

"Do you like it when people help you parent your kids?"

Rachette rubbed his ear. "No."

She closed her eyes and focused on getting her breathing under control, listening to the silence, feeling the heat of the seat against her back.

Rachette started up the SUV and reversed out. "I'm sorry," he said. "It was stupid of me."

She shook her head. "I didn't know that about Tommy."

A few seconds later, Rachette cleared his throat. "He's not really. But I've read about it. And it can be bad not knowing."

She closed her eyes again. "Drive fast please."

20

Wolf waited in the reception area of the restaurant for Jorel to emerge from the back. Five minutes in, he resisted the urge to leave. Truth was, he wanted to hear what the man had to say.

He spent the time watching the employees reverse the work they had done earlier. Faith and her daughter were still there, but their tasks hadn't changed. While her daughter scribbled on her paper, Faith continued rolling silverware, apparently for another day.

Sandy bobbed and weaved behind the bar, eyeing Wolf without discretion. Tyson spent a lot of time unseen in the back, while Kylie moved about mostly in the front of the house, generally acting as if Wolf didn't exist.

Jorel finally pushed through the kitchen's swivel doors and walked over.

"You ready?" he asked.

"For what?"

"I have something to show you in my vehicle."

Wolf motioned to the door, and Jorel led the way out, striding fast across the parking lot.

Eyes squinting against the bright sun, Wolf worked to keep up with the man's pace. Thankfully, the ache in his legs from the previous two days' strain had dissipated somewhat.

Jorel's Range Rover was parked at the far southern end of the lot, pointed at the bow in the river below.

"Please," Jorel said, opening the passenger side door and walking around the front of his vehicle to the driver's side.

Wolf climbed up onto a soft, warm leather seat. The interior was spotless and smelled of tasteful cologne.

Jorel pushed a few buttons, and the air conditioning kicked on. The vents whispered as he stared out the windshield.

"Seventy-fifth, right?" Jorel said at last.

Wolf grunted in the affirmative.

"You get a chance to deploy?"

"Two tours to Afghanistan. Helmand and Kunduz. And some other interesting deployments with our Tier 1 brothers. You?"

"Two tours to Afghanistan as well. Kunduz and Nuristan." Jorel looked past Wolf into another time.

"And now you're working for one of the richest men in the world."

"Yes, I am."

"Must be interesting."

"I thought of becoming a cop after I got out. Even went to the academy in Chicago. But that's where I met a guy in private security. And I realized being a cop wasn't for me. No offense."

"What do you have for me, Jorel?"

Jorel flicked his eyes to the rearview. A man got into his

sedan a few spots away and drove off. "Mr. Thatcher wants to make sure you guys aren't investigating him."

"Or you."

Jorel met his gaze directly for the first time that day, his blue eyes narrowing. "You don't think we're actually involved in this in any way, do you?"

Wolf noticed the man had a lengthy scar along one cheek, made almost invisible by dark stubble.

"We're searching for a motive, and we're having trouble seeing past the guy with the daughter with an adulterous fiancé. The guy who stood to lose face, and money, letting Brock Wendel into his family.

"Then again," Wolf continued, "murder is the riskiest kind of business. Roland Thatcher doesn't seem to be that dumb. Especially when it would have been simplest to get rid of Brock Wendel by paying him off. You know, give him a million and tell him to scram for life, or else."

"Which is exactly what we did."

"What?"

"You were right. It was us who called Brock seven days before his disappearance. Me, to be precise. I called him and told him we knew about his affairs on Gemma and the scam he was running on her. I said we wouldn't stand for either, then offered him two million dollars to, as you put it, 'scram for life,' or we would cut him off, reveal the truth, and he would get nothing."

"Wait, what scam?" Wolf asked, frowning.

Jorel sighed. "When we began to suspect Brock was cheating, I looked deep into their finances and learned he'd been taking investments from Gemma for years to help run an internet company he'd set up to sell digital products, like guides on how to triple your net worth. As far as I could tell, the company was a front. He never made any income doing it. He just took money from her and spent it on other women and vacations around the globe."

"Why didn't you tell us about this earlier?"

"I'm telling you now."

"What did he say when you called him?"

"What could he say? I showed him our evidence."

Jorel reached across Wolf's lap, unlatching the glove compartment. It fell open, revealing a ZEV OZ9 combat pistol lying atop a manila folder. He pulled out the folder, shut the compartment, and placed it on Wolf's lap.

Wolf found a set of photographs inside. The top photo had been taken through a window by a telephoto lens, and it displayed two naked people in mid-action on a bed. Upon closer inspection, Wolf recognized the exterior of Brock's apartment building.

"This is . . . Clara Abraham?"

"Yes. And the second is Kylie Jones."

Wolf flipped to the next photo. Same place, same angle, same lens, same guy, different woman.

"Like I said, I showed him these, plus evidence of his financial misappropriations, and I told him to get lost. We'd give him one million upon leaving, and one million after a year of staying lost."

"And he agreed."

"Wholeheartedly."

"And this was seven days before his disappearance?"

"Yes."

"And you didn't give him the money?"

"No. He was getting his affairs in order. Perhaps literally.

We were going to send the initial payment to him on the first of the month. That's when he said he planned to leave. But then he and Clara stole the paintings and disappeared."

"Why would he steal those paintings and put the two million you offered him at risk?" Wolf asked. "Selling them wouldn't have netted him more money. Gemma said they'd be worth five to eight hundred K per. Is that true?"

"Yes."

"And that's at auction, not the black market," Wolf said. "Offloading them to a fence, he would take a big hit, not making nearly as much as two million."

"Exactly." Jorel shrugged.

"It doesn't make any sense."

"Maybe Brock was just stupid. Or maybe whoever killed Clara and Brock put them up to it."

Wolf frowned. "You know anybody else who would want to steal those paintings?"

"No."

"And you've asked Roland that same question?"

"I have. He has no clue."

Wolf wasn't sure if he believed Jorel. He sounded genuine, but being the head of security for a billionaire, he probably knew a thing or two about lying convincingly.

"Back to your conversation with Brock. Why not just expose the infidelity?" Wolf asked. "Why not tell Gemma the truth and kick Brock out on his ass, broke?"

"It was Mr. Thatcher's wish to keep it secret. He tends to think of his daughter as fragile. I personally thought she could use the news as a growth opportunity, but Mr. Thatcher saw otherwise. Brock was supposed to break it off with Gemma and leave peacefully."

Wolf shut the manila folder. "But he went rogue, stealing the paintings with one of his girlfriends, and then got himself killed. By whom?"

"That's the question now," Jorel said. "What leads do you guys have? We heard there was no spatter in Brock's vehicle. Somebody lifted him into the trunk. Probably had to be two people, right?"

"Or one strong guy." Wolf looked at him.

Jorel shook his head.

"And that wasn't public knowledge," Wolf said. "How did you hear about the spatter?"

"We have our sources."

Wolf thought of all the men and women who had been gathered in the woods not more than an hour and a half ago, watching those vehicles coming out of the ground. Lorber wouldn't have disclosed anything, but the rest of his team? Any of them could have talked, with or without a hefty payment from Roland. Gossip was human nature, especially in this small valley in the middle of Colorado.

"Maybe Roland found out Brock was going rogue and decided he didn't want to pay the money to him after all," Wolf said. "Maybe he killed Brock and sold the paintings to a black-market dealer. Or somebody on his security team did. Two million dollars is a lot to save."

"Two million is nothing for him. Thatcher's bank account has fluctuated tens of millions of dollars as I spoke this sentence. He doesn't think about money like we do. I'm telling you. It wasn't him. It wasn't me."

An employee fired up their car, backed out, and left the parking lot.

"You're shutting down the restaurant. What's that about?"

"There could be cold-blooded killers in that building. That would put them close to Gemma Thatcher. It's my job to protect all that Roland Thatcher holds dear."

"And so you're helping us now."

Jorel nodded.

"You can't go around intimidating civilians. You know that, right?"

"I wouldn't think of it." Jorel smiled, showing a sliver of humor. "You keep those photographs. Look into Kylie Jones."

Wolf narrowed his eyes. "Why should I look into her when you already have? Just tell me what you found."

"She's from Denver. Only child of rich parents. Relatively rich, of course. Moved up here last fall to become a ski bum. Lives in Points. Got a job with the restaurant over the winter. Got involved with Brock pretty much immediately. She's also with Tyson."

"Any large financial transactions lately?" Wolf asked.

"I haven't looked yet. We didn't know Brock and Clara were dead until a couple hours ago, so I had no reason to."

"What about Tyson?"

"I haven't looked into him yet, either. Again, no reason to until now."

"Anyone else I should keep my eye on?"

"Not that I'm aware of. But I'm happy to be of service to you and your team if you need anything. Here's my number." Jorel handed Wolf a card, then opened his door. "Now, if you'll excuse me, I have an establishment to shut down."

Wolf exited the vehicle. "I hope you'll keep me posted about anything you find in your investigation," he said, putting away Jorel's card and pulling out his own.

"I already have your number." Jorel strode away, locking his vehicle with a chirp.

Wolf put the card back in his pocket. "Of course you do."

He walked to his SUV, watching Jorel disappear inside.

And through the tinted windows of the restaurant, he saw Kylie Jones. She peered at him for a few moments, then turned and vanished into the reflections.

21

"Whoa . . . that's uh . . . can I have a copy of this one?"

Yates snatched the picture from Rachette's hand and whistled softly. "Yeah, this is a good one."

"Okay," Wolf said, raking the stack of photographs off the desk and out of Yates's hand. He put them back in the folder. "The point is, Brock was definitely involved with Kylie Jones as well as Clara. Let's move on to the implications. I want everything we can get on her, and on Tyson Lennox."

He stood up and looked out of his office window. Below, Main Street bustled with people and rush-hour cars passing by. Sunrays slanted down between the resort and the mountain next to it, giving another few minutes of light to the bottom of the valley before the sun ducked out of sight.

"We'll get on it," Yates said, leaning back in his chair.

"You think this Jorel guy is telling the truth?" Rachette asked. "That Brock died before they gave him the money?"

"He seemed to be. And we already know Brock's financial

transactions were minimal around the time of his disappearance."

"They could have paid him in crypto," Rachette said. "And
then somebody stole the digital wallet, or whatever the hell it's
called."

"A digital wallet," Yates said. "If they did that, then we'd
never know."

Rachette scoffed. "It doesn't make any sense that Brock
would have the two-million deal going with Roland, and then
risk it all by stealing those paintings with Clara."

"Maybe Brock was trying to milk all he could out of Roland
before he left town," Wolf said. "He thought that if Clara was
the one who took the paintings, Roland and Jorel wouldn't
realize he had played a part in the theft, so he'd still get his
payoff. Then he could have his cake and eat it, too. Maybe
another friend was in on it, and the friend turned on them."

"No way. Too risky. He hadn't even gotten the first payoff
from Roland yet," Yates said. "Nobody's that much of a moron,
right? He must have known Jorel and Roland would see the
security footage and see how he stayed in the kitchen. That
they would find out he cut the servers early and left the front
door wide open for somebody to waltz in and take the paintings. He had to have known they would suspect him."

"Yeah," Wolf said, still staring out the window.

"Somebody put Brock and Clara up to it," Yates said. "Had
to be. No way he risked his payday when selling the paintings
on the black market wouldn't have made up the potential
loss."

Rachette nodded. "And then those people took the paintings from him and killed him and Clara to shut them up. Or
maybe Jorel is blowing smoke up our ass for some unknown

reason. Roland's a billionaire. How do you even get to that level unless you're a genius? The dude probably has us tricked five different ways, and we don't even know it."

"Yeah," Wolf repeated. He rubbed his neck, pushing hard on a knot that was forming above his shoulder blade. He saw a young couple holding hands on the sidewalk, talking close with one another.

"Pull up Tyson Lennox's socials," Wolf said.

Yates tapped the keys of his laptop. "Here's his Instagram. It's private. Checking his others. Facebook . . . He's not there. LinkedIn? Not active. Private here . . ."

"How about our bartender, Sandy?" Wolf asked, thinking of her blatant staring.

"Sandy Eggleston," Yates said, typing. He scrolled through the search results, shaking his head. "She's not looking active, either. No Instagram account, and her Facebook profile . . . well, she has a few pictures from years ago. Wait. Wow. Okay, well, you're not going to believe this." He pointed at the screen.

There was a photo of a group of seven people gathered around a sign that read, *Silver Vein Wilderness Area*. All but one of the hikers were The Oxbow employees.

Rachette leaned in. "You're shitting me. We've got Tyson Lennox tagged, Clara Abraham, Brock Wendel, Faith Orton, Sandy Eggleston, Gemma Thatcher, and some guy named Chad Westerberg."

"No Kylie," Yates said. "She hadn't moved up here yet."

They stared at the picture for another few seconds until Yates threw up his hands and pushed away from the desk. "So, everyone's spending time up there at the scene of the murder. And we've got a roster of forty-two people who worked at that restaurant at the time of their deaths. You ever worked at a restaurant before?"

"No," Rachette said. "Why?"

"Because those places are relationship mega-factories. Who's screwing who this week? Who's got the hots for who today? Who just shot down who last night? We don't just have forty-two people to look into, we have forty-two people's multiple relationships to look into. It's like a math problem from hell. And who's to say the killers even work in the restaurant? They could be anybody."

The knot in Wolf's neck tightened. His mood was dropping fast. He needed food.

"What's our plan here?" Yates asked.

"Start at the top and make our way down to the bottom," Rachette said.

"I think we start with where that zoom lens was pointing," Wolf said.

"Kylie Jones?" Yates asked.

Wolf nodded. "We figure out if Jorel was telling the truth about her and Tyson being involved, and then we go from there. Maybe Kylie and Tyson decided to manipulate Brock, blackmailing him with proof he was screwing around. 'Steal the paintings for us, or else we'll tell Gemma, and you'll be out of a lucrative marriage.'" Wolf shrugged. "Something like that."

"That would fit," Yates said.

"We look into both of them," Wolf said, "and if that's a dead end, then we look into all of the employees until we figure it out. But it's been a long day. You guys head home. And I'm sorry, but it looks like we're working the weekend, so I'll see you tomorrow."

The two detectives stood up. Yates closed and stuffed his computer into his bag, and they left out the door.

"See you tomorrow, Chief," Yates called over his shoulder.

"See you tomorrow."

Wolf pulled out his cell phone with a sigh, typing out a message.

Hey, how's it going?

He sent the text to Piper and watched the screen dumbly, waiting for an answer. When she didn't immediately reply, his stomach reminded him it was empty. He put on his sweatshirt and left his office, dialing the phone number of a nearby restaurant to place a to-go order, happy he could solve at least one problem for the day.

22

Wolf strolled along the sidewalk of Main Street, taking in the sights, sounds, and scents of a bustling Friday night. Down the road, live music flowed out of a tavern. Once upon a time, the only place to catch a live band would have been Beer Goggles. Now, three new establishments on Rocky Points' main thoroughfare drew impressive weekend crowds.

One of those places was Cheep's, located in a freshly renovated building near the coffee shop. They served sandwiches and entrees and had a large bar that was very popular. He was going there now to pick up the sandwich he'd ordered, which he would take back to the office to eat before making his way home. Or he'd drive home first, staving off his hunger, and enjoy the meal in front of the television. He hadn't decided yet.

A woman crossing the street caught his eye, and he realized it was Piper. She was dressed smartly in a gray pantsuit that draped close to her lithe figure. Her dark hair flowed over her shoulders as she walked and laughed. The sound was instantly recognizable to Wolf's ears, making his heart skip a beat.

Wolf slowed to a stop when he noticed the man walking next to her was Austin. He was dressed in power-lawyer attire, and he was also laughing. His teeth glowed like a light strip on his tanned face.

A half dozen other people surrounded them, clearly a group from her office out to get a drink together after a long week.

He watched as they crossed the street and turned toward him, still locked in their conversation. But before they reached him, they turned again. Austin rushed forward and opened the door to Cheep's, holding it ajar for the group. Piper hung back, taking the last spot in the train and thanking Austin on the way in. Austin's eyes, and then body, followed her inside.

Wolf continued up the sidewalk, though at a considerably slower pace now, his thoughts turning cold as he replayed the way Austin had looked at Piper. He pulled out his phone and saw she had not yet responded to his text message. Which was normal, he told himself. She had probably been walking with the large group when he'd texted. It had only been a few minutes ago. Besides, he didn't expect her to be at his beck and call.

He was hungry.

As he drew closer to Cheep's, he looked through the restaurant's windows and spotted them inside. Austin was still talking to Piper, handing her a glass of wine. The other members of their group surrounded them, but they seemed to be keeping to themselves.

Or that last part could have been Wolf's imagination, as another man came up and joined their conversation.

Wolf kept walking, wondering if he was getting jealous. It was a strange, rare sensation, one he couldn't recall having since Sarah. After the end of their relationship, and especially after breaking up with Lauren, he'd forgotten how to get knotted up in pointless, petty mind games with himself over a woman. He'd moved light-years beyond that. Right?

Then why was he getting upset about this Austin guy?

He was hungry. That was why. At least, that was a good explanation for now.

The door opened right when he reached for the handle, and somebody came out, barging into him.

"Oh, I'm so sorry—David?" It was Piper. She let out an astonished laugh, stumbling back. Her phone was in her hand. "What the heck? What are you doing here?"

She grabbed his arm and pulled him to the side, letting in a man trying to get past.

"Hey," he said. "I'm just getting some dinner. I ordered a sandwich."

"I just saw your text," she said, raising her phone. "I was going to call you."

"Oh."

She looked up at him, the joy in her eyes morphing to concern. "How was your day?"

"It was good. How about you?"

"Good." She reached up and kissed him on the lips.

The simple gesture evaporated every negative thought that had been swimming through his mind. He leaned forward and kissed her back, and they hugged, her embrace strong around his neck as she balanced on her toes.

When they parted, she said, "I'm in there with some coworkers and a prospective client."

"Oh, cool."

"So, you're coming in?"

"Yeah."

"Great. You can say hi to everyone. And I was actually going to ask you a question when I called you, but I'll have Austin do it."

Wolf had no clue what that meant, but she had already started walking to the door, tugging him by the hand after her.

They entered a raucous atmosphere smelling of alcohol and bar food. Her thin hand keeping a firm grasp on his, she led him through the crowd and straight to Austin.

"Look who I found outside!" Piper said, poking Austin's shoulder.

Austin broke from a conversation and turned around, smiling wide. "Hey! David! How are you doing?"

Wolf returned the grin despite himself and shook hands.

"This is Thomas McMahon, one of our partners at the firm. Tom, this is Piper's significant other, David Wolf. He's a detective with the sheriff's department."

After smiling through another few introductions, Piper grabbed Wolf by the arm.

"Tell him about tomorrow night," she said to Austin.

Austin frowned. "You haven't asked him yet?"

"No."

"Asked me what?"

"Tomorrow night, my fiancée and I would like to have you two over for dinner."

Piper nodded. "Her name's Ashley."

"Oh." Wolf raised his eyebrows. He glanced down and saw the way Piper was hanging on his next words, her face frozen in a brittle-looking smile. "Yeah. Okay, that sounds good."

Piper's smile relaxed, and she squeezed his arm, sliding her hand down to grab his hand.

"That's great. See you two at six, then." Austin looked around. "So, what were you doing outside? You were just hanging around? You don't drink, do you?"

"No. I was just on my way in here to get a meal to go. In fact, I'd better try and figure out where that is now."

"We look forward to seeing you tomorrow, David." Austin turned around.

Wolf nodded and broke away from the group. Piper stuck by him as he went to the edge of the bar and told the bartender about his order.

While the food was being retrieved, Piper said nothing. Conversation was nearly impossible due to the din, anyway. Instead, she hung out next to him and sipped her wine, like she was truly content just to be together. He realized he felt the same way, and the thought made him smile. It was amazing the one-eighty the last few minutes had taken.

After he got his sandwich, Piper walked him out.

"Thanks," she said.

"For what?"

"For saying yes to tomorrow. It was super late notice, I know. I'm just glad you're coming. I think it's kind of important you get to know Austin."

Why? he thought, but he nodded. "Yeah. Of course. It will be fun."

"It probably won't be fun. It may be excruciating. But thanks."

He nodded again.

"Kind of like this happy hour," she said. "Our prospective client likes to go out and have fun. He said so at the meeting this afternoon, and everyone's gung ho to appease him. I'll be heading home soon. I'm tired. But I'm rambling. I'll let you get to your food."

Wolf laughed. "I'll pick you up tomorrow."

"Okay. Say five thirty?"

"It's a date."

"Bye." She reached up and pecked his lips again, then went back inside.

He walked down the sidewalk toward headquarters, wondering why he'd ever hesitated to give her that ring.

23

Heather Patterson scrubbed the dish under the running water, cocking her head toward her youngest son.

"And it's because it's not . . ." Lucas hesitated, his seven-year-old brain struggling to find the word.

"Fun?"

"No!" He waved his hand, shooshing her. "It's not . . . satisfying."

She smiled, surprised at how much she'd underestimated the upcoming end of the sentence.

"That's a great word there," she said.

Her son left the kitchen, ignoring her compliment.

Scott laughed, placing a dish in the sink. "He's getting sophisticated with his vocabulary."

"You can . . . exclaim that again."

"Nice try."

Her cell vibrated in her pocket. She turned off the faucet, wiped her hands on a towel, and pulled out her phone, reading a number she recognized.

"Important?" Scott asked.

"Maybe. I have to answer this."

"Go," he said, taking over the dishes.

"This is Heather."

"I've found some things," James Long, the private investigator from Bend, Oregon, said.

Patterson stepped inside the home office and shut the door behind her, a rush of blood coming to her ears. "Yeah? And?"

"And he inherited twenty-six million from his wife's death."

She raised her eyebrows, looking out the window at the fading sunset. The snow-covered peaks to the north were alight with alpenglow.

"That's more than I thought," she said. Margaret had once told her it was six. Not that six million was anything to scoff at, but twenty-six seemed like a whole new realm of rich to Patterson. "And the donations to his campaign? He still hasn't filed anything."

"It doesn't look like he's taken a dime from a lobbyist group called Alpine Heights. I can't find anything. I looked from both sides. My contact in DC says Waze is donating to them, not the other way around."

"And what about from other groups?" she asked.

"Nothing."

"Okay. And from Roland Thatcher? His company? Or any subsidiaries?"

"Listen. I don't want to tell you how I know. And you don't want to know how I know. But I know he hasn't taken anything from anybody."

She exhaled. "Okay."

"There is something, though. I did some *discreet* interviewing and research."

Patterson's stomach churned at his tone. She sensed that what he was about to say could land her in jail someday.

"You know his wife was killed by a drunk driver?"

"Yes."

James Long began disclosing the rest of the information he'd learned.

At one point, Patterson pulled the phone away from her ear, not wanting to hear any more. She felt disgusting for prying into the man's broken, mangled family. But after a moment, she put the phone back because she'd asked for this information.

Patterson let out an involuntary sigh. "You're sure?"

He was. He had uncovered and verified irrefutable proof, which he described to her in detail.

That could explain the absence of Waze's daughter in his life, she thought. Maybe his daughter knew the devastating secret. Maybe she blamed her father for her mother's death.

"Thank you," Patterson said. "I appreciate your work. You can send me the bill. And, please, if you would keep our work confidential, even with my aunt, I would appreciate it."

"Of course. Give me an email address to send the bill to."

She gave her personal email, said goodbye, and hung up, picturing the eternal taint on her soul for making the transaction.

She went back out into the kitchen.

"Everything okay?" Scott asked.

A tear escaped her eye, running down her cheek.

"What is it?" He wrapped her in a hug.

"Nothing."

But it wasn't nothing. Now she had dirt on Waze, and she felt slimy each time the thought cycled in her mind. Everything she had been afraid of, everything she'd warned Margaret about, had come true.

She smiled to relieve Scott's concern. "I'm just tired. I'm going to bed."

"Okay," he said, but he knew something was up. And he also knew to let it go for now.

She smiled weakly, kissed him, and went upstairs.

24

Wolf sat behind the wheel, watching the condominium complex.

Another vehicle drove into the lot and parked. Two young people stepped out, pulling vape pens from their pockets, mouths wisping smoke as they laughed and made their way up a flight of stairs.

Kylie Jones reappeared at the third-floor window of unit 38B: her rented condo, according to public records. She was dressed in a skimpy pair of shorts and a tank top as she put her hands to the glass to see out beyond the glare.

It was almost as if she were looking back at Wolf. At first, he'd wondered, but now, sitting in his unmarked SUV at the corner of the lot, submerged in the black shadows pooling beneath a set of tall pines, he concluded she was waiting for somebody.

He finished the last bite of his Cheep's meatball sandwich, savoring the chewy bread, then sipped his drink, watching as Kylie turned away and moved out of sight.

A cloud passed in front of the almost-full moon, causing its edges to glow silver. A spray of stars glinted overhead.

He could climb the stairs to go talk to her. Ask her about Brock Wendel and her whereabouts on the night of his death. But bringing her in for formal questioning during standard business hours was the right move. Then his detectives would be there for the interrogation, and he could record it.

Right now, he was just here out of curiosity. He wanted to see what this woman was up to on the night after Brock's and Clara's bodies had been discovered.

His phone chimed, and a message popped onscreen.

Good night. I can't wait to see you tomorrow.

Wolf smiled at Piper's text. He thought about the way she had looked at him earlier at the bar, waiting for him to answer Austin's invitation to come over. She seemed desperate to bring Wolf behind the scenes. For him to get to know her boss. Wolf was still asking himself why. Maybe she hoped the two of them would become friends.

He typed out his reply.

Good night. I can't wait either.

Fatigue wrapped him like a warm blanket, and he stretched his mouth in a wide yawn. He needed to get some good sleep. The last few nights, he'd been late to get to sleep and early to rise, as often happened during a case.

He wished he were the kind of detective who could shut off his mind each night and get back to it the next morning, but he wasn't. Questions had been churning in his head ever since they had found Clara's bones. There were killers out there who'd gotten away with the worst crime, and now they were being pushed into a corner. They would be dangerous.

Reaching to press the SUV's ignition button, he paused as another vehicle pulled into the lot.

Music hummed out of the truck, which sped between parked cars and came to a rocking halt a few spots away from Wolf.

The music shut off, along with the lights, and Tyson Lennox stepped out, his phone pressed to his ear.

Wolf was still holding his own phone, so he turned on his video camera, careful to shut off the flash first.

Half through the screen of his phone and half through the SUV's windshield, he watched Tyson take the stairs two at a time to the third floor, walking straight to Kylie Jones's place. When he got close, he ducked low.

Kylie appeared at her window again, speaking into her phone.

Tyson lurched into view, scaring her. With an awe-shucks smile, she went to the door and opened it, then launched herself into Tyson's arms, her legs wrapping around his waist.

Tyson groped her, and they kissed passionately, stumbling into the condo and shutting the door behind them.

Wolf blinked. Keeping the recording going, he stepped outside and walked to Tyson's vehicle, getting a shot of the license plate for good measure. He climbed back into his SUV and propped up his phone on the dash, aiming it at unit 38B. But the two of them never came into view of the one uncovered window. They were undoubtedly too busy in another room at that moment.

Shutting off the video recorder, he wondered—how capable of murder were these young lovers?

He yawned again, pressing the ignition button, deciding the answer would have to come later.

25

Xavier Jorel silently scoped the nearby setting.

The single-story ranch home was out in the middle of nowhere by any definition of the phrase. The nearest neighbor was over a mile away in any direction.

Behind him, the valley sprawled south, out all the way to the distant Cave Creek hills. The waxing moon's rays set the sage- and juniper-covered ground alight. But not where he stood. A passing stream of clouds had obscured the overhead glow, dousing him in inky darkness, removing any need for him to hide.

Somewhere to his left, an owl hooted, joining the mournful call of a dove.

Far to the north, a storm raged on some high peaks, flashing and booming, barely audible even in the desolate silence of his surroundings.

Much closer, a different kind of storm had been going for some time now, and he returned his attention to it with heightened interest.

The two women inside the house were arguing at the

kitchen table, their voices hushed. But every once in a while, a snippet would carry outside to Jorel's front-yard observation point.

One woman was older, in her late fifties or early sixties, dressed in a flannel set of pajamas. He assumed she was the mother of the younger woman, who he knew was thirty-three years old, thanks to the restaurant's records. Wearing a T-shirt and sweatpants, the daughter had her face smothered in her hands.

Jorel had always thought the employee was pretty. Now, in her vulnerable state, he thought she was especially so.

They appeared to be having a life-and-death exchange of words. Everything the daughter said, the mother took with a look of horror and a hand over her mouth.

He could imagine what they were talking about: the discovery of the bodies, and how they were doomed.

The evidence pointed to them. The cops just didn't know it yet.

I should turn myself in, the younger woman was probably saying.

Or maybe they were talking about how they were going to shoot their way out of the situation. If his hunch was right—and he was 95 percent sure it was—then he had to remember he was staring at two ruthless killers right now.

The storm rumbled in the distance, louder this time. The clouds must have been moving south toward him.

He deliberated his next move. He needed solid proof.

After the theft of the paintings, he'd installed some microphones in the restaurant. A couple hours ago, while going through the day's security footage, he'd spotted an employee tucked away in a dim corner of the restaurant, whispering into her phone. Upon cranking the volume, he'd been able to decipher her side of the conversation.

"They're here again . . . I know, I know . . . Bye . . ."

That's all the woman had said, but it had been enough to rouse his suspicion, bringing him to this run-down house in the dead of night.

More thunder rolled low. He turned his head to glance at the clouds, but his eyes caught on a prick of light in his peripheral vision instead. He realized the noise was coming from a vehicle traveling down the road toward the house, not the storm.

Damn it.

It was still a good quarter mile away, so when the lights flicked out of view behind a rise, he walked casually to the two cars parked in the driveway, ducking between them. At any moment, the approaching vehicle would pass his Range Rover, which he had parked up the hill, just out of sight of the house, near a tall stand of junipers.

The sound of squealing brakes broke the silence. He couldn't see up the road anymore, his view blocked by a lone old-growth pine standing sentinel in the front field, but he could hear the rumbling engine quiet to an idle. The newcomer was checking his vehicle.

And then the engine revved, and the rumbling resumed, tires crackling on the dirt road. A spray of high beams preceded the vehicle's arrival in the driveway.

He moved to the side of the house and bent down behind two trash cans.

Another squeal of brakes. The headlights raked over and across his hiding spot. Jorel held frozen, and they passed him by, sliding to the front of the house.

The vehicle parked, and the driver shut off the engine and lights. Their door popped open, then slammed closed, and he pictured somebody stepping out.

He heard footsteps leading away from him, and then the sound of the front door opening.

"Hey," a female voice said. "What's going—"

The front door closed, snuffing out the rest of the woman's words.

Jorel stayed crouched, breathing slowly, eyes narrowed, straining to hear all that was happening around him.

He felt the weight of his ZEV holstered to his hip.

Slowly, he straightened and went to the corner of the house to listen. There was commotion inside, the sound of clanking plates and pots and pans, as if the woman entering the house had spurred a bout of deep cleaning.

Frowning, he questioned what his plan was now. They were probably onto him, given that his Range Rover had been seen, and maybe even recognized, by the woman who'd driven in. Perhaps he should knock on the front door. Maybe a little intimidation would push them over the edge, and they'd fess up.

Or maybe he was wrong about the situation altogether, and these women were innocent.

No. His gut had steered him unscathed through numerous intense firefights on the battlefield, and his gut had brought him here tonight. These women were who he was after. Who they were all after.

"Freeze," a woman said from behind him.

He remained still.

"Show me your hands."

Putting his hands out to his sides, he turned around smoothly.

The cloud covering the moon moved on, and light shone down on a woman he recognized well. She was ten paces away, holding a gun pointed at his chest. He hadn't heard her come up on his rear. But how could he have with all that racket happening in the house?

His insides curled at the thought, and at the sight of her perfectly interlaced hands clutching the revolver, the barrel dead steady in its aim.

"What are you doing here?" she asked.

He smiled, shrugging. "I was just hoping we could talk."

"So you came over here, parked your car down the road, and snuck up on us? Looks like you wanted to spy on us."

He was only a foot from the driveway. He could lunge around the corner, pulling his ZEV at the same time, and take shelter behind one of the vehicles.

But he never got the chance, because the revolver's barrel flashed, and searing heat punched into his chest. And then he was on the ground, looking up.

Footsteps sounded nearby.

A woman cried out, and there was an answer, this one much closer.

It was all meaningless noise in Jorel's ears. His mind was in shock as he stared at the radiant silver orb in the sky, barely recognizing the smoking barrel pointing down at him.

There was another flash, and the moon went out.

26

Wolf sipped his first cup of coffee of the morning, savoring the hit of caffeine as he leaned back in his office chair. Out of habit, he set down the mug and reached inside a desk drawer, fetching the familiar box. He opened it, staring again at the ring inside.

On his computer screen, Austin Lethbridge's address was pulled up on Google Maps, the display zoomed all the way in. The home was large and faced west for maximum views. It was located on an expansive lot in the same area as MacLean's property, butting up against a swath of forest. All the math added up to the place costing a boatload of money.

There were two knocks on the door, and Rachette poked his head inside.

Wolf shut the ring box and dropped it in his open drawer, then grabbed his computer mouse.

"Top of the morning," Rachette said, sipping his own coffee. If he had noticed the ring, he made no show of it, which told Wolf he hadn't seen squat.

"It's ten a.m.," Yates said, following Rachette inside.

"On a Saturday. So, yeah. Top of the morning."

Yates and Rachette sat down, Rachette on the loveseat, Yates across from Wolf.

"What's with the garment bag?" Yates asked, pointing to the hanging zip bag holding Wolf's change of pants and shirt.

"I have a date tonight."

"Aha."

Wolf shut the drawer. "I stopped by Kylie Jones's place on the way home last night and saw something interesting."

"Please tell me we can see more pictures," Rachette said.

Wolf raised an eyebrow. "It's a video."

"Oh good."

"But not that kind of video."

He handed Yates his phone, and Rachette rose from the couch, coming closer to watch Tyson Lennox arrive at Kylie Jones's condo and disappear inside.

"So they are together." Yates pulled his laptop out of his shoulder bag and put it on Wolf's desk, opening it and turning it on.

"Look at that truck he's driving," Rachette said. "That thing's brand new. Maybe paid for by a few paintings sold on the black market."

"Could be he's responsible with his money." Yates poked his trackpad. "Could be Mom and Dad paying for it. We'll have to get the warrants to find out. And we'll have to talk to both of them, of course. I took the liberty of creating a spreadsheet last night for our interview process."

He turned the screen for them to see. "I've got the names here, position at the restaurant, years worked there, alibi, and

I've made it possible to track relationships with others at the restaurant via a pivot table I created."

"Wait, wait." Rachette turned to his partner. "You sat at home on a Friday night making a spreadsheet?"

"Yeah."

"I don't mean to be rude, but that's absolutely pathetic."

"Eat it."

"Why aren't you going out on the town?"

"I'm in my forties. I don't go out on the town."

"Plenty of people in their forties go out on the town. You do spreadsheets."

"You don't know what's going on in my life."

"I know you're not getting laid."

"Oh, is that so?"

"Wait. You are? Who?"

"Please." Wolf put up a hand.

His two detectives backed down. Rachette returned to the couch, and Yates resumed tapping the keys of his laptop, looking red in the face.

"Rachette, why don't you get started on the warrants for Tyson's and Kylie's financials?" Wolf said. "Yates, you can try and schedule interviews with them. And then we may as well start looking through everyone's socials right here and now, splitting the list and figuring out what we can."

Yates and Rachette went to the squad room to work, leaving Wolf alone in his office.

He spent the next few hours studying the online lives of The Oxbow's employees, coming up with both obvious and vague connections between them. The process of sifting through social media accounts, though necessary, interested

Wolf in the least, especially since even when it was all done, they would still have to talk to each and every one of the employees to cover all their bases. In the end, it always came down to pounding the pavement—or the dirt, as it were in Sluice-Byron County.

He took a long lunch, eating only a little to save room for whatever meal Austin had planned later, and then worked some more. As afternoon sunrays began reaching into his office, Wolf's eyelids started to feel heavy.

His cell phone vibrated on his desk, jolting him awake.

He pressed the answer button. "Wolf here."

"Detective Wolf, this is Roland Thatcher."

"Hello, Mr. Thatcher. What can I help you with?"

"Jorel is missing."

Wolf stood from his chair, stretching an arm overhead as he took in the view out the window.

"He never came back to the house last night, and he's been gone all day."

"Is that abnormal for him to not come back to the house?"

"No. He often spends time with friends or . . . women. But he's not returning my calls. Which is very abnormal."

"Maybe he's busy."

"It's his job to return my calls."

"Okay," Wolf said. "When's the last time you two spoke?"

"Last night. He said he had a lead that he was going to follow, and that he would be late to return to the house."

"A lead with the case?"

"Yes."

"What lead?"

Roland exhaled into the receiver. "He never said."

"Why not?"

"It's not his way, our way, of working. He knew I wouldn't want to hear any theories or conjecture. I want to see the results, not be involved in every step of the work."

"Especially if he's using means you don't want to know about to get those results."

Roland said nothing.

Wolf sat back down. "Maybe he needs more time to get the results."

"But he's not answering my calls," Roland repeated, voice rising.

"There are a lot of places in this county that are cell phone dead zones. Maybe he's tracking down something in one of those spots."

"You spoke to him yesterday," Roland said. "Did he mention any of these spots to you?"

"No. He didn't."

"I don't like it," Roland said. "I've called him several times, and there has been no answer. His phone goes to voicemail, like it's shut off. No way he does that. Not when he knows I'll be looking for him."

"Even on a weekend?" Wolf asked.

"Even on a weekend."

Wolf retrieved a notebook and pen out of his desk drawer. "He's driving the Range Rover, I take it?"

"That's right."

"What's the model and license plate?"

Roland spent a few minutes shuffling his phone, then came back and gave the information.

Wolf pulled out the card that Jorel had given him the day

before and read off the phone number. "Is this his cell number?"

"Yes. That's it. But you're not going to be able to get any information from it. I mean, there's no way to track it, if that's what you're thinking of doing."

Wolf wasn't thinking of doing that yet, but asked, "Why's that?"

"That's also part of Jorel's job: to keep anything electronic on me or him or Gemma un-trackable. The same will go for the vehicle."

Wolf felt the billionaire's anxiety like a vibration coming through the phone. He clearly was worried. Perhaps he had grown to count on Jorel for too much, and now he was concerned for himself. Then again, maybe they were friends.

"I'll put the word out and see what I can come up with."

"And you'll keep me posted? You can call me at this number."

"I'll keep you posted."

Wolf hung up, grabbed his desk phone, and called in Yates and Rachette.

They arrived a minute later.

"Jorel is missing." Wolf recapped Roland's call.

"What do you need?" Yates asked.

"Why don't you two go back to the squad room and see if any patrol units have come across his vehicle overnight or this morning?"

"On it," Rachette and Yates said, already moving.

Ten minutes later, they strode back in, shaking their heads.

Wolf picked up his desk phone again and dialed the state patrol's number. The captain was off work for the weekend, so he reached the section commander instead.

"This is Sergeant Allen speaking, sir."

"This is Detective Wolf with SBCSD. I'm looking for an SUV. It's gone missing overnight. I'm wondering if any of your officers have come across it for some reason or another." Wolf read off Jorel's vehicle information.

"I'll have to call you back."

Wolf hung up.

"What now?" Yates asked.

Hand still on the receiver, Wolf picked it up and dialed, then pressed the speakerphone button and set the receiver down on his desk.

"Brushing Police Department."

"Hi, this is Detective Wolf with SBCSD. Could I speak to the patrol supervisor on duty?"

"Let me connect you. One moment."

The phone clicked.

After a few seconds, a husky male voice answered, "Lieutenant Davis here."

Wolf and Davis exchanged small talk for a bit, then Wolf asked about Jorel's vehicle.

"Well, funny you should bring that up. We got a call from a rancher a couple hours ago. He saw your vehicle nearby his ranch. He's been trying to get it towed, but the allotted time hasn't passed, so it will remain for another day or so until we can deem it abandoned."

"Any sign of foul play?"

"Uh, none that I'm aware of, no. But it is a strange place to put a vehicle. It's tucked in the trees. There are no hiking trails nearby, and only private land. We had a patrol check with the two neighboring properties, and they came up with no leads as to why it was there."

Wolf eyed his watch, then the two men in his office. "Thank you. My detectives, Rachette and Yates, will be right there." He hung up.

Rachette and Yates looked at each other.

"What are you going to do?" Yates asked.

Wolf nodded to the garment bag, then the clock, which read 4:10 p.m. "I told you—I have a date. But keep me posted."

27

Patterson reclined in her chair on her rear deck, watching Lucas and Tommy chase each other through the yard, giggling uncontrollably. Lucas slashed with a foam sword while his older brother squealed in delight.

"You want a glass of wine?" Scott asked, his head appearing on the other side of the screen door.

"Yeah. Sure," she said, whiffing the charcoal smoke coming out of the barbecue.

As the early evening sun warmed her face, she wondered how she could feel so out of sorts when everything around her was so perfect.

The reason was of her own making. She had crossed the line, and now she had to deal with the mental consequences.

Scott came out and set a glass of pinot grigio in front of her, then went to the grill and flipped the burgers. "What's going on?" he asked, but she knew what he meant: *what's wrong?*

She shook her head, debating exactly how to answer in a way that didn't make her feel more ashamed.

Her phone vibrated in her pocket, and she pulled it out,

reading MacLean's name onscreen. Of course. How had she not thought about him yet?

In a flash, she realized her solution might lie in a conversation with the man on the other end of the line. She needed to speak to somebody who had been in this arena many times before and come out on top. Somebody who could give her a mental slap and help her see the situation differently.

"I'm sorry. I—"

"Go ahead."

"Hello?"

"Heather, it's Will."

She smiled, walking into the house. "Yeah. I know. It said so on my phone."

"Right. Yeah." He seemed preoccupied with something. "Listen. I was hoping you could come over. I have something to tell you. I know it's late notice . . . but it's important."

"Oh," she said, considering. She was desperate to speak to him, and she didn't want to bring all this up in front of the boys, anyway. Besides, she certainly wasn't going to enjoy dinner with her mind the way it was now. "Yeah. Okay. I'll be over in a few minutes."

When she went to Scott and hugged him, he set down his spatula and faced her. "What is it?"

"I'm going to leave for a while. I need to go talk to MacLean about something that's going on in the campaign."

Scott nodded, turning back to the burgers. "What about dinner?"

"Can you save me one? I'll heat it up later."

"And this is something you can't talk to me about?"

"No. I can't. Not yet."

He raised an eyebrow. "Well, okay then."

"I tell you what, I'll pick up some ice cream on the way home to make it up to you guys."

"In that case, get the hell out of here."

She kissed him, gathered her things, and got in her SUV, then made her way down the road toward 734.

MacLean lived straight north on the highway, about a ten-minute drive from her place, but as far as property values went, his estate might as well have been in another galaxy. There, the land was less severe, featuring wide-open meadows dotted with wildflowers and sprawling houses with views of snow-capped peaks.

Going over the conversation with James Long in her head, she parked in front of MacLean's house, oblivious to the breathtaking beauty of his acres of manicured grass and towering pines—and to the vehicle she had parked beside.

At the front door, she rang the bell, and MacLean answered shortly.

"Come in."

"Should I take off my shoes?" she asked, stopping in the entryway. She glanced outside, now noticing the truck next to hers. It was familiar, but she couldn't place it.

MacLean shut the door. "You can keep them on. Come on back." He led the way into his house and down the hall.

Patterson followed, trying to figure out where she had seen the truck before.

They entered his home office, and she stopped at the sight of the man rising from the couch.

"Hello, Sheriff." Gregory Waze stood with his hands clasped in front of him. "It's good to see you."

28

Wolf turned off the main road, following an asphalt driveway that dipped down and curled around a flat meadow, bringing Austin Lethbridge's house into view. It was immeasurably more impressive than the overhead and street images on Google Maps had portrayed.

Piper paid no attention, pulling down the visor and using the mirror to put on lipstick. Dressed in a sheer black top and white pants, with dangling earrings and a couple bracelets slinking up her tanned arm, she could have come straight out of a fashion magazine.

"You look good," he said.

She smiled. "You told me that at the house when you started groping me."

"Sorry about that."

"No, you're not."

Wolf pinched the fabric of his pants and tugged down, feeling intensely uncomfortable as his clothing bunched in places he wasn't used to. He was wearing some black slacks that Margaret Hitchens had thrust on him last year before a charity event Patterson had spoken at. The tight fit in his legs and backside was the latest style, according to Piper. The button-up shirt, also a donation from the mayor, was too sheen for his liking, but he had to admit he looked decent in it.

Piper reached over and squeezed his leg. "Thanks for coming."

He eyed the house again. It was two stories, jutting in right angles, covered in glass and steel, and lit warmly within. It looked like a jewel nestled against a wall of pine trees.

"This place is a dump," he said.

"Yeah," Piper said. "You'd think with a place like this, he'd spend more time at home and less time in the office. I guess Ashley will help with that once she moves in."

"You said she's from Aspen?" Wolf asked.

"Yeah. I'm not sure what stage of the move they're in. I guess we'll find out."

He parked next to an obsidian-black Porsche SUV.

The air was warm, perfectly still. A white strip of smoke rose from the other side of the house, and the aroma of spiced meat mingled with the scents of pine and cut grass.

They walked across the driveway, past the luxury automobile, shoes scratching on the asphalt. Soft jazz emanated from hidden outdoor speakers as they stepped up onto a spacious porch.

A massive front door made of wood swung open. Austin stood on the other side with a glass of white wine. "Welcome!"

Piper went in first, kissing Austin's cheeks before passing him a bottle of wine. Wolf followed, shaking Austin's hand.

Inside, the air was cooler, the music somewhat louder, the origin of the sound waves just as vague. The smell of cooking food was stronger, mouthwatering, and the home's interior was more impressive than its exterior, a perfect marriage of chic architecture and panoramic windows.

Austin showed them to a kitchen covered in polished stone and dark wood and matte chrome. A huge island was centered in the space, appetizers spread out around its perimeter. A woman wearing a black and white dress, who Wolf pegged as in her mid-fifties, was putting a silver platter into one of two ovens.

"Ashley!"

"What?" said a woman from somewhere down a long hall.

For a moment, Wolf was confused. But then he realized the woman in the kitchen must be a private chef.

Austin turned to Wolf, a conspiratorial smile arching across his impossibly smooth face. "Women, eh?" he said, setting down the bottle of wine on the kitchen island. "We can put a man on the moon, but we can't figure out how to get a woman ready in under an hour."

Wolf saw Piper's face go slack. She looked at him with one raised eyebrow, silently saying, *See what I have to put up with*?

Wolf smiled at her, which encouraged Austin.

"You know what I'm talking about," Austin said, slapping Wolf on the shoulder. "You want a ginger beer? A sparkling water? A non-alcoholic beer? I've got it all. Name your poison."

"The first thing you said."

"You got it. Mary? You got that?"

The woman in the kitchen handed over a cold bottle of golden ginger beer, which tasted spicy and sweet.

"There," Austin said. "It's about time, for Chrissakes, Ashley." He winked at Wolf.

Wolf turned around, seeing a wafer-thin, bejeweled

woman in a billowing red and yellow dress that was so bright Wolf felt like squinting. He had expected her to look irritated, but instead, her pretty face was stretched into a wide smile, as if she'd just heard the funniest joke of her life.

"It's nice to finally meet you," Ashley said, taking Wolf's hand and pulling close to him. She reached up and kissed one of his cheeks, then the other. "Wow, he is hunky, isn't he?"

Wolf stood stunned.

Piper's slack face held a sliver of enjoyment at his discomfort. When Ashley spun toward her, Piper smiled radiantly, and they shared hugs and kisses like Wolf had seen Italians do.

"My God, you're radiant," Ashley said. "Even more so than the last time I saw you. It's been, what? Two months, right?"

"I think so," Piper said.

"Why don't we head out onto the back porch?" Austin said. "Piper, Ashley, how about you get yourselves a drink and meet us out there? You like cigars, David?"

Wolf followed Austin outside through an open glass partition. "No, I'm not a fan."

Austin frowned. "Seriously?"

Wolf shrugged.

"Okay, well. That's no big deal. No drinking. No cigars. What do you do for . . . ?" He let the sentence trail off.

"What are my vices?"

Austin snapped a finger. "Yes. That's it."

"Not exercising enough?"

"Ha! You're hilarious. Please, sit. Make yourself comfortable. Mary! Can you start bringing out the appetizers to the table?"

Wolf sipped his drink and took a seat on one of the plush

chairs placed around a neatly set stone table, steeling his mind for the long night ahead.

Piper walked out, Ashley telling a story at her side.

"Oh, that's great," Piper said. "David, she's moving in next week. We were wondering about that on the drive in."

They all joined him at the table, clinking their drinks and passing food around.

Piper rested a hand on Wolf's leg, and he watched her engage in effortless conversation. Austin and Ashley clung to her every word, laughing uproariously at punchlines pulled out of the thin mountain air. Even Mary got in on the action, smiling and chiming in with comments here and there as she moved between the house and the porch to bring them more delectable dishes.

Wolf smiled, spoke when he was spoken to, and found he enjoyed watching Piper work her magic. If she was half as good at the office as she was here, he understood why Austin was so enthralled with her.

As the sun lowered on the jagged horizon, warming the high clouds to a glow, Mary brought out the main course—steak with a medley of colorful cooked vegetables.

"Oh my," Piper said. "This looks amazing. And smells amazing. Thank you, Mary."

Mary laid the platters on the table and served Piper.

"Oh, I can get it," Piper said.

"Nonsense," Austin said. "With what I'm paying her for this meal? She can get it." He winked at Wolf again. "Mmm. Looks delicious."

They sat patiently as Mary doled out the food and then left.

Piper squeezed Wolf's leg one last time before picking up her utensils.

The meal was perfectly cooked, tasting as impressive as anything at a five-star restaurant.

"These green peppers are amazing," Austin said.

Ashley smiled. "They're red peppers, honey."

"Oh." Austin kept his eyes on the plate, his face turning red.

"Shall I get the glasses for you?"

"Uh, yeah, sure."

Ashley rose from the table and walked away.

Wolf exchanged a glance with Piper.

"Austin is colorblind," Piper said.

"I have mild deuteranomaly," Austin said. "A type of red-green colorblindness. It's hard for me to differentiate colors. I mean, I see most of them as muted shades of what you might think of as green. Red's green. Orange is green. I'm used to it, though."

Ashley came back a minute later carrying a pair of black-rimmed glasses with grayish-blue lenses. Making a show of it, she sat down, looked over at Austin, and put them on his face.

Austin all but ignored her, continuing to chew his food.

"Well?"

"Yeah." He set down his fork and knife. "Wow. There's a lot of color on this plate."

Ashley beamed at Wolf and Piper, tears forming in her eyes. "I was so glad these worked when I got them for him. The glasses don't help everyone, you know. He is lucky."

"Holy crap, is that what you're wearing?" Austin scanned Ashley up and down. "You look like a piñata. Is her outfit as bright to you guys as it is to me right now?"

Wolf gave an ambiguous shrug of his shoulders, mumbling something unintelligible.

Austin's words passed through Ashley like a neutrino. She smiled ever wider, striking a pose, ruffling her sleeve.

"So, you can see color now?" Piper asked.

"Yeah. It's crazy."

"Why don't you ever bring those to work?"

Austin shrugged. "I'm used to how I've always seen."

"May I try them on?" Piper asked.

Austin took the glasses off and handed them over.

Piper put them on, turning her head left and right. "Wow, everything is so saturated now."

"You can give them a go, David," Ashley said.

Wolf took the glasses and looked through one lens, seeing everything on the table was a shade brighter.

"When did you learn you were colorblind?" Wolf asked, thinking of Rachette's unbidden prying into the little girl's possible affliction the day prior.

"When I was a kid. I remember a doctor showing me some pictures and telling my mom I was colorblind. And how devastated she was. She wanted to have them give me an eye transplant."

"Are you serious?" Ashley asked.

"No."

She slapped him on the shoulder, then leaned into him like he was a sofa.

"But I remember being like, 'Finally, I understand what's going on.' I, literally, could never see what people were describing when they pointed out different colors."

"And now, with the glasses, he gets to try wearing colors. Right, honey?"

Austin stabbed a piece of steak. "I'll let you wear them for me."

"You know him, Piper," Ashley said. "He wears black or gray. Gray or black. White if he's feeling adventurous. He used to have an excuse for it, but not anymore. Now he can experiment and not be worried."

"I don't understand," Piper said.

"He's been afraid to wear colors his whole life," Ashley said.

Austin held up a hand, silencing Ashley. "I'm not *afraid*. I just had a few bad experiences in college. Mismatched socks. Hideously clashing outfits. It's easier to avoid color altogether."

"He had a bad date, so he decided to dress like he's at a funeral for the rest of his life."

Wolf paused, setting down his fork, looking up, thinking of the row of clothing in Brock Wendel's closet. *The guy dressed like an undertaker.*

"What?" Piper said, reading Wolf's face. She squeezed his leg. "Everything okay?"

"What's wrong?" Austin peered at him. "Are you choking?"

"What did I say?" Ashley asked.

Wolf shook his head. "Sorry, no. Nothing. It's just that I'm working a case, and what you're saying may be very important."

Austin and Ashley perked up.

"About being colorblind?" Austin asked.

Wolf nodded. "Do you happen to know how colorblindness is passed down to a child? From the mother? Or the father?"

"It's usually passed down from the mother. I think. Wait . . . maybe it's both." Austin shrugged, smiling sheepishly. "I don't know. I'm not an expert."

Wolf remembered how Faith Orton had point-blank told

Rachette she herself was not colorblind. So, if Haley really had the condition, what did that imply?

"Do you mind excusing me for a few minutes?" he asked. "I have to make some quick phone calls."

"Of course," Austin said. "You can use my study if you want."

"No, it's okay. I'll just go around the corner if you don't mind."

"Sure."

Wolf walked along the wraparound deck to the side of the house. Sitting on some steps leading off to the lawn, he called Yates.

The detective picked up after only one ring. "Hey."

"Can you give me Gemma's phone number, please?"

"I'll send it over to you."

"Thanks." Wolf hung up.

A few moments later, he received the number and dialed.

"Hello?" Gemma answered, her tone cautious.

"Hi, Gemma. This is Detective David Wolf."

"Oh, hi. What's going on?"

"I wanted to ask you a question. Was Brock colorblind?"

"Yes. He was. Red-green colorblind. Why?"

"It's just something I was wondering. I saw his clothing . . . and I wondered."

"Yes. He couldn't distinguish between many colors, so he usually wore black or gray."

"I'm sorry. I have to go now. But thank you for the information."

"Wait. Why? Why did you want to know about the clothing? Or about his colorblindness? Does it matter?"

"I have to get going. I'll fill you in when I'm able, okay?"

"Okay. Yeah. Fine."

Wolf ended the call, then dialed another contact. Staring out into the trees, he waited.

"Just a second," Lorber said. Loud music was playing in the background. He turned down the volume. "What's up?"

"I need to know about red-green colorblindness. How it's passed down to the next generation."

"You think I just know the answer to that off the top of my head?"

"Do you?"

"Of course. But it's complicated."

"Try me."

"Why do you want to know, anyway?"

"It might have to do with the case. Please. Time could be a factor here."

"Okay. Well, a male has an X and Y chromosome, while a female has two Xs. When a child is conceived, the parents each pass one of their two chromosomes on to the child. Red-green colorblindness is a recessive trait, and the gene mutation that causes it is passed on the X chromosome.

"In order for a female to be born red-green colorblind, both of the X chromosomes she receives must contain the gene mutation. In other words, her father must be red-green color-blind, and her mother must either be red-green colorblind or a carrier of the gene mutation. A woman is a carrier if she has one X with the gene mutation instead of two. Got it?"

"Yeah. And for a male?"

"Since we only have one X, it only takes one X with the gene mutation for us to be born red-green colorblind. Males always receive their single X chromosome from their mother, so they inherit red-green colorblindness solely from her. The father's genetics don't matter. That's why males are much more prone."

Wolf shook his head, losing the thread of logic just as he grasped it. "Let's try another way. Brock Wendel was red-green colorblind. I just learned that from Gemma Thatcher."

"Okay."

"And a woman working at The Oxbow named Faith Orton has a young daughter who appears to be red-green colorblind, too."

"Ahhh. And you want to know if this Faith woman's daughter is Brock Wendel's. If we can somehow prove the kid is his daughter just by her condition."

"Right."

"Only a DNA test can prove that, of course. But, if the girl truly is red-green colorblind, then her father must be, too. If the girl's father was not red-green colorblind, there would be no way she could be. The odds would drop to zero because of how genes are passed on."

"You're sure?"

"Yeah. One hundred percent positive."

Wolf said nothing.

"Listen, I can draw you a diagram and save us some words," Lorber said. "Otherwise, does this kid look like Brock Wendel?"

Wolf pictured Haley Orton's smile. Now, as he thought about it, he could see the way it resembled the one on Brock's face in the photo of him on that boat in the Mediterranean.

"Maybe," he said. "Thanks, Doc."

"No sweat. Keep me posted."

Wolf hung up.

"What's happening?" Piper asked, appearing behind him. "All done with your calls?"

He stood up, looking down at his phone. "Unfortunately, I think I've just begun."

"Are you telling me we have a valid excuse to leave now?"

"Yes."

She looked over her shoulder at Ashley, who was now sitting on Austin's lap, feeding him by hand. "Oh darn."

29

"Please, Sheriff. Take a seat."

Patterson remained still in the entrance to MacLean's home office, feeling like a roped animal.

MacLean sat behind his leather-topped desk, motioning to the chair across from Waze's couch.

Waze sat down, and Patterson put her butt in the indicated chair. "What is this?"

"This is a conversation we should have had a long time ago," MacLean said. "Can I get you a drink?"

"No." She crossed a leg over the other. "What conversation, exactly?"

"Well, I'm going to get myself one." MacLean stood and went to a bar cart, pouring copper liquor from a carafe into a glass. "Greg?"

"No, thank you."

"Right. You guys are driving." He picked up his drink and returned to his desk.

Folding her arms and settling in, she decided there was no sense getting angry. Yet.

"Heather, I've called you here because four months ago, I was too scared to explain something to you. Do you remember that time in the diner? I was going to tell you something as you were leaving, but I didn't because Roland Thatcher was waiting in your office to talk to you."

"Sure."

MacLean tilted the glass back, swallowing down all the liquid. With a quivering exhale, he leaned forward on his elbows. "Heather, I brought Gregory Waze here to run against you."

Patterson blinked, her eyes closing for a few moments as the madness of the statement sank in. "Excuse me?"

MacLean stared at her. "I knew Greg growing up. We went to the police academy together. I was once a patrol officer with him in Portland."

"I thought you . . ." Patterson dug in her mind for MacLean's history file, realizing for the first time just how little she knew of MacLean's early life. "You were down south. In southern Colorado."

"I spent two years in Portland before that. Then, you're right, I went to Alamosa for my first real stint in a department. After ten years, I moved up to Ashland, where I became sheriff." MacLean chuckled, getting up from his desk to pour himself another few fingers of liquor. "I never told you about me being up in Portland at the same time as Waze, but I've been waiting for you to make that connection."

She had researched Waze, but she had never looked into MacLean's past. Why would she have?

A wave of anger washed over her. "You lied to me, then."

"By omission?" he asked. "Sure. I guess I did. But I also did worse."

"You brought Waze in to run against me. What do you mean by that?"

MacLean looked at Waze, then at Patterson again. "I became your friend months prior to my invitation. Heather, when we started going out to lunches, I learned just how great of a woman you are. You've done a better job in that office than I ever could have, and in a much shorter time."

"And so you bring in somebody to kick me out?"

"Let me finish, please."

She scoffed.

"I brought him in because I saw what the job was doing to you."

Her face heated. "What do you mean?"

"Do you even realize how much you despise what you do?"

She said nothing.

"Every time we speak, it is the same song and dance: you telling me how tedious your days are. You tell me again and again that you hate all the lunch appointments except for the ones with me. That you hate the county council's meetings, and their constant demands on your time, and the way they want to hear how you're managing the budget and stream-lining efficiency and cutting staff while expanding scope—all that bullshit rhetoric you absolutely loathe. Stop me when I start lying to you here."

She said nothing.

MacLean sucked back his second drink, coughing loudly and setting the glass down on his desk as he took his chair. "But heck, you're shackled to this job for life because God forbid you, a woman, give up your role—your dead-end role by your own admission—and let those bigot, sexist assholes think they are right. Can't have them saying you quit because you couldn't handle a man's job."

"So you brought in a man to take it over for me."

"No!" MacLean put his head in his hands for a moment, then stood up, rounded his desk, and sat on the front edge of the wood. "I had a friend who lost his wife to a drunk driver. A friend who was devastated, with no direction in life. A friend who is a good, decent man. Somebody who needed a new mission after he retired from his department, lost his wife, and now sat in—I'm sorry to say it, Greg—in misery. I had a friend who needed meaning."

MacLean raised a hand toward Patterson. "I had another friend who was miserable in her job but wouldn't admit it to herself, no matter how I tried to help her see it. And so, I brought one friend in to take another friend's job. And the burden that comes with it."

"You could have just told me," she said, unfolding her arms. "Don't you get that? How psychotic that is? How dishonest?"

"I told you dozens of times that the job put me in the cancer ward. Gave me a death sentence that somehow, I miraculously survived. I told you, dozens of times, that you could walk away. And you didn't listen. I'm not sorry for what I did, Heather. Not for one moment. Not if it means helping you out of the job that's going to kill you, even if you don't see it yet. Not if it gives Greg a new lease on life. He thrives in the environment we despise. And not if it gives him an opportunity to come over here to Rocky Points, Colorado, the place I've grown to love, so he can work with great people like you and your team of detectives."

Patterson pulled her eyebrows together. "You mean Wolf's team of detectives?"

Waze cleared his throat. "You are clearly more qualified to head up the division. If you wanted to."

"So that's it? I roll over and you take sheriff, and I get chief detective?"

Waze and MacLean said nothing. They clearly didn't like the way she had put it.

"And Wolf?" she asked.

"He would, of course, stay on the detective squad."

She snorted. "Jeez, I . . . don't know what to say . . . except that sounds like the biggest crock of horse shit I've ever heard."

"Heather," MacLean said.

"Do you know where this man was the night his wife was killed?"

The office turned deadly quiet.

"He was out screwing another woman. Cheating on his wife. Being *dishonest*, unlike the kind of guy you're telling me he is."

Waze looked down at his hands, and a stream of tears came tumbling out of his eyes.

Patterson sighed, feeling instant regret for what she had said. But Gregory Waze's suffering wasn't her fault. He had brought it upon himself.

"I know," MacLean said. "He told me."

Waze sobbed silently.

"And he regrets it."

"And now you're both liars." She shook her head, standing up. "Don't you see how I'm never, ever going to give up this race? Don't you see the kind of hypocrisy I have to shield the people of this county from?"

Leaving both men with their heads bowed, she turned and walked out of the office, down the hall, and outside.

Once she was driving toward the highway, visor down to block the bright sunset, she dialed Margaret's phone number.

"Yeah."

"Hey, it's me. I want you to set up a press conference for Monday morning."

"Monday is bad. Already an event happening down in Ashland that I have to be at. Tuesday would be better."

"Fine, Tuesday. Whatever."

"What for?"

"It's time we bury Waze."

"And how are we going to do that?"

"With the dirt I have on him."

30

Rachette spat on the ground, listening to the Brushing PD officer talk as they walked over to a group of uniforms circled up at the shoulder of the dirt road.

"I tell you, it's not a normal place to park a vehicle," Officer Kensington said. "I'd believe the guy's gone missing. Looks fishy to me. Looked fishy the first time I saw it."

They reached the four other police officers, who cut their conversation and faced Rachette and Yates. Rachette recognized two of them. They all shook hands and turned to view the new-model Range Rover.

Two ruts from spinning tires cut through cocoa-colored earth toward the vehicle, which was parked up a slope off the road, behind a clump of oak bushes growing at the foot of some pines. From certain vantages, the SUV was invisible, but from here, the hiding spot was plain as day. The Range Rover's clean black paint reflected the red sunset behind them.

"See what I mean?" Kensington said. "It looks concealed. Not parked."

"Could be the driver tried to hide the vehicle," another

officer said, "because he didn't want people messing with it while he went on a hike."

"But they're saying he's gone missing."

"That true?" the officer asked.

Rachette nodded. "We can't get hold of him." He walked up the slope, checking the ground, seeing dozens of tracks. "Let's keep off this area here."

"That's not us," another officer said. "Those are probably Chaffee's. And then the tow truck driver's. He was called in, but he wouldn't tow it out because it's not technically abandoned yet, you know."

"Who's Chaffee?"

"The rancher that's been trying to get this vehicle towed all day."

"Stay here, please," Yates said to the officers, heading up to join Rachette by the Range Rover.

Rachette spotted nothing past the dark tint of the windows. He snapped on a latex glove and tried the driver's side door. It opened, letting out the scent of cologne.

"Unlock it," Yates said, moving to the passenger side.

Rachette pressed the unlock button on the interior control panel, and Yates popped open the front door.

"No phone anywhere," Rachette said, closing the sliding mechanism of the center console.

"Got some ammo in the glove compartment," Yates said. "No gun."

"Some dirt on the floorboards over here," Rachette said.

"Is that seat pulled forward?"

Rachette climbed in and sat down. At five foot six, he was anything but a tall man, and yet even for him, the steering wheel seemed close. "It's pulled way forward. Jorel was short."

"Not as short as you. Let's get some prints." Yates stepped back. "I'll get the kit."

They shut the doors and came down the slope. The officers once again stopped talking.

"Okay." Rachette spat, shifting the Copenhagen snuff in his lip. "Let's keep our distance. The situation is fluid right now. We might be looking at a crime scene."

"Yes, sir."

"I wanna know everyone that's been—" Rachette's phone rang in his pocket, cutting him off. He took it out and saw Wolf's name. "Excuse me for a second." He walked away, hitting the answer button. "Hey."

Rachette relayed what he and Yates had learned so far, then listened to Wolf share the revelation he'd had this evening. He smiled as the puzzle pieces snapped into place.

"I'm on my way up to Faith Orton's now," Wolf said. "I'll send you two the address."

"We're a lot closer than you. You want us to go knock on the door?"

Wolf sighed. "I don't like how this is looking. She may be dangerous. Also, I figured out she lives with her sister and mother."

"We've always thought there were multiple people involved," Rachette said. "It's looking like she might fit."

Wolf said nothing for a beat. "Get over there and keep your distance. Call me when you're in position."

With ultimate satisfaction curling his mouth into a smile, Rachette strolled back down the dirt road toward Yates, who was holding the print kit he'd fished out of the SUV.

"Was that Wolf?"

"Yeah.

"What are you smiling about?"

"He had some interesting news."

"What's that?"

Rachette hesitated for effect.

"Spit it out, Lassie."

"Brock Wendel was colorblind."

"O-kay . . . and?"

"And who else did we notice was colorblind? Or, wait, I guess I should say, who else did *I* notice?"

"That little girl. Faith's daughter." Yates's eyes narrowed. "You're saying we think that kid is Brock Wendel's?"

Rachette shrugged. "If she is, that ties Faith Orton awfully close with Brock Wendel."

"Like . . . secret kid?"

"Did you hear Gemma introducing her as Brock's kid? Yeah, secret kid."

Yates turned around, eyeing Jorel's vehicle.

Both Rachette's and Yates's phones chimed at the same time. They pulled them out and saw an address sent over text by Wolf.

"That's Faith Orton's address," Rachette said. "Wolf is on his way up. In the meantime, we're supposed to head over there and get eyes on the place."

"What about the prints?"

"Lorber can get them when the tow truck brings it to his office."

Yates read the text. "This address is close to here."

Rachette nodded. "Let's get these guys to wrap this place up tight, and then we need to go."

31

Faith Orton sucked in a breath, wiping sweat off her face as she lifted her head from the pillow. It was dark. Only soft orange light spilled in through her west-facing window.

What time is it? Night?

The skin of her hands was sore and blistered. Her arms were tight, and her lower back, too, as if she had done a difficult workout.

She sat up, shifting to the edge of the bed, and then froze. All at once, she remembered everything: The man's glistening, hollowed-out skull. The never-ending drive. The weight of the muscular corpse as they had dragged it beneath the moonlight. The shoveling.

Now, she wished she were back asleep. She had woken into the nightmare.

She took off her clothes and put on some sweatpants and a sweatshirt. The blood-red numbers of her digital clock read 9:08 p.m. Her phone battery was down to only a few percent, but it was enough for her to check the date: Saturday, June 16.

Her time was running out.

Clanging and sizzling, along with the aroma of eggs and bacon, came from the kitchen. She almost gagged, thinking of trying to eat while the phantom smell of blood coated her nostrils.

Still, she hurried into the kitchen, eager to see Haley, cursing herself for sleeping the entire day.

Her mother was sitting at the table with Haley on her lap, looking at a colorful puzzle. "Red . . . blue . . . yellow . . ."

Her sister was hovering over the range, seasoning a pan of scrambled eggs and vegetables. "Hey, you're awake." She smiled as if nothing were out of the ordinary, as if they were on a vacation in the Bahamas. "You want some food?"

"I do!" Haley yelled.

"Oh, I know you do. Who wants bacon?"

"I want bacon, too!"

Faith closed her eyes, just stopping herself from vomiting. "Go outside and play."

Her mother looked at her, then out the window at the sunset. "It's nine p.m. We've been outside playing all day while you've been sleeping."

"Please go . . . somewhere else. I have to speak to Skylar alone."

Skylar stirred the eggs, watching them over her shoulder.

"Now, Mom."

"Mommy, what's wrong?"

"Nothing, honey. I just need to speak to Aunty Sky alone for a minute."

Her mother rose, lifting Haley up with her. "Okay. We'll watch the sun go down behind the mountains. Maybe we can see the bats!"

Faith and Skylar stood in silence, watching their mother put Haley in a hooded sweatshirt and take her outside.

Cool air flowed in through the screen door.

Skylar shut off the range.

"So, what happened?" Faith asked. "Did he call? Why are we still here?"

"He didn't answer yet."

"You have to be kidding me. It's after nine. You haven't heard from him all day? Why didn't you wake me up?"

"Because I hadn't heard from him. And you needed the sleep."

"I don't need sleep. I need money. Which I can't get because it's in a safe deposit box at the bank. Which isn't open again until Monday morning. Which is a very big problem because my sister decided to murder somebody last night and I need to leave this godforsaken place before the cops figure it out and lock us away for the rest of our lives. I don't need to sleep. I need money!"

"Relax. He'll call soon," Skylar said. "For twenty percent on the payout? He'll call."

"Why hasn't he, then?"

"He's nocturnal like you. He never answers his phone during the day. He'll call."

Faith squeezed her hands, grimacing at the pain, and at the overconfident air of her sister.

"Why are you so worried?" Skylar tilted her head. "The evidence is gone. Nobody will come to us."

"If they track his cell phone, they'll be able to see the GPS coordinates of where he was last. They'll know he was here."

"They'll wait days to do that."

"He works for a billionaire. They might have ways that are much quicker than law enforcement."

"This isn't the movies. They don't just say, 'Oh, a grown man is missing. Let's track him by his phone.' They wait for him to come back. For days. Then they start looking for him. It's not even been twenty-four hours yet."

Faith checked the wall clock. They were only an hour or so from reaching that mark. And the more time that passed, the more she stayed in this house, the more her mind-bending stress ratcheted up.

Faith sat down at the kitchen table and put her face in her hands.

"If Roland Thatcher knew anything, they'd be all over our asses right now."

She ignored her sister.

"Look at me."

She looked.

"Did you hear me? If Roland Thatcher knew anything, then we'd be in jail right now. But we're not. Why? Because they don't know shit. Because they don't even know that Jorel guy is missing yet."

"His name was Xavier. Jorel's his last name."

"What? Whatever. I don't give a shit." Skylar wiped her hands on a towel. "By the time they pull their heads out of their asses, we'll be in Mexico."

"My daughter will be a fugitive."

"Or she'll have a new mom. Which one do you want?"

Haley giggled outside as her grandmother chased her across the lawn.

"Wait! Stay over here, honey!" Faith's mother said, steering Haley away from the side of the house.

"Call him again."

Skylar made a noise in her throat.

"Call him again!" Faith slammed the table with her open hand, causing her blistered palm to burn. "Call him again! Call him again!"

"Okay, holy shit, calm down."

Skylar went to the counter, picked up her phone, and tapped the screen.

A long twenty seconds passed before she hung up with a shake of her head.

"Call him again."

Skylar did. Several rings in, she straightened.

"Hey. What the hell? I've been calling you all day. . .. Because, well, we need to ask a favor. . .. Remember the money we got for those paintings? . . . Yeah, we're looking for an immediate loan against it. . .. Because we need it now. Tonight. Tomorrow morning at the latest. And the bank deposit box we put it in is—" A disturbed smile twisted her lips. "That's right, twenty percent. . .. Okay, fine, whatever. Forty?" She looked at Faith.

Faith nodded.

"Yeah, okay. Forty percent."

She rubbed her face. Their plan was desperate and stupid, and she could only imagine what the hardened criminal on the other end of the line was saying right now.

"We'll exchange the key for the money. You would just have to go to the bank and—" Skylar paused, then said, "Hello?" She lowered the phone and put it on the counter.

"Oh my God," Faith said. "I told you it was a—"

"Shut up," her sister said, cutting her off. "I know you said it was a bad idea to use a safe deposit box and"—she switched to a whiny, mimicking tone—"'subject ourselves to banking hours.' You say it again, and I'll bash your skull in."

It was also a bad idea to kill a man on a Friday night, Faith thought.

"We had to lock up the money," Skylar continued, pacing. "You don't know the guys I know. They're dangerous. They knew we sold the paintings. They knew we had cash. They could have come for it. Hell, they could still come. Tonight, for all we know."

"Let's leave without the money," Faith said. "It's time to cut and run."

"We're not leaving. You have to calm down."

"You have to face the facts. We're in danger."

"If we leave now, then all this is for nothing. The killing. The planning. The years you spent believing all Brock's lies, watching him ignore you and Haley while he screwed around on other women right in front of you. All the late nights you came crying to me. All the lost sleep."

Faith shook her head. "I never wanted this."

"Then he shouldn't have fucked with my sister." Skylar stirred the cooling eggs, her eyes narrowing with rage, her jaw jutting out. "He was just like Dad. He deserved to be shoved in that trunk and shoved down that hole. He deserved worse."

"I never wanted this," Faith said again.

Her sister stared at her with a sour smile. "Suck it up, bitch. What are you going to do? Cry? You going to sit there and let the world do what it wants to you? You gonna let some piece-of-shit peeping Tom come over here, spy on us in the middle of the night, and tell us we're caught? No. You're gonna kill the bastard and shove his body in a shallow grave."

Skylar stepped close to her. "You gonna let Daddy put

those onion-smelling hands of his all over you again? Exploring down your pants?"

Faith shut her eyes, swaying on the chair as the memory kicked her off balance.

"No, you're not," Skylar said, her voice low, sounding just like their father's used to all those years ago. "You're gonna go in and slit his throat."

"That's what you did." She kept her eyes closed, trying not to picture her father's body lying in a bed stained crimson, her mother screaming in agony. "I didn't do that."

"You wanted to!"

Faith jumped at the closeness of the shout.

Skylar grabbed her by the shoulders, touching her lips to her ear. "But you were too scared. Mamma wanted to. But she was too chicken." She let go and returned to the range, picking up the skillet and throwing it against the wall. The cast iron clanged to the floor, sending eggs flying every which way. Slimy, pale-yellow pieces slid down the wall. "You wanted me to!" She put her hands on her head and let out a larynx-shredding scream.

Faith covered her ears, pulling her legs up, curling into a ball.

When Skylar ran out of breath, she sagged to the floor.

"Mommy?" Haley cried.

Faith hurried to the screen door and stepped outside. "Yes, honey. It's okay. I'm okay." She ran to her daughter, whose wide, perfectly innocent eyes were filled with heart-breaking concern.

She kneeled, grasping Haley's tiny body in her arms, and stood.

"What's wrong, Mommy?"

"It's okay, honey. Everything's okay." She mustered all the conviction she could and infused it into her voice, rubbing Haley's back.

"What the hell's going on in here?" her mother said, standing by the screen door.

"Forget it, Mamma," her sister said from inside.

"This is absolute insanity. What have you two girls gotten us into?"

Faith couldn't make out her sister's response, but her tone sounded evil. Ominous.

She faced Haley away from the house, putting a hand on the back of her head to keep her from seeing, just in case her sister did something else. Skylar was beyond controlling. The slide she had started twenty years ago was coming to a dramatic, catastrophic halt, like an explosive collision with a rock wall. Faith didn't want Haley or herself to become part of the collateral damage.

She came up with a rudimentary plan right there on the spot. It was simple, with one step: get out with Haley right now, this instant.

Through the window, she saw that her sister was sitting at the kitchen table. Her mother stood above her, rubbing her shoulders, pushing the psychotic episode away with soothing words, deluding herself that their plans, their lives, were salvageable once again.

Faith climbed the concrete step, pulled open the screen door, and walked into the kitchen, still holding Haley.

Skylar slumped over the table, forehead to her forearms. Her mother ceased her motions, watching Faith.

"I'm leaving for Mexico with Haley," she said.

Skylar raised her head.

"You two can follow us on Monday after you go into the bank and get the money." Faith spoke quickly. "Haley and I will go down now. We can set up. We can figure out some stuff before you get there, like where we're going to stay. And we'll . . . I don't know, we'll get some groceries. When you guys get there, we'll have a great meal. We'll take a walk on the beach. You guys won't have to worry about anything. You just show up." She swallowed, nodding. "We'll take care of the beforehand stuff. You guys will get the money."

"Where you gonna go, Faith?" Skylar gave her that pitying, mocking look. The one she always gave Faith when she thought her little sister was getting too big for her britches.

Faith's eyes narrowed on her sister's curled lip. Her vision iced over. She raised a clenched fist, fingernails digging into her palm, and bared her teeth. "Me and Haley are leaving. Now."

Haley began to cry, burrowing her head in Faith's shoulder.

Faith leaned toward her sister, fist still raised, daring her to protest. Blood from a ripped-open blister trickled down her wrist and forearm.

"Let us pray," her mother said.

"Oh shut up, old woman," Skylar said, locking her gaze on Faith's.

I'm leaving for Mexico, and you're staying here to gamble with your life. If you make it, you make it. If you don't, you don't, Faith silently told her.

Skylar looked at the blood dripping on the table, then back at her.

"I think that's a good idea," her mother said.

Skylar's eyes glazed over, like she was thinking long and hard. And then she nodded. "Goodbye, Faith."

"Hold her." Faith handed Haley to her mother.

Her mother took her daughter and went out the front door, the sound of her soft singing dissipating to silence as she walked farther into the yard.

Faith turned on the faucet and put her hand underneath, washing the blood into the sink. Tears brimmed in her eyes and fell, swirling with the blood in the drain.

Her sister rose from the table and picked up the frying pan off the floor.

Faith held her breath and closed her eyes, waiting for the blow.

But instead of hitting her, Skylar placed the pan gently into the sink, then unspooled some paper towels, shut off the water, and held her little sister's hand, patting the blood and water dry. She wiped Faith's tears from her cheeks before wrapping her in a warm embrace.

"It's okay," she whispered in Faith's ear. This time, her voice sounded like their mother's. "It's okay."

Faith reached her arms around her sister and squeezed.

"It's a good idea," Skylar said. "Me and Mom will stay here and wait for the bank to open Monday morning. We'll get in and out right at opening time. And then we're on your ass faster than . . . I don't know . . . me in high school."

Faith laughed, a fresh batch of tears falling from her eyes. Strength welled up inside her, filling her so much that it spilled out in intense sobs.

"It's okay," Skylar said again, hugging her for another minute before releasing her. She looked at Faith with an earnest glare that said, *Okay?*

Faith nodded in response.

"Now go pack up and get the hell out of here. And don't forget your bathing suit."

As her big sister got busy cleaning the eggs off the floor and walls, Faith hurried to her bedroom, wondering what in the world she wanted to take from this miserable life into the next.

32

Rachette raised the binoculars to his face and glassed the scene below.

"What do you see?"

"Nothing yet. Hold your horses." He put his elbows on the SUV's hood, steadying the view.

Faith Orton's house sat at the bottom of a long dip in the valley floor. Without the binoculars, it looked like a cluster of three lights, but with the magnification, the structure came into better relief.

It was a small, rectangular, one-story ranch house. He guessed it had been pulled in on a trailer sometime in the distant past and made into a permanent home. There was a large pine tree out front, obscuring some of the structure and the driveway, but the rest of the place was relatively exposed, apart from some surrounding native shrubs.

"A car is out front. They have the rear hatch open."

Rachette continued narrating to Yates as a woman came into view, leaving the house with a piece of luggage. She put the bag in the back of the vehicle, then disappeared into the house again.

"They're packing up?" Yates asked.

"I guess so. Looks like it."

"How many vehicles are out there?"

"I just see the one. But there's a big tree blocking the driveway. Could be another one."

"What's the make of the car outside?"

"I don't know. Maybe a Mazda? It's too far. Too dark."

"Give me those." Yates wrestled the binoculars from Rachette's hands and put them to his face.

Rachette scoffed, turning around and looking the opposite direction. A nearly full moon was climbing above the eastern mountains, illuminating a desolate stretch of dirt road. Miles away, pinprick lights traveled along 734, weaving into the Cave Creek hills to the south or heading north toward Vail.

A few minutes ago, just as they had turned off the highway and onto the county road leading here, they had passed a vehicle, one that neither of them had paid any attention to until shortly after, when they had gotten the vehicle information for Faith Orton. Had the car they'd passed been a two-year-old Mazda CX-5?

"Yeah, damn it," Yates said. "I can't tell what it is, either. Shit."

"I just wish you would have seen it," Rachette said.

"And why not you?" Yates lowered the binoculars. "You were right there."

"I was driving. Give me those." He leaned on his hood again and peered through the eyepieces. The house bobbed into view as the woman reemerged with a garbage bag, which she also tossed into the back of the vehicle. "They're definitely packing up. Looks like they're ready to get moving."

"How far out is Wolf?"

"I don't know. Call him."

Yates pulled out his phone and dialed. "Sir. We've got eyes on the house. We can see that they're packing up a vehicle. It looks like they might be ready to leave."

"How far is he?" Rachette repeated.

Yates ignored him for a moment, listening, and then said, "Twenty-five minutes."

"Shit."

"Yes, sir. . . .. Okay. . . .. Oh, we'll be careful. . . .. Yes, sir. Okay." Yates hung up.

"Well?"

"He says it's up to us. If they get in their vehicle, this could turn into a chase."

"And we would be putting innocent lives at risk while we pursue their asses," Rachette said.

"He authorizes us going in. But he says be safe. Otherwise, we can wait it out."

Rachette looked through the binoculars. "I see somebody else. She's older. She's got a bag with her, too."

"How much older?"

"Okay, screw this. I say we head down there."

"Driving? They'll see us coming. It might spook them."

Rachette smiled to himself, flexing his recently acquired leg muscles under his pants. For the first time in a few years, he felt joy at the prospect of going a half mile on foot. "Keep up with me."

· · ·

Rachette took the lead, running on the balls of his feet, his steps light and silent as they hit the dirt road. Yates sounded like a wounded, hoofed animal jogging behind him, and Rachette had to shush him twice.

As they approached the house, they slowed to a walk and got off the road, sticking close to a barbed-wire fence. Light from the halogen porch lamp flitted in and out of view behind shrubs, and the big pine marking the driveway grew until it towered over them. They took position behind a ball-shaped juniper, crouching in the shadow cast by the colossal trunk of the pine.

There were no people in the dirt driveway, just two vehicles: a beat-up Toyota sedan parked with its front bumper to the house, and behind it, a Chevy crossover SUV with its hatch still wide open.

A mourning dove cooed, filling the quiet of the barren countryside. A single light shone over a mile down the winding road, marking the nearest neighbor.

"They're inside," Yates said.

The living room window of the house was illuminated, showing two women walking back and forth. One of them was older, clearly the mother. Rachette couldn't tell if the other was Faith. Probably not, since Faith's vehicle was gone.

"Wolf mentioned the sister lives here, too," he said. "That must be her."

"Damn it," Yates said. "We gotta tell Wolf we missed Faith."

The front screen door squeaked, and the older woman came out holding a duffle bag.

"What?" she called, pausing as she cocked an ear. "Yeah."

Head down, seemingly distracted in thought, she walked

to the Chevy, slung the bag into the rear, and closed the hatch. Then she stopped, lifting her gaze to examine the wilderness stretched out before the house, and tilted her nose to the air.

It was at that moment Rachette realized how strong Yates's cologne was. It looked like this woman was getting a whiff of it. Face inked out by shadow, she rotated her head toward the tree.

Rachette flicked his eyes down and saw a sliver of his pants was painted visible by the halogen. He remained frozen.

Almost imperceptibly, the woman jerked, as if with realization, as if she'd seen Rachette, and then she pivoted and hurried for the house.

"Excuse me, ma'am!" Rachette moved out from under the tree.

The woman acted like she hadn't heard him.

"I got your six," Yates said, hanging back.

"Excuse me, ma'am. Sheriff's department."

That slowed her to a halt. She turned around.

"That's right. My name is Detective Tom Rachette. I just want to speak to you for a bit."

Her eyes were wide, mouth agape.

"Where are you going?" Rachette came closer, smiling, keeping his tone light and his hand on the butt of his holstered Glock. He glanced past her, at the window, and saw a quick, indistinct movement inside. And then nothing.

"Oh, I . . ." The woman shook her head, turning away. "No. No, thank you."

"I'm not selling anything, ma'am. I'm with the sheriff's department."

Rachette quickly stepped in front of her, blocking her access to the door.

She backed up, looking through the window, which was now behind him.

His partner had it covered. With his gun out, Yates walked ahead in a crouch.

"Here. Here's my badge." Rachette flashed his shield. "See? Says right there: Detective Rachette. Is Faith inside? Or is it her sister in there?" He pocketed the badge. "What's her name?"

The mother said nothing.

"Did Faith leave?"

The woman shook her head. Her eyes transformed, becoming cool and defiant. Right then, Rachette knew they were dealing with a cunning trio of women. They might be in immediate danger. If these women were guilty, that meant they had killed Brock and Clara. And maybe Jorel, too. The thought spiked his body with adrenaline.

He pulled his gun, holding it by his hip.

"Where's your daughter?" He snapped his finger and pointed to the side of the house.

Yates moved, understanding. The sister could be escaping out the back right now.

Two shots popped. Instinctively, Rachette fell to a knee, raising his weapon.

Holy shit. What was Yates doing firing so fast? He hadn't even—

And then he saw Yates come into view by the two vehicles, stumbling backward, away from the house, hitting hard off the front bumper of the Chevy. Blood stained his shirt. He fell on his face and remained motionless.

"What the fuck?"

"He's at the front door!" the old woman yelled. "He's got a gun out!"

Just then, the younger woman, whose face he still did not recognize in person, came sprinting around the corner of the house, pointing a gun at him with one hand. She fired again and again.

Bullets zipped past him, feet from his head. He ducked and lunged forward, putting the Toyota between him and the shooter.

The old woman went back inside, the slap of the screen door making Rachette jump.

The Chevy started.

He rose and fired three times into the windshield.

His bullets punched into the glass, sending white cracks webbing outward.

The Chevy's engine revved, and the vehicle surged backward, turning, bouncing as it missed the end of the driveway and hit the drainage ditch.

Rachette took up a Weaver stance, aiming carefully at the Chevy's side windows and firing, seeing his still-unmoving partner lying on the ground in his peripheral vision.

The glass shattered away as the vehicle halted its backward movement and started rolling forward, the gears catching late as the engine once again revved hard.

Rachette emptied all fifteen rounds, then changed the magazine and continued to fire, Swiss-cheesing the door and flattening both wheels.

The engine moaned as the vehicle continued up the road, carrying off into the moonlight, jerking side to side.

With his hearing washed out and the Chevy past the effective range of his Glock, Rachette gritted his teeth and looked back at Yates, forgetting the woman for now. He must have hit her half a dozen times. She wouldn't get far.

Moving toward his partner, he dove to the ground as yet another shot rang out, this one coming from the other side of the house's screen front door. He rolled as a bullet hit the ground nearby, ricocheting into the distance behind him.

With cold, lightning-fast calculation, he aimed and shot three rounds into the door.

The old woman tumbled outside, landing hard on her chest, appearing dead on impact.

"Yates!"

He kneeled by his partner.

Yates's eyes were open, mouth leaking blood. A wound on his chest flowed crimson, soaking his shirt. "Shit. Hey! You okay? Yates!"

Yates's gaze swiveled to him.

"You hang in there, buddy!" He pulled out his phone and called for medical aid, stressing the need for a helicopter, then hung up and dialed Wolf.

33

"She shot Yates! Consider her extremely dangerous."

"Understood. Get that pressure back on his wound. They're sending a medevac from Brushing. It will be there in a few minutes."

Police units were also on their way. Wolf had overheard the chatter on the radio.

On cue, a bright light appeared in the sky. A minute later, a helicopter rushed overhead, its navigation lights blinking, its rotors drowning out the rumbling of the SUV's tires on the dirt road.

"I don't know if I can do it, Wolf. I don't know if I can keep him alive."

"They just flew over me. They'll be right there."

"Oh. Yeah. I see it. Shit. He's cold."

The helicopter descended as it passed, disappearing over a hill.

Ahead, the road swept to the left in a long arc, like a backward C, climbing up to the point where he'd lost sight of the helicopter. It was there, near the top, that he saw a thin trail of fumes rising into the air, pale against the dark landscape. The source of the smoke looked to be a car that had gone off the road, careened down the slope, and hurtled into some rocks below.

"I see her vehicle. She's crashed."

"Be careful. I filled that car with twenty holes, and she kept on driving. Okay. They're here. They're landing."

Wolf shut off his lights and slowed, pulling to the shoulder. "I gotta go."

"Be careful."

"I will."

He ended the call, cut the engine, and got out.

The air was cool and still, smelling of juniper, sage, and greasewood, all overlaid by the earthy scent of the dust his SUV had kicked up. Thumping rotors echoed through the night, then quieted, leaving him in dead silence.

He stared hard at the vehicle wrecked in the bushes and trees, its front end wedged against a cluster of boulders. He estimated it to be two hundred yards up the road, down off the shoulder.

How long ago had she crashed? Probably right after Rachette had called in the shooting, which had in turn lit up the radio waves with frenzied activity. That had been—he checked his watch—no more than ten minutes ago.

But one could travel a long way in ten minutes on foot.

Pulling his Glock, he aimed away from his vehicle and blinked on the tactical light mounted under the barrel, checking that it worked. It did, blasting the area in front of him with five hundred lumens. Quickly shutting it off, he turned and stood on the relatively high ground of the road, planning a route through the foliage below before making his way down the shoulder.

His work boots scraped on hard rock at first, and then the soil became sandy and soft, each step sounding to him like the crunch of a potato chip bag. The moonlight made navigation easy, so he chose his route carefully, avoiding dry twigs and branches that would snap and announce his presence.

He'd covered over half the ground between his vehicle and the crash when the helicopter lifted into view and passed overhead, washing the area with noise.

Ducking behind a juniper tree, he watched the chopper vanish over the horizon, giving a wordless prayer that Yates would be okay. Ignoring the pang in his heart, he cocked an ear, listening hard as the area plunged back into silence.

And that's when he heard a woman grunt, curse, and then cough.

Wolf considered the distance to the crash site. The woman had sounded much closer. She was out of the vehicle and on foot. Or on hands and knees.

With heightened senses, he rose from his position and looked around, straining his ears.

There was a scrape, and then the cracking of a twig, and he pinpointed the source to be directly behind him, and very close.

"Help me," whispered a woman's voice. Her words were barely audible and didn't seem to be directed at him. More like she was speaking to a higher power for assistance. "Help me. Help me. Please, help me . . ." She said something else, something too faint to hear.

He turned in place, spotting movement between two squat

junipers ten or so yards to his right. His eyes zeroed in on the location, and he caught the silhouette of a hunched woman, one of her legs dragging behind her with each labored step she took forward.

"Come on," she said. "Move it, bitch. Move it."

He raised his gun in front of him and followed after her, eyeing the ground before each footfall, trying to remain quiet. He put his index finger on the tactical light switch but dared not depress it. No need to give away his position yet. Not when he could still get closer.

"Who's that?" the woman said. "Whose car is that?" And then she yelled, "Who's there? Who is that? Help!" She coughed again, this time uncontrollably, and it sounded wet, like she had advanced pneumonia.

Bushes rattled loudly as the woman fell, cracking sticks upon impact. "Shit!" she said, grunting.

Taking advantage of the chaos, he moved faster, rounding a set of bushes. He clicked on the tactical light, illuminating the area like it was suddenly midday, and found the woman sprawled on her back inside a large sage bush, squinting against the light.

Wolf didn't recognize her, but it would have been difficult to recognize his own mother in the shape she was in. She had multiple wounds on her face, including a cut above her eye that was pouring blood, and more along her side—all bullet strikes from Rachette's discharges. Glistening red blood streaked the entire length of her body.

"Show me your hands," he said.

"Who are you? Who is that?"

"Sheriff's department. Freeze and show me your hands."

"Oh, you again." She ignored him, struggling to stand up.

One of her hands was visible, the other in the bush and out of sight.

"I said freeze! Stop moving!"

She smiled, revealing pink, blood-tinged teeth. "What are you going to do?"

"You're going to climb your ass out of there, and I'm going to arrest you. Now get up."

"Where's my sister?"

"That's a good question."

She said nothing, now motionless in the bush.

Wolf stepped sideways, rounding her body to get a view of her concealed hand. "Show me both of your hands. Now."

"My other hand has a gun in it. I'm about to pull it and shoot you. Just like I did to that other asshole pig a few minutes ago. I missed that other prick. But I got one of you guys good."

Wolf knew what she was doing. She was priming him to shoot. Suicide by cop.

Thinking of Yates flying away in that helicopter with a hole in his chest, he was obliged to help her out. He just needed a look at the gun first.

And then she bucked, thrashing the bushes, pulling a handgun into view like a striking snake.

He fired first.

34

Heather Patterson exited the ice cream shop carrying a gallon of rocky road.

A woman walked past, laughing hysterically into the phone pressed against her ear, and bumped into her.

"Oh. I'm sorry," the woman said.

Patterson stopped, staring at her until she moved on.

"Jeez. Just ran into a . . ." The woman said something that sounded like it rhymed with itch.

Patterson continued down the sidewalk of Main, passing a stream of young adults out enjoying a night on the town.

She had driven straight home after MacLean's house, knowing Scott and the kids would understand if she didn't have the energy to go into town to get the promised ice cream, but then she had realized she wasn't ready to face her family yet. She was still too riled up. So, here she was.

"Hi, Sheriff."

Patterson failed to recognize the voice, and she didn't bother looking or responding.

I brought Gregory Waze here to run against you.

All she could think about was the betrayal, and all she could feel was the rejection.

She'd just gotten the equivalent of a parting kiss on the forehead from MacLean, her mentor-turned-traitor. She should have known he was a lying bastard.

He still wasn't telling her the truth now. He was pretending he brought in Gregory Waze to take over for her own sake, like he was some savior, like she needed someone to watch over her, to keep her safe from herself.

What a joke. She knew, all the way down in the depths of her soul, that she was a fantastic sheriff. She was competent. Strong. Fair. Not drowning in her responsibilities like he had accused. She wouldn't let him make her doubt herself.

"Piece of shit," she said out loud. A passing couple looked at her, but she paid them no mind.

She would show MacLean and Waze how capable Heather Patterson was. She'd been stepped on, looked around, and dismissed her whole life. It was how she thrived. Little did they know, they'd just stoked the fire, and it was about to get real hot for them.

Her phone vibrated in her pocket. It wasn't somebody calling her, it was an emergency alert. The obnoxious beeping yanked her from the torment of her mind. She took out her phone and saw an Amber Alert had just been issued.

Child Abduction—Sluice-Byron County Sheriff's Department.

Victim: Haley Orton. Age 4. Blond hair, blue eyes.

Suspect: Faith Orton. Age 33. Brown hair, blue eyes, 5 foot 6 inches, 150 pounds.

Vehicle: Red Mazda CX-5 with Colorado plates.

Last seen near Brushing, Colorado.

If observed, call 911.

She then noticed she had two unread messages and three missed calls. They were from Rachette and Wolf. Her adrenaline spiked.

She pressed Wolf's name to dial, not bothering to read any of the messages.

"Sheriff," Wolf said, his voice loud.

"What's going on?"

"It was Faith Orton. It was Faith and her sister. And their mother."

She shook her head, trying to comprehend.

"They did it all. They killed Brock Wendel and Clara Abraham. And it's looking like they killed Xavier Jorel."

"Shit. Okay. What happened? What's going on?"

"Yates is shot."

"What?" The bag fell from her hand. "Is he okay?"

"He's in surgery up in Brushing. Rachette and I are on our way there now."

"I'll be right up."

"Wait!"

"What?"

"Faith is on the run."

"Okay. Yeah. I saw the Amber Alert. What's going on with the sister and mother?"

"They're both dead. Rachette shot the mother. I shot the sister."

"My God." She reached down and picked up her bag, seeing the ice cream had opened and tipped out inside the plastic. She didn't bother fixing it. "Okay."

"Where are you?" Wolf asked.

"I'm in town. I'm on my way up."

"Okay. I'll see you soon."

"Wait, Wolf."

"Yeah."

"How bad is it?"

"He was hit in the chest. But he's in surgery."

"Right," she said, walking faster. Passing a trash can, she deposited the bag of ice cream. "Okay. I'm coming."

She hung up and dialed Scott, telling him the news, and that she would be driving to Brushing, so he shouldn't wait up for her. They said goodbye, and then she pocketed her phone.

She jogged the rest of the way down the block and climbed into her SUV. Once inside, she fired up the engine and pulled out, turning around and speeding north.

"Damn it. Damn it. Come on, Yates. You can make it. Please, God, watch over him. Please let him survive."

Her phone rang through the speakers, and the screen showed Wolf was calling.

"Oh, now you take calls? Stupid car." She poked the answer button. "Yeah?"

"Faith's been spotted at the Mackery gas station. An attendant just got the Amber Alert and called it in. They said so over the radio. You're in town?"

"Yes. Is she still there?"

"She's filling up now."

"I'm right here," Patterson said, checking her mirrors. "I just passed it."

"Every available unit is on its way," Wolf said. "But they were all heading to the action up here when the call came through, so it'll probably be a few minutes."

"Copy that." She made a sharp U-turn, ignoring a honking driver. "I'll try to keep an eye on her."

"You want me to stay on with you?"

"I'm here now." She pulled up to the bright lights of the Mackery gas station, parking on Main Street, eyes searching the pumps under the awning. "I see her."

Faith's red Mazda sat unattended, and she saw the girl waiting in the back, her face lit aglow by the screen of a tablet computer.

Patterson looked toward the gas station's convenience store, seeing Faith was coming out, holding a bag and staring at her phone. Her face was stricken.

"What's happening?" Wolf asked.

"I'm moving." Patterson dropped her phone in the center console and jumped out, rounding the front of her SUV as fast as she could.

Faith spotted her. Without hesitating, she sprinted to her vehicle.

"Wait!" Patterson yelled. She hopped over a strip of landscaping, hurdling a bush, and landed hard on a rock on the other side. Her left ankle twisted, and she went down to the pavement. "Ah!"

The vehicle revved hard. Tires squealing, the Mazda launched out into traffic, drawing honks from other drivers.

Patterson scrambled up on her good leg and watched Faith speed down Main, a gas hose dangling from her tank, splashing gasoline.

"Hey!" A gas station attendant came running out. "Was that her?"

Patterson ignored the attendant, turning and hobbling toward her SUV. Pain burned up her leg, lancing hot with each step, but she gritted her teeth, pushing through the bushes, and made it back to her vehicle.

She climbed inside, shifted out of park, and drove fast.

"You there? Hey! What's going on?" Wolf's voice was muffled, coming out of the center console.

She retrieved her phone. "I'm following her now. She saw me, and now she's running. I have to make calls."

She hung up and dialed 911.

Tammy Granger answered, and Patterson cut her off before she could get the greeting out.

"It's Patterson. I'm following Faith Orton. She's driving down Main right now. She'll be passing the building in a few seconds."

"Holy shit," Tammy said. "Yeah, she just flew by. Almost killed some people."

"Call Ashland. Get anybody south of the pass to head north now. Tell them to set up a roadblock."

"Yes, ma'am." Tammy clicked off.

Patterson clenched the wheel with both hands, concentrating on the road as she swerved dangerously between cars and rolled through the stop sign in front of headquarters. She had no siren, no lights. She was driving the family SUV, and it was slow compared to other new-model vehicles. She mashed down the gas and pushed the engine's limits.

A minute later, she was out of the south end of town. She navigated a sweeping corner, and the taillights of a red vehicle came into view. It was far away, but even from a distance, as it rounded to the right, she saw the hose still dangling. There were no cars between them.

Patterson's speedometer crept up on seventy-five miles per hour, but she gained no ground.

"Damn it." She slapped the wheel. "Her kid's inside. What's she doing?"

Patterson leaned forward, jaw set, eyes locked, hands

opening and closing. The road inclined, twisting to match the path of the river below. She dropped her speed as the curves tightened and the road rose higher above the flowing water. She wasn't about to careen into a ravine.

She passed the turnoff for the bridge that ultimately led to Wolf's property, then a sign reading, *Williams Pass, 4 miles.*

For several agonizing minutes, she contemplated what to do. If she sped up, risking her own life and limb to get closer, she would be endangering the little girl as well. She had to hope units on the other side of the pass were acting quickly.

But even if they succeeded in getting a block up in time, what then? How would Faith react? She had already driven away with a gas hose sticking out of her car. Wolf and Rachette had shot and killed her sister and mother. And her sister had shot Yates.

Yates. Thinking of the detective made her feel light-headed. *Come on, Yates. You can pull through. Hang on.*

Her phone rang again.

"Answer!" she told the car, not daring to break her focus from the road.

"It's Tammy. We have two units on the south side of the pass. They're speeding toward you right now."

"Okay. Tell them to pick somewhere narrow and block the road. Keep me posted, please."

The phone call ended with a click.

She tried moving her left ankle, wincing at the renewed pain that popped up her leg.

The road inclined some more, narrowing as the surrounding forest thickened, and the slope down to the river grew steeper and taller until it was sheer cliff in places.

Turning a tight corner, she sucked in a breath and jammed

the brakes. Her heart leaped into her throat as she steadied the wheel with white knuckles, halting her vehicle only ten yards from Faith's car.

The red Mazda idled in the middle of the road, a gentle puff of exhaust coming out of its tailpipe. It was pointed sideways, facing the river.

She let out a breath. "Oh, what the hell, Faith?"

Illuminated by Patterson's headlights, Faith Orton stared through her windshield and into the abyss, ruminating on something dreadful.

Patterson eyed the edge of the road, then the bugs swirling in the empty space above the ravine.

"Shit," she breathed, shifting into park and flicking on her hazard lights.

Hoping nobody was coming up on her rear, she cranked the parking brake, shut off the engine, and opened her door.

Gingerly, she stepped down onto the road, favoring her good leg, and limped up to her SUV's front bumper.

Rushing water echoed up from her left, washing out the noise of Faith's vehicle.

She saw the little girl sleeping peacefully in her car seat on the rear passenger side, oblivious to her mother's anguish.

Patterson stepped into her headlight beams, keeping toward the shoulder of the road, trying to pull Faith's attention to her.

"Faith," she said, putting her hands up to show they were empty.

She could barely hear her own voice over the roaring river below. They were near Greenwater Rapids, a vicious stretch of the Chautauqua with vertical bluffs that ascended between forty and fifty feet to meet the road. Guardrails lined many of the sharpest turns along the river, but not here. If someone went over the edge in this spot, there would be no surviving.

"Faith! It's me! Sheriff Patterson! Can you roll down your window?"

Faith sat frozen behind the glass for a long moment before complying. The girl stirred as the driver's window came down.

What was her name? Patterson tried to remember. It came to her in a flash.

"Faith. Don't do this to Haley. She doesn't deserve this."

Faith's lips moved, but the river drowned out her words.

"I'm going to come close," she said. "I can't hear you, and I want to hear what you're saying. I'm unarmed."

Faith finally met her gaze, but only for a moment. Her eyes were accusing, bloodshot and rimmed red from crying.

"I'm not going to come too close." Patterson stopped, hands still raised. "I don't have a gun or anything. I just want to talk. Okay? I'm going to stay right here, and we'll talk."

Light swept across the trees along the road, and Patterson looked over her shoulder, watching as a vehicle easily halted behind hers. Its high beams remained on, and a second later, its hazard lights started flashing. A man got out.

"You okay?" he asked, hollering.

Patterson waved him off, turning her attention back to Faith.

The man persisted. "What the hell's going on?"

Patterson waved once more.

"You guys need a tow truck?"

When Patterson didn't respond, he went silent, thankfully reading the situation for what it was.

"Faith. You don't have to do this."

Again, Faith's lips moved inaudibly.

"I can't hear you, Faith."

Faith whipped to face Patterson, raising her voice to a shout as she said, "It's too late!"

Haley jolted awake behind her mother and began crying.

"No," Patterson said. "It's not too late."

Tears streaked out of Faith's eyes.

"Let me get Haley out of the back," Patterson said.

"No. Don't you touch her. You stay there."

Patterson froze, realizing that she had stepped closer. She softened her tone as she said, "You don't have to do this. It's not too late. It's never too late."

Haley's cries morphed into wails.

Faith gazed out the windshield. "It is too late. I've already screwed everything up. There's no point anymore."

"Yes, there is. There's Haley. There's keeping Haley alive, and then keeping yourself alive for Haley."

"There's no life left for us."

"Yes, there is. Listen, Faith. Just because you went down a certain road for as long as you did, doesn't mean you can't turn around. You can. You can turn around now. You can shut off the car and put on the parking brake. You can step out and take a ride with me and Haley back into town."

"Where's my sister?"

"She's . . ." Patterson hesitated as she tried to come up with a lie.

Faith looked at her. "Where's my sister?"

She said nothing, letting her silence speak for her.

Faith closed her eyes.

Patterson considered diving in through the window and switching off the ignition, but the image of her two boys standing at her funeral stopped her.

"I'm already so far down the road," Faith said.

"No. It's never too late. Look. Look at what you did tonight. You were driving away from me, and you stopped. You stopped, Faith. And now you can turn around and get back on the right track. Let's start by shutting off your engine."

Oh, damn it.

Another vehicle approached, from up the road this time, brakes squeaking as it came to a halt. It stopped thirty yards away, and its lights pierced right into them, making Patterson squint.

The door of the new vehicle opened, and another man stepped out. "Everyone all right?"

"Sheriff's department!" Patterson said. "Please stay in your vehicle!"

Haley was wailing harder now, on the path to hyperventilating. Faith closed her eyes, looking like her patience for life had worn through.

"Faith. Look at me again."

Faith opened her eyes.

"Forget about them." She gestured toward the two vehicles. "Forget about Haley right now. Just look at me and listen. It's time to stop the car. Go ahead. Push the button. Or turn the key. Or whatever it is that this vehicle does. Just . . . shut off the car."

Faith blinked, and then she reached her hand along the center console, clasping the gearshift.

The car lurched. Patterson's heart stopped.

"No—" She swallowed her words because the Mazda backed up, rotating to align with the shoulder of the uphill lane, then rocked to a stop, pointing downhill.

The two waiting vehicles took turns using the open lane.

Soon, they had both disappeared around their respective bends, leaving the women and child alone on the dark road.

Patterson went to the back passenger door and pulled on the handle. It was locked, but a click sounded, so she tried it again. It opened this time. Quickly, she undid Haley's harness and picked her out of her car seat.

She rocked Haley in her arms, but the girl stared at her in confusion, crying unabated, her hands pushing against Patterson's chest in a request to be freed.

"Come on, Faith. Shut off the engine. Let's go back down to town."

Faith cranked the wheel, and the engine revved high. The Mazda sped through the headlights of Patterson's vehicle and dumped over the edge, falling into the dark void, scattering the swirling bugs.

Over Haley's crying and the rush of water, Patterson heard the rent of steel and the explosion of glass as Faith collided with the rocks below.

35

Waking from a dreamless sleep, Wolf realized somebody had tapped his shoulder.

He sat up from the row of plastic chairs he was lying on, finding Patterson looking down at him, carrying two Styrofoam cups. She had puffy, sleep-deprived eyes.

"What's up?" he asked. The question took on a whole new meaning when memories of the night's action came back to him. He had heard the story about Patterson and Faith Orton down on Williams Pass secondhand from Deputy Nelson a few hours prior. Or maybe it was more than a few hours. He had no clue. "How are you doing?"

Patterson took the chair next to him, handing over a steaming cup of coffee. "Black. Like you like it."

"Thanks."

Beyond the windows of the hospital waiting room, the horizon was unfamiliar, but pleasant all the same. The mountains lining the eastern outskirts of Brushing, lower than the ones in Rocky Points, climbed against a rose-tinted sky.

"What time is it?" he asked, checking his watch.

"The butt crack of dawn," she said.

"Any news?" Wolf saw that Rachette was absent from the waiting room.

"He's still in surgery."

They went silent, sipping their cups, watching the sun top the hills and spill its rays across the verdant Brushing Valley. It was more agricultural up here, with green checkerboard fields in the distance being watered by huge sprinkler systems, the backlit sprays shimmering like white fire.

"The mother is still alive," Patterson said. "Agatha Orton. They have her in surgery as well."

Wolf shook his head, barely believing it. He had seen the woman lying in a pool of blood at the bottom of a step outside the house. Her pulse had been weak when Wolf had arrived on-scene.

"She'd better survive," he said.

"What happened?" Patterson asked.

Wolf told his story about finding and killing Skylar Orton, then shrugged. "I still haven't had the heart to ask Rachette what happened at the house, so I'm not sure what went down." He looked at Patterson. "How about you? Everything okay?"

She nodded. "Faith gave up. At least she let me take the kid out of the car first."

Wolf exhaled long. "Poor kid."

"Yeah."

They stared outside until the elevator chimed and Rachette came barging out.

He walked to them, stopped, and nodded. "They're done. He's stable. I just got word from a nurse. The doctor's on his way up." Rachette smiled, breaking into tears.

They stood and embraced three ways.

A few minutes later, the elevator opened again, and a man dressed in blue scrubs came out. He spotted them and strode over.

"I'm Dr. Powell. I performed the surgery on Detective Yates." He nodded. "Sheriff."

"How did it go?" Rachette asked.

"The procedure went well, considering he was shot in the chest. The bullet missed his heart, grazing his right lung. I had to repair some blood vessel damage, remove some damaged tissue, and repair the chest plate. But it could have been much, much worse. He lost a lot of blood, but he was strong throughout the procedure. No complications, and he seems to be doing well now."

"That's good," Rachette said.

"How . . . long?" Patterson asked.

"He'll be in here for at least a couple weeks, depending on how well he heals."

"He'll be out in fourteen days or less," Rachette said. "The dude has always been a fast healer."

Dr. Powell smiled. "I hope you're right, Detective."

"When can we see him?" Rachette asked.

"The next forty-eight hours will be important, and I'll recommend not allowing visitors during that time, giving him time to rest and recover. Then we can talk about going in and visiting him."

Rachette looked down.

"But he's alive," Patterson said.

"Yeah." Rachette nodded. "He's alive."

"What about long term?" Wolf asked.

Dr. Powell shook his head. "There's been no damage to the

heart. Minimal damage to the lungs. I'll of course be cautiously optimistic, but it's not out of the realm of possibility for him to make a full recovery. It will depend on the coming days."

They said goodbye, and Dr. Powell left.

Patterson turned to them. "We'll all need a formal debrief."

"Today?" Rachette asked.

"Hell no," she said. "Today, we rest. We hug our families. Rachette," she said. "Go home."

"Charlotte's on her way," he said.

"Good. Go home with her."

"I've got my fleet vehicle."

"Give me the keys. I'll have somebody drive it back."

Rachette handed them over. "Xavier Jorel is still missing."

"They found dried blood on the side of the Orton's house," Wolf said. "And when they were towing out Jorel's Range Rover last night, they found some blood in the rear. Daphne verified both are Jorel's. The Ortons also had a couple shovels leaning up against the side of the house, one with a bit of his blood on it, too. It's clear he's dead and they buried him somewhere."

"We can ask Momma Psycho when she wakes up," Rachette said. "Barring she, God forbid, dies in surgery."

"We could check Faith's and Skylar's phone GPS data," Wolf said.

"They were smart ladies," Rachette said. "They probably turned their phones off before they went out and buried him. But sure, we can take a look."

Patterson put her hands on Rachette's chest. "Go. Home."

"Yeah. Okay. And you two?"

"We'll be on your heels," Patterson said.

Rachette left, stepping back into the elevator.

Patterson gazed out the window, her face troubled.

"What's on your mind?" he asked her.

"What do you think about the whole Waze situation?"

Wolf frowned. "Honestly?"

"Yeah, honestly. Tell me the truth, not what you think I want to hear."

"I don't know. What do you think about it?"

She looked at him, rolling her eyes. "What? Are you a psychiatrist now?"

He smiled. "I've spoken to a couple people up in Bend. He was a good chief for the PD, from what I can gather. People liked him. He's competent. Does that mean we would like him? That's another story."

"You've spoken to people up in Bend?"

"Yeah."

"When were you going to tell me about that?"

"I'm telling you now."

She blew air from her lips.

"Why?" he asked. "What are you thinking?"

Her eyes glazed over, like she had gone somewhere else in her head. "I think I've traveled very far down a road. One that's narrowed around me. So much so that I'm not sure if I can turn around or not. Because if I do, I might fall off the side to my death."

Wolf frowned. "Excuse me?"

She blinked. "Nothing. Never mind. I have to go." She walked away.

Wolf watched her for a second, and then abruptly, he understood. He hurried after her, grabbing her shoulder.

She pivoted. "What?"

"You know that if you turn around on that road—which

you can—you could come driving straight back to us, right? To me, and to Rachette, and to Yates. You could park your car right in the center of the garage. Right in one of the spots reserved for the detectives."

She smiled, shaking her head. Her eyes filled, and she turned around, putting her back to him. Wiping her tears away, she said, "Thanks. I appreciate it."

"You're welcome. Of course."

She went to the elevator, pressed the button, and faced him, revealing her expression was stoic and strong once again. "Now go hug Piper," she said. "And call your son. And your grandson."

He followed her inside the elevator, smiling at his new assignment. "I will."

36

Heather Patterson ducked her head inside the media room to get a peek at the gathered reporters. There were at least a dozen of them, and they were talking softly as they situated themselves on the row of benches.

"They're all here," Margaret said behind her. "Sentinel's here. Denver Post. Fox. CBS . . . Everybody. You ready?"

Patterson looked at her aunt, who looked back, unblinking, with a hint of a smile on her lips.

"Yep."

"Then let's give 'em hell. We're ready." Margaret snapped her fingers, getting the attention of Wilson, who nodded and went to the lectern.

Scott watched Patterson from a few feet away, leaning against the back wall. She turned to her husband and gave him a quick smile. He returned the gesture.

Tapping the microphone in front of him, Wilson cleared his throat. "Ladies and gentlemen of the press, thank you for attending this morning."

Patterson glanced over at her aunt. Margaret was beaming, her lips frozen in a satisfied smile. She had been giddy upon hearing the dirt Patterson had extracted from the private investigator about Gregory Waze, and since that moment, the mayor of Rocky Points had been beside herself with anticipation of a hard-won campaign.

"Sheriff, all yours." Wilson stepped aside.

Patterson straightened her formal uniform jacket, running a finger across her hat as she walked to the stage and stood behind the lectern.

Cameras clicked. Somebody cleared their throat.

"Thank you for coming to this press conference I've called on this bright and beautiful Tuesday morning."

A couple of reporters chuckled. It was forty-five degrees and raining outside.

"I wanted to start by addressing our very own Detective Reginald Yates getting shot in the chest Saturday night north of Cave Creek. As we mentioned this weekend in our statements, he has undergone surgery, and the latest word is that he's doing well. His recovery is underway."

Somebody clapped, and she nodded.

"I've also called you here to make an announcement." She paused, ensuring she had everyone's full attention. "When my term as interim sheriff is complete, I will vacate the position. I am officially, from this point forward, no longer running for sheriff of Sluice-Byron County."

Astonished murmurs filled the media room. Patterson slid her gaze past Margaret, who had her hands up in a what-the-hell gesture.

"I want to thank the people of Sluice-Byron County for letting me serve as your interim sheriff. My team and I have accomplished much since I was appointed to office, from streamlining communication between our numerous county departments with the new online portal we launched last fall, to protecting our community by drawing down the rate of group A crimes committed county-wide."

She smiled, standing even taller. "I am proud of what I have achieved as your interim sheriff, but I simply enjoy being a detective more. That's what I did before I accepted this position, and that's how I'll continue to serve this great county in this beautiful state I love moving forward. Thank you very much."

She nodded curtly, stepped away from the lectern, and exited the room with her head held high. On the way out, she looked at Scott, who gave her a thumbs-up, grinning proudly. He joined her in the hallway, along with Wilson. They made their way to the first-floor stairwell to head back up to her office.

"Heather!"

She slowed, turning to confront her aunt.

Margaret's heels clicked fast as she hurried toward them.

"What was that?" Margaret said, staring at her.

"That was me doing what I needed to. I'm sorry."

"For what?"

"For letting you down."

Margaret smiled, but it looked more like a spasm. "By not being sheriff? You think I care about that?"

"Yeah."

"Okay, yeah. I do. But . . . why didn't you tell me?" Margaret glanced between her, Wilson, and Scott.

Wilson and Scott looked away.

"I didn't want you to try to talk me out of it," Patterson said. "I wasn't going to change my mind."

Margaret closed her eyes, rubbing a temple with bony fingers.

"I had myself convinced I wanted to be sheriff until this weekend," Patterson said. "But things changed."

She thought of her pleas to Faith Orton. She thought of holding the sobbing child while watching the despondent woman launch herself into the abyss, succumbing to the poor decisions she had made instead of trying to right them going forward.

"I realized I didn't want to be sheriff. I've never wanted to be sheriff. It was a path that other people put me on. I've been following it for years, afraid to question if it is right for me. But now I'm turning around before it's too late, Margaret. And I don't care what you, or anybody else, thinks. I'm an investigator. I've always been one. I'm meant to be a detective."

Margaret twisted her neck to view the reporters streaming out of the room.

Patterson saw Cindy from the Chautauqua Sentinel come into the hallway.

"They're going to say, 'I told you so,'" Margaret said.

"Let them. I don't care."

"And what about you?" Margaret asked Wilson. "You're going to be Waze's undersheriff?"

Wilson shrugged. "Sounds like it."

"What do you think about that?"

"I don't know. We'll see when the time comes," he said, a hint of a smile curling his mustache.

Margaret sighed loudly. To Patterson, she said, "You're a

pain in my ass. But you're my niece. And you know I love you still. I'm behind your decision. One hundred percent."

Patterson nodded. "Thank you."

Patterson's phone chimed in her pocket. She pulled it out and read the screen. "We have to go upstairs." She kissed Scott. "Thank you for coming."

"Of course," he said.

She and Wilson stepped into the stairwell. As the door shut behind them, she felt a heavy weight lift from her shoulders. She took the steps two at a time, chuffing up to the next landing.

"Easy there, killer," Wilson said.

"Come on, Wilson. You can go faster than that!"

She continued climbing, leaving him in her dust. Breathing hard as she barged through the door to the third floor, she gave a couple of deputies standing by the elevators a nod.

"Deputies."

"Sheriff."

She adjusted her jacket and milled about in the hallway, waiting for the undersheriff to emerge. When he did, sweat glistened on his forehead.

"What took you so long?"

"The weakness of my legs," he said. "The fat on my gut."

They walked to Wolf's office, and she knocked.

"Come in!"

She opened the door and went in, Wilson trailing behind. "Hey."

Wolf clicked his computer mouse, sitting back in his chair. "Good job. I just watched the press conference online. Short. Sweet. To the point."

"Just like me," she said, taking a chair at Wolf's desk.

"I'll give you short," Wilson said, sitting next to her.

She eyed the wall clock, which read 11:40 a.m. "You're back fast."

"We left at seven."

"Oh, I guess it's been a while then."

"How's Yates?" Wilson asked.

"He was awake when we got there. Spoke to us for a while. Ate a popsicle. Smiled some. Told Rachette to shut up a couple times."

"So, he's doing well," Patterson said.

Wolf smiled. "Rachette's still up there."

"I think I'll go up later today," Wilson said.

"I'll join you," Patterson said. She crossed a leg. "So? Did you talk to Agatha Orton?"

Faith and Skylar's mother, Haley's grandmother, had sustained two gunshot wounds from Rachette's gun—one in her shoulder, and one in her abdomen. The third bullet discharged from Rachette's weapon had missed. Her surgery had gone smoothly, and she was reportedly recovering without issue. Brushing PD had on-site units keeping her constrained to her room, making sure she didn't try to escape while they gathered the charges against her.

"We did," Wolf said.

"And what did Momma Orton say? Did she talk?"

Wolf nodded.

"She didn't want a lawyer?"

"Rachette might have promised we'd have Haley come visit her if she told us everything."

"Well, I'm not sure that's going to happen," she said.

Wolf shrugged.

"What did she say?"

"Rachette got it all on audio. You can listen to the whole thing when he gets back later."

"Give us the CliffsNotes," Patterson said.

"Okay." Wolf crossed his arms, collecting his thoughts for a moment. "Five years ago, Faith and her mother lived up at the same ranch house. Skylar wasn't there yet. She was living down in Albuquerque, doing drugs and hanging out with criminals.

"Brock had just moved into town from Oregon and started working at the restaurant. He pretty much immediately began dating Gemma. Faith got a job there around the same time. According to Agatha, they all became friends right away. Then Faith began spending the night with Brock up at the house."

"Behind Gemma's back," Wilson said. "What a great friendship."

"Yeah. Agatha told us this went on for a number of months. She said Brock used to sit down at the kitchen table with her and Faith and tell them about Gemma's money. How much there was of it. How little she cared about it. How easy it was for him to get it when he was with her. Said that all he had to do was ask, and Gemma would give him thousands of dollars in cash."

"Really? Wow," Patterson said. "Gemma never seemed that gullible to me."

"Jorel told me Brock had an internet business that he'd somehow convinced Gemma to help him with. A business he never made any money from. One that needed a constant inflow of cash. More likely, that cash was used for Brock's other extra-curricular activities. He was a con artist. A good one, apparently."

"Go on," Patterson said.

Wolf took a sip of his coffee, then continued, "So, this went on for a time, and then one day, Faith got pregnant. And when Faith didn't want to have an abortion, Brock told her to keep it secret, to tell Gemma somebody else was the father. He told her he wanted to help, and the best way was by getting more money from Gemma. But that would only work if Gemma never knew the truth."

Patterson raised an eyebrow at him.

"I'm just reporting it," Wolf said. "Anyway, Agatha said it started as Brock providing them with two thousand dollars every month during the pregnancy to help cover doctor bills. But, as Faith got more skeptical of the grand scheme, he upped it to three thousand. And then when she finally had the baby, he kept paying her but stopped coming around."

"Oh, imagine that," Patterson said.

"Faith was apparently upset with this hands-off approach. His solution was to up the payment to four thousand per month. She was still not happy about that. She wanted a father for Haley. Faith threatened to come out with the truth numerous times, but Agatha said Brock was a good talker. He kept promising he had larger plans for them if she was just patient. And he also reminded her that if he was outed, then there would be no more money. If that happened, he would leave them with nothing, and Haley would never have a father."

"What larger plans?" Patterson asked.

"Marrying Gemma Thatcher," Wolf said. "His plan was to propose to Gemma. Then he'd have control over part of the Thatcher fortune himself."

"How could Faith go along with . . .?" Patterson pressed her palms into her eyes.

She thought again about Faith driving off the edge of the road. The woman hadn't just been hopeless for her future, she'd been ashamed of what she'd done in her past. For what she had been duped into doing.

"So that continued for three years," Wolf said. "The payments, and Brock keeping his distance from his child. Meanwhile, he proposed to Gemma, and they were engaged when Haley was one year old."

"This is crazy," Wilson said.

"The crazy really starts when Skylar comes home from Albuquerque, moving in with Faith, Haley, and their mother," Wolf said. "Skylar was a hardened criminal by this time, and not so much of a pushover as her sister and mother. She saw the bullshit going on for what it was.

"She began going into town to stalk Brock, and that's when Skylar figured out that he was screwing around with all sorts of other women, not just Gemma and Faith. So, she decided to confront Brock and up the blackmail by a few thousand dollars per month. He conceded the higher amount, which he easily sourced from Gemma and paid.

"That went on for about a year, bringing us up to four months ago, when Roland and Jorel finally noticed the cheating and the money being passed from Gemma to Brock. Jorel called Brock and told him to get lost for two million dollars or else."

"So, Jorel was telling you the truth," Patterson said.

"Yeah," Wolf said. "He left a detail out, though. Apparently, Jorel froze the money coming from Gemma, preventing Brock from paying Faith and her family that month."

"Oh boy," Wilson said. "Bet Skylar wasn't happy about that."

"She was not. She made Brock come over to the house and explain, and then she pulled a gun on him. She told him to pay or else he was dead. He came clean about the deal he'd made with Jorel. He told them he was going to be paid one million at the beginning of the next month. Skylar demanded half the money—and the paintings from The Oxbow. He had no choice but to take the deal."

"How many layers of blackmail is that now?" Patterson asked.

"Three," Wolf said. "I think. Four, counting Jorel and Roland paying off Brock? I have no idea."

"Why did she want the paintings?" Wilson asked. "That seems like such an odd request."

"Skylar had it all thought out, apparently," Wolf said. "She knew there was no way Brock was going to pay them the half million. He had already lied to them countless times. Once he had the money, he would cut and run, and they'd never track him down. So, the paintings were going to be their real payday. Skylar had been eyeing them for a while. She knew they were worth a fortune and didn't have alarms, and she had friends who were fences and could help her offload them."

"Ah, I see," Wilson said. "By including the couple million in paintings in the deal, the Ortons were putting their destiny in their own hands. If Brock surprised them and held true to his word, paying them the half million, all the better."

"Exactly," Wolf said. "To make sure Brock followed through with the theft once the gun was no longer to his head, Skylar threatened to tell Roland and Gemma about his secret daughter—blowing the whole thing up and leaving him out on his ass with nothing—if he showed any signs of deviating from the plan."

"Then Brock set up the painting heist with Clara," Patterson said. "Why with Clara?"

"Clara was the new girl smitten with Brock. Remember that woman, Tricia, that I called four months ago when they first disappeared? Clara's friend? She said Clara was involved with a new man, her boss, and planning to go away with him. Brock must have talked her into doing the theft and skipping town with him."

"This guy was the Picasso of con artists," Wilson said.

"Yeah. In any case, they did it," Wolf continued. "They stole the paintings and met Skylar and Faith at the Silver Vein Wilderness lower parking lot to hand over the art. According to Agatha, Skylar didn't intend to kill Brock and Clara, but she had . . . issues. A nasty temper. Things got heated, and she snapped and shot Brock. She killed Clara to cover her tracks."

Patterson frowned. "If it wasn't premeditated, why was there chemical cleaner residue in Brock's car? And why'd they pick a meeting location near a mine shaft?"

"I asked Agatha the same questions. She said Faith kept disinfectant wipes in her car for Haley's messes. They used those to try to remove their prints. And they picked the location because it was a remote place they were all familiar with. They all hiked there frequently."

"What about Agatha?" Patterson asked. "Was she there?"

"No. She was home, watching Haley."

"That makes sense I guess," she said. "Did they end up selling the paintings?"

"Yes."

"How much did they get?"

"One hundred thousand."

"Each?"

"Total."

Patterson closed her eyes, sighing deeply. She stood up. "Well, I think I'll go vomit in my office."

"I'll write up the report."

"Thanks."

They said goodbye to Wolf, and Wilson followed her out. They walked in silence, Wilson struggling to keep up with Patterson's strides despite his longer legs.

"Thanks for understanding," she said.

"About what?"

"I mean, it must have been kind of a shock when I called and told you I was quitting last night."

Wilson said nothing.

"I hope I didn't mess anything up for you," she said.

"For me? Like what?"

"I don't know. Maybe you wanted to work with me some more, and I'm screwing up those plans. Aren't you going to miss having me as a boss?"

"Not in the least. I can finally breathe a sigh of relief."

She grimaced. "Okay, well, just remember, I'm your boss for six more months."

He smiled. "Yeah, fine. I'll miss you. But Waze is a decent enough guy."

"How do you know?"

"He took me to lunch once a couple months ago. Seemed professional. Likeable. I told him I was backing you, one hundred percent. To his credit, he said he understood, and that my job would be safe if he won the election. He called me this morning to confirm that was still the case. He's a man of his word."

"You went to lunch with him? A couple months ago?" She

slowed to a stop, folding her arms across her chest. "When were you going to tell me this?"

He shrugged, stopping, too.

She shook her head. "I don't want to talk to you anymore."

"Good, 'cause I have to use the bathroom." He turned around and disappeared into the men's room.

She walked to her glass-enclosed office and sat behind the gargantuan wooden desk.

Looking at the squad room beyond the windows, knowing she would be back out there soon, a smile tugged at her lips.

37

THREE DAYS LATER . . .

"Almost there."

Wolf followed Piper. The trail snaked through a dense set of pines, switching back and forth along a steep slope. The soil beneath their feet was dark brown, like the color of coffee grounds, and eroded by water and years of hikers frequenting the path.

Wolf's legs were burning, his lungs pumping for air. He had to strain to keep up with Piper, who had been hiking effortlessly since they had parked the car miles below.

"I can't believe you haven't been here before," she said. "But I guess it makes sense, it being south of the pass. Now that I'm in Rocky Points, I feel like I don't spend enough time down here."

Wolf noted her breathing barely accelerated as she spoke.

"Here we go. We're here."

The trail opened up to the west, the dark ground giving way to bleached-white rock.

"Wow," Wolf said. Each step he took into the clearing atop the mountain exposed more of the valley below.

Piper looped her arm through his, leaning against his shoulder. "It's great, right?"

A fresh breeze wicked the sweat from his face and neck. The sun was high, the sky bright blue and cloudless, apart from a faint wisp far to the south. To the north, Williams Pass rose like a furry green lump. Farther to the west, Cold Lake shone blue among the never-ending layers of forest. At the foot of the mountain stood the shimmering town of Ashland, impossibly small and silent from such a distance.

"Yeah." He smiled down at her. "It is great."

She stretched up and kissed him on the cheek. "Come on. I want to show you this."

He followed her, curious.

"Look at those rocks."

Wolf tracked her pointed finger to a large formation located within a cluster of pine trees a few hundred feet below. It comprised two cylindrical spires formed from the same white rock they stood on.

"Now, I haven't seen that before," Wolf said, astonished. He had been born and raised in this county. Had lived here his whole life. How had he missed it?

Piper's eyes brightened. "You know what they call it?"

"No. What?"

"The Proposer."

He frowned. "What?"

"Yeah. See how the one on the left is shorter? Kind of looks like a man kneeling down? A proposer? And the one on the right looks like, you know, the proposee?"

He squinted, trying to see it, his chest constricting as he thought of the ring box stuffed in his pants pocket.

"I . . ." he said.

"You what?"

He shook his head, gathering himself. "I don't see it."

"You don't?" She reached around his waist and put her palm over his pants pocket, feeling the box, then slid her hand up to rest on his hip.

He looked down at her.

She kept her eyes on the view.

He turned his gaze back to the valley, not seeing any of it now. The moment he had proposed to Lauren flashed in his mind. He stood frozen, trying to return to the present, unable to shake painful memories of the past.

"I'm sorry," she said, facing him. "Wait. No, I'm not."

She fished her fingers into his front pocket. He stepped away, and she stepped with him, pulling out the ring box.

"Wait," he said.

But she had already opened the box and was looking inside. She stared at the ring, twisting the box so the diamonds caught the sunlight, nodding. "It's beautiful."

His horror began to wear off, leaving his body tingling. His mind empty.

"Can I put it on?" she asked, glancing up at him.

He nodded.

But she didn't. Instead, she just looked at the ring some more, then snapped the box closed, handing it back to him.

He took it, holding it dumbly in his palm.

"I've seen that ring before, you know. Back in January."

He narrowed his eyes. "How?"

"You were staying over. You had it in your pocket back

then, just like you have for months since. I was going to the bathroom, and I stepped on your jeans, and I felt it. And I pulled it out of your pocket. And I looked at it. It was dark, though. It looks much more beautiful in the light."

He closed his eyes and lifted his face to the sun. "I'm sorry," he said.

"For what?"

"For not . . ."

"Not asking me to marry you?"

He eyed the box perched in his hand. "Why did you pull this out of my pocket?"

"Because I can't keep looking at it." She sighed. "I didn't do it to make you ask me. I just want to . . . I don't know. I want to talk about it. About what that ring represents. We don't have to get married, but every second I see you walking around with that thing in your pocket and not proposing, well . . . it sure doesn't fill me with confidence about us."

He said nothing.

"I thought it was Austin. That maybe you were jealous of him or something. And then, well, you met him and saw he's not a guy I'd ever be into. At least, I hope you did. And then . . . and then you still carried that ring box around in your pocket. And you never pulled it out. Why?"

He swallowed. "I don't know why."

"Yes, you do. So why don't you tell me?"

"I guess I'm afraid."

"Of marrying me?" Her voice was gentle, but hurt flickered in her eyes.

He shook his head. "No."

"Of asking me?"

He shook his head. "No."

"Then what? What are you afraid of?"

"I guess I'm afraid of losing you."

She raised her eyebrows. "You're afraid of losing me, so you don't ask me to spend the rest of my life with you?"

"Yeah. It doesn't make much sense in my brain, either."

She looked at the rock formation again, and in that moment, he got the feeling she was contemplating a new future. Without him.

"Okay, yeah," he said. "Maybe I was a little scared of asking you, too. But I've never, ever been scared of marrying you. Not since the first time I laid eyes on you."

She peered up at him.

"Piper Cain." He kneeled, opening the box. "Will you marry me?"

She held his gaze. Tears welled in her eyes. "David. I swear I didn't pull that out of your pocket to demand you ask me. That's not what I was doing."

"I know. I was going to do it today, anyway. I was holding it in my pocket for five months so I could do it today. Here and now. Just like this. Don't you see?"

She blinked, and the tears rolled down her cheeks. She ignored the proffered ring, pushing the box aside as she dropped down and threw her arms around his neck. "Of course I will."

They lingered in a timeless clutch, holding one another so close he thought they might merge.

And then Wolf said, "Can you please take this ring now? I'm sick of holding it."

She laughed, unwrapping herself from him. Wolf took the ring from the box and put it on her finger. And then they hugged, and kissed, and stood looking out on the rock formation below.

"I still don't see it," Wolf said.

"What?"

"It really doesn't look like a guy proposing to a woman."

"Oh yeah, I lied about that. I was trying to find a way to bring up the whole ring subject, and it just came out of my mouth. I think it's called Donkey Kick Chimney."

Wolf tilted his head.

"See how it's a donkey?" She pointed. "Kicking a chimney?"

"Ah. Beautiful."

38

FOUR MONTHS LATER...

Wolf pulled to the side of the dirt road, watching a swirl of leaves and dust pass by the SUV. He checked the address on the mailbox against the one he'd logged into his mobile data terminal, verifying they were the same.

The map on the MDT looked like it had shorted out and forgotten to load the pixels for the terrain. Really, there was nothing to display aside from the vertical line representing the road he was on. Shooting off the line was a tiny, nearly imperceptible squiggle signifying the driveway leading to the property he'd come to visit.

A two-story house, modest in size, sat a hundred or so yards ahead. Behind it stood a huge wall of oaks shedding yellow leaves. Between the edge of the road and the home grew an expanse of waving brown grass.

The land here in southeastern Colorado, as far as the eye could see in any direction, was board-flat. A line of windmills churned in the distance, eating the breeze and spitting out electricity.

Next to his vehicle, a carved pumpkin sat on top of the mailbox. Beside the mailbox, a scarecrow with zombie hands fluttered in the wind.

What a place to live, he thought. It was solitary, surrounded by nature. He would give it that.

He released the brake and turned into the driveway, squinting as the evening sun reflected off the mirrors, searing his retinas.

A woman was outside, carrying a bucket from a barn-style outbuilding to the house. She stopped and put her hand in front of her face to block the sun, watching Wolf approach.

He drove up slowly, parked a non-threatening distance away, and got out. Before he shut the door, he reached over and plucked the present off the passenger seat. The gift wrap covering the box featured rainbows and unicorns.

"Ahoy!" the woman said. "You must be Wolf."

"Yes, ma'am."

She smiled warmly, placing the bucket on the ground, and came toward him, her cowboy boots scratching on the dusty driveway.

Wolf walked to meet her, noticing the plastic play equipment that had been erected around the property: slides and swings, a low table with tiny chairs, a pink lawnmower, and a foot-powered plastic car.

"David Wolf."

"Whinny Miles."

"Nice to meet you, Whinny."

They shook hands. Whinny's were covered in dried mud, and she made no apologies about it, just wiped them on her overalls. She wore a pink Kansas City Royals baseball cap pushed down on her head of sandy-blond hair, shading her tanned, freckled face. Her eyes looked kind.

"Jim!" she called at the house.

"Yep!"

"Come outside! The . . . David Wolf is here!"

A few seconds later, the front door opened, and a tall man dressed in sweatpants and a T-shirt stepped out. He turned around and said, "Come on, honey."

A girl with messy blond hair poked her head through the doorway shyly, then walked onto the covered wooden porch and down the stairs.

"Come on over, Haley," Whinny said.

Wolf watched with more than a little surprise as the girl ran to Whinny without hesitation, latching onto her leg, aiming a smile at Wolf.

"Who's that?" Haley asked, looking at him.

"Hi, Haley," he said. "I'm David."

"David?"

Wolf smiled.

Jim came over, and they shook hands. The man was much like his wife in the way that his face was tanned and covered in freckles. He also had kind eyes.

"Hello," Jim said, his voice deep and soft. "I take it your drive was uneventful? And I mean that in the literal sense. There isn't much between here and Denver. Or Rocky Points, I guess." He almost whispered the words *Rocky Points*.

Wolf chuckled.

Haley pointed at the box in Wolf's hand. "What's that? Is that for me?"

"Oh, this?" He looked at Whinny. "Um. This is technically for her. But I wanted to run it by you two first."

Wolf gave the box to Jim. "Do you think we could talk in private for a moment? It's about the box. I mean, what's in it."

Jim nodded, gesturing for Wolf to follow him.

When they got a few yards away, Jim stopped. "What's up?"

"A few of us at the department chipped in to get these. I'm not sure if she's old enough to use them yet or not. I know she's four years old. They say five and up."

"What are they?"

Wolf told him, and Jim smiled. "Well, she's damn good with words and shapes and numbers. I think she'd be ready. But I'd better run it by the boss first. Just a second. Whin."

Jim walked to Whinny and whispered in her ear. Whinny shrugged, smiled, and waved Wolf back over.

"I don't even know if they will work for her," Wolf said. "There's a chance they won't."

Jim handed the box to Wolf. "I guess we'll find out."

Wolf handed the box to Haley. "For you."

Haley's face lit up, and she ripped open the paper, tossing the discarded pieces to Whinny. The four-year-old was confused when she uncovered a box with a pair of glasses pictured on the front. She went silent, her excitement waning as she tried to pry the cardboard apart with her tiny fingers. Whinny helped open the box, removing the pouch holding the spectacles.

"We've heard of these," Whinny said. "We just . . . We haven't given them a try."

Wolf suddenly felt like they had done a very bad thing. What if they didn't work?

"What are these?" Haley asked.

"They're just some fun glasses," Whinny said, apparently thinking along the same lines as Wolf and not wanting to set up any expectations. She gave Haley the pouch. "Let's give them a try, shall we?"

Intrigued now, Haley took out the glasses and put them on.

Wolf motioned toward the wrapping paper in Whinny's hand.

Whinny held it up. "Can you see anything different about this paper?"

Haley straightened, sucking in a breath. Frowning, she lifted the glasses off her nose to look underneath them, then dropped them back into place. Her mouth opened. "What the heck?"

She snatched the paper from Whinny's hand, raising and lowering the glasses as she stared at it.

"Can you see anything different?" Jim asked.

"Is this color?" Haley glanced up at them. "Is this color? What the heck?"

They watched, all of them smiling, as Haley studied the paper with the lenses now firmly planted on her face.

"There's . . . more color or some-sing."

Whinny put a hand over her mouth, tears brimming in her eyes. She pointed at one of the rainbow stripes on the wrapping paper. "What do you see here?"

"Oh my goodness! That's bright. What is that?"

"That's red."

Haley considered Jim's sweatpants, which were also red. "That's like those!"

"She's never been able to pick out red," Whinny said to

Wolf. She looked back at Haley and tapped her hat. "What about this color? What color is this?"

"I don't know."

"Oh, I guess that makes sense," Jim said. "She doesn't know colors because she hasn't seen them before."

"That's like this." Haley pointed at a unicorn's pink eyeball.

Whinny shook her head. "That's amazing." She met Wolf's eyes. "Thank you."

"You're welcome," he said.

"Tell everyone thank you."

"I will."

Haley mesmerized herself with color for another few minutes before Jim steered her inside, leaving Wolf alone with Whinny.

"How's she doing?" he asked as they slowly started walking toward his SUV.

"She's doing better. She was really shy at first. It took us a while to get her to talk. She doesn't mention her mother anymore. I'm not sure if that's a happy or sad thing."

He listened in silence, unsure how to respond to something so intense.

"As for the adoption process, it's going well. The foster people are telling us it's all but a done deal. We just have to wait until it's official. She's going to daycare a couple times a week up in Lamar, just for a few hours while I do some shopping, just to get her to socialize. Oh, she's going to love showing off those glasses."

Wolf smiled, relieved the present had worked out.

"But she's showered with love," Whinny said. "I never knew it would be possible"—she started crying—"to love a child so much when it wasn't yours, you know?"

Wolf nodded.

"But she's just a blessing for us."

Wolf nodded again. "That's great. I'm glad to hear everything is going well for everyone."

"Thank you."

They reached Wolf's SUV and stopped.

"Goodbye," he said, eyeing the house one last time, catching a glimpse of Haley peeking out the door. He waved. "And good luck."

"Bye. And same to you. Thank you for coming."

He shook Whinny Miles's hand and slid into the SUV.

Turning up the heater, he directed his vehicle north and started covering the few miles to Lamar, where he would be staying the night.

He picked up his phone and called Patterson, listening to the ring through the speakers.

"Hey, it's me," he said when she picked up.

"Well?" she said at the same time.

"She's doing good."

"She is?"

"Yeah. She really is."

"What are they like?"

"They're nice, loving people. She has toys all over the place. She looks happy. She was smiling. Talking. She's doing well."

Patterson went quiet for half a minute, sniffing at first, then blowing her nose. "Thanks for going down there."

"You're welcome."

"How did the glasses work out?"

"They worked."

"Really?" Patterson asked loudly.

"She was identifying colors. She was very excited."

"That's awesome." After another moment of silence, she said, "Thank you."

"You already said that."

"Where are you staying tonight?"

"Holiday Inn Express."

"Awesome."

"I don't mind it."

"Don't get too used to it," she said.

"I'll be back tomorrow."

"Good. We had a bar fight over at The Mustang last night. The owner came in this morning. Yates and Rachette are pissing me off with it already."

Wolf smiled. "Well, luckily you're sheriff, for another few weeks at least, so you can reprimand them accordingly."

She said nothing.

"But you don't want to rock the boat right before you rejoin the team," he said.

"Bingo. You're such a good detective. Just give them a call tomorrow and ask how they're handling the interviews. You'll see what I mean."

"Can't wait."

"Bye." She hung up.

Stopping at the turnoff for the highway, Wolf saw he had missed a text from Piper. There were no other cars for miles, so he checked the message.

I sent you an email with the revised cost. Can we elope instead?

He grinned, knowing there was no way in hell he was going to do anything but a full-out wedding with everyone invited.

We'll just have to get creative, he wrote.

A few seconds later, she answered.

I hope you have a peaceful night down there in the sticks.

He stared at the wind farm on the horizon, watching the day's final light slant across the land, thinking about what lay ahead in his future, and the future of the little girl behind him.

He tapped out his reply.

I will.

ALSO BY JEFF CARSON

The David Wolf Series

Gut Decision (A David Wolf Short Story) – Sign up for the new release newsletter at http://www.jeffcarson.co/p/newsletter.html and receive a complimentary copy.

Foreign Deceit (David Wolf Book 1)

The Silversmith (David Wolf Book 2)

Alive and Killing (David Wolf Book 3)

Deadly Conditions (David Wolf Book 4)

Cold Lake (David Wolf Book 5)

Smoked Out (David Wolf Book 6)

To the Bone (David Wolf Book 7)

Dire (David Wolf Book 8)

Signature (David Wolf Book 9)

Dark Mountain (David Wolf Book 10)

Rain (David Wolf Book 11)

Drifted (David Wolf Book 12)

Divided Sky (David Wolf Book 13)

In the Ground (David Wolf Book 14)

High Road (David Wolf Book 15)

Dead Canyon (David Wolf Book 16)

NEW Echoes Fade (David Wolf Book 17)

The Ali Falco Series

The Como Falcon (Ali Falco Book 1)

Made in United States
Orlando, FL
13 February 2024

43617490R00186